LOVE IN THE TIME OF SERIAL KILLERS

ALICIA THOMPSON

JOVE

New York

A JOVE BOOK
Published by Berkley
An imprint of Penguin Random House LLC
penguinrandomhouse.com

Library of Congress Cataloging-in-Publication Data

Names: Thompson, Alicia, 1984– author.
Title: Love in the time of serial killers / Alicia Thompson.
Description: First Edition. | New York: Jove, 2022.
Identifiers: LCCN 2021054444 (print) | LCCN 2021054445 (ebook) |
ISBN 9780593438657 (trade paperback) | ISBN 9780593438664 (ebook)
Subjects: LCGFT: Romance fiction.
Classification: LCC PS3620.H64775 L68 2022 (print) |
LCC PS3620.H64775 (ebook) | DDC 813/.6—dc23/eng/20211116
LC record available at https://lccn.loc.gov/2021054444
LC ebook record available at https://lccn.loc.gov/2021054445

First Edition: August 2022

Printed in the United States of America
8th Printing

Book design by Daniel Brount

LOVE IN THE TIME OF SERIAL KILLERS

For my sister Brittany
because I love you, and because you get it

AUTHOR'S NOTE

This story contains some themes of grief, memories of a neglected/emotionally abusive childhood, and past suicidal ideation. While there are many true crime references throughout, there is no on-the-page violence or active killing in this book.

LOVE IN THE TIME OF SERIAL KILLERS

ONE

OBVIOUSLY A TWO-HUNDRED-POUND Victorian writing desk wasn't made to be moved all by yourself. But it also hadn't come with those incomprehensible IKEA instructions showing a blocky illustrated guy getting help from a buddy, so. There wasn't anything saying not to try it.

I took a step back, assessing the desk where it was strapped to the roof of my car. It was the only piece of furniture I'd brought with me, and it was a monstrosity. My old landlord in North Carolina had helped me load it onto my car in the first place, and it had been the reason I'd made the drive to Florida in one straight shot, stopping only briefly at rest areas and a Taco Bell in Starke.

If I undid the straps, it was possible the desk would slide right off the car. I had an image of trying to catch it and ending up flattened into a pancake like a cartoon character under a piano. But I could brace it against my body, maybe, ease it to the ground. Then I could penguin-walk it up the driveway to the house.

I turned to survey my dad's old house, which had been sitting empty for the last six months, since he'd died back in January. I guessed it was my and my little brother's house now, technically. But this house hadn't felt like mine since the day my mother and I had moved out when I was thirteen, maybe not since before then.

My brother, Conner, could still be awake, even though my phone screen showed that it was already two in the morning. He'd always been a big gamer, and would stay up all hours trying a level one more time or trying to beat the last boss. But that had been before he and Shani had moved in together, before he'd gotten his first postcollege job at a call center. And anyway, I wasn't going to text him to come help me with something as stupid as a desk.

Conner and I weren't that close. We'd barely grown up together, for one thing—when our parents divorced, he'd chosen to stay with our dad, while I'd gone with our mom. He was also seven years younger, twenty-three to my thirty, although that fact alone couldn't fully explain his optimistic exuberance in contrast to my jaded cynicism. We'd spent time together during holidays and select weekends, of course, but still when I thought of him I mostly remembered the way he would eat ketchup by the bowlful when he was six years old.

I typed how to move heavy furniture by yourself into a search on my phone, and scrolled through the results. Ads for moving companies, an article about how to use moving straps and dollies and other equipment I didn't have, another couple of articles that basically boiled down to *don't*.

"Need a hand?" a voice came from behind me, and I jumped

and gave a little scream. My phone flew out of my hand and hit the pavement with a sickening *crack*.

I spun around, coming face-to-face with the random dude who'd spoken. He was standing on the sidewalk, a decent distance away from me, but still. He'd come out of nowhere. He had dark, shaggy hair and was wearing jeans and a T-shirt that had a huge rip in the collar. When I glanced down, I saw that his feet were bare.

"What the fuck?" I said, as much about the bare feet as about the fact that he'd addressed me at all.

He took a step backward, as if *he* were scared of *me*, and shoved his hands deep into his pockets. "It just seemed . . ."

"Well, it's not," I snapped. I reached down to pick up my phone, which, yup, totally had a cracked screen now. Great. My search results for how to move heavy furniture by yourself glowed brightly through the spiderweb of lines, and I had the irrational thought that he'd totally seen them, that they'd called him here like some sort of Bat-Signal to creepy nocturnal dudes looking to accost isolated women in the suburbs.

And now he knew where I lived. I was tempted to get back in the car, to drive to a local gas station and sit in the parking lot for one full podcast episode, then circle the block a few times before pulling into the driveway again. Although, to be fair, it was probably the podcast episodes that were making me so paranoid in the first place. I could rationally recognize that with one part of my brain while the other part of my brain screamed, *This is the exact scenario two post-Evanescence goth podcasters will one day use for their cold open.*

"This isn't my home," I blurted.

He blinked at me, obviously confused. The more he stood there in his stupid bare feet, the more harmless he seemed. He was only a few inches taller than me, I realized. And he probably weighed less, all wiry and lean where I was curvier.

But wasn't that exactly how guys like him broke through your defenses? By appearing helpful, like the Zodiac Killer telling you your wheel was wobbling and offering to "fix" it for you, only to sabotage your car and take you hostage. Or by appearing helpless, like Ted Bundy with his fake casts, needing help carrying something to his car.

Fuck that. I'd rather be seen as a little rude than risk being taken to a second location.

He gestured toward the desk. "That looks heavy," he said.

Driving ten hours straight must've scrambled my brain, because his words made me snort and then break into full-out laughter. It was absurd—this random conversation that barely hit polysyllables, the giant desk strapped to my Camry, the fact that I was here at all, standing in front of a house that I had very few fond memories of. It was two in the morning and I was wearing coffee-stained pajama pants because I'd thought it would be brilliant to dress so I could roll right into bed when I arrived, only I hadn't factored in my stunning inability to drink from the right side of a to-go cup.

"My dude," I said. "If you think this desk looks heavy, you should see my trigger finger on my Mace in about five seconds if you don't back off."

He looked at me for a moment, almost as if he were about to say something else. And maybe it was coming up on time to reread *The Gift of Fear* again, because I realized that the butterflies in my stomach weren't from anxiety but from . . . anticipation. Like there was some quiet watchfulness in his expression that pierced through my armor, and I wanted to know what he saw there.

But instead I turned back toward the desk, making a show of tightening a strap even though that was the opposite of what I was trying to do. When I glanced over my shoulder a minute later, he was gone, as stealthily as he'd arrived.

My forehead dropped to the roof of the car, my grip around the legs of the desk relaxing. I was so tired. I doubted anyone would be interested in stealing a desk, and it wasn't supposed to rain that night. I should go inside and go to bed and let this be a problem for rested, freshly caffeinated future me to solve in the morning.

I grabbed my backpack out of the passenger side, hauled my bigger duffel out of the back seat, and locked up the car. My dad's neighborhood was older, somehow escaping the homeowners association restrictions that would regulate things like streetlights, so it was dark, too. I gave one last sweeping glance around the street—to the left, where an outside cat looked up from its position laid out on my neighbor's driveway, to the house to the right, where a single light still shone through one window. Satisfied I was alone, I headed up to the front door of my dad's house.

The first thing that hit me was the smell. Musty, like a damp towel that had been left on the bathroom floor too long, with a slight antiseptic undercurrent like that same towel had been sprayed with Windex a couple times. This must've been what Conner meant when he said he'd been coming by once a week to "clean."

The place sure didn't look clean. That wasn't completely Conner's fault, I knew—my dad had been a bit of a pack rat, not so bad they'd put him on a TV show but definitely hoarder-adjacent. Even as I walked in, I stubbed my toe on a plastic tub filled with magazines and mail in the entryway, and then knocked a broom to the floor. The bristles of the broom were covered with cobwebs, lest I think Conner had been using it.

I set my bags down on the first empty expanse of floor I could find in the living room. My dad's room was to the left, but there was no way I could sleep in there. He hadn't died in there or anything—it had been a heart attack at the grocery store, mercifully quick, the doctors had told us—but still. It was my *dad's* room.

I opened the door anyway, just to see inside. More magazines, stacked next to the bed and fanning out from where they'd toppled over. What had it been with him and magazines? I'd never even thought of him as much of a reader. But he'd been such a sucker for those commemorative magazines at the checkout aisle in particular, *100 Greatest Films* or *Remembering D-Day* or *Photographs That Changed the World*.

Next, I checked out the kitchen, not expecting anything edible, but just hoping that there wasn't some open bag of sugar that had fallen over in the pantry and been allowed to attract ants for the last six months. When I opened the fridge, it was surprisingly clean—and with a large bag of Kit Kats and a twenty-four pack of Mountain Dew inside.

There was a Post-it stuck to the Mountain Dew: **WELCOME BACK, PHOEBE!** written in sloppy capital letters. It wasn't signed, but of course, there was only one other person who had keys to this place. And only one person who loved Mountain Dew so much he'd been arrested once trying to steal a six-foot-tall cardboard cutout of a two-liter from a gas station. He'd wanted it for his dorm room, he said.

I smiled to myself, shaking my head as I closed the fridge. It was actually kind of sweet that Conner had thought to leave me something. *Sweet* being the operative word, since I'd be in a sugar spiral in five seconds if I tried to subsist on his gifts alone. I'd have to go shopping in the morning.

But for now, I was exhausted, and all I wanted to do was peel off these coffee-stained pajama pants and fall into bed. I only hoped that my dad had kept the bed in my brother's or my old room. My brother had lived in this house more recently than I had, leaving only three years ago when he'd transferred from community college to a campus a few hours away. But when I checked out his room, I saw that he must've taken his bed with him at some point, or else my dad had gotten rid of it. There were still some signs that he'd lived there, like the huge *Red Dead Redemption* poster he had hanging on one wall, but otherwise it was just an old table pushed to one corner, a couple laundry baskets filled with household items and not a piece of laundry in sight, and the pieces of a computer laid out on the floor like someone had been interrupted in the middle of putting it together.

It did something to me, seeing the computer like that. I could picture my dad working on it, could imagine him trying to explain to Conner how some of the parts went together and then getting impatient when Conner kept asking questions about some aspect of the process my dad hadn't gotten around to explaining yet.

For all I knew, it hadn't happened like that at all. But for a moment, I could see it as clearly as if he were still alive and in this room. My dad, smiling gently as he described what a microprocessing chip did or whatever. My dad, slinging the motherboard across the room and leaving a dent in the drywall as he yelled at Conner to *listen*, just fucking *listen*.

I took a deep breath before opening up the door to my old room. I hadn't stepped foot inside it for fifteen years, not since I was fifteen and said I wouldn't come here for weekend visitation anymore. My dad wasn't the type to want a home gym or even a guest room, since he'd eschewed most physical activity and never welcomed a single guest. I had no idea what to expect.

It was exactly the same. My twin bed with the wrought iron frame, the blue-and-yellow quilt from Walmart, the black painted walls, the collages of eyes I'd cut out from magazines and tacked up everywhere. A desk in the corner where I'd spent most of my time, chatting with friends on my laptop. A vase of dried flowers on my dresser, a stack of my favorite movies on DVD. So that was where my copy of *Heathers* had gone.

I found some more sheets in the linen closet—they had that closed-up scent of mothballs and neglect, but they had to be better than what was on the bed—and changed them out. Then I carried my bags into the room, plopped them on the floor, and made as quick work as I could of brushing my teeth and getting ready for bed.

The last thing I did before clicking off the light was rip every single eye collage off the walls. If I had to deal with old *America's Next Top Model* rejects staring down at me as I slept, I'd have nightmares of Tyra trying to "edge" me out by bleaching my eyebrows.

Well, the second-to-last thing. After I lay in bed for a few minutes, I sat up again, switching on the nightstand lamp and reaching down into my backpack for my bullet journal, where I'd been writing all my dissertation notes.

Encounter w/ strange man June 3, approx. 2 a.m. White, 5'9", slightly scruffy, shaggy brown hair. Ripped T-shirt, jeans, no shoes. Origin and destination unknown, believed to be night wanderer.

I chewed on the end of the pen, wondering if I should include any other details. It had been too dark to tell what color his eyes were. His voice had been deep, with a rasp, almost . . . but I couldn't write that. If my body was found in the woods behind the house, and investigators were competent enough to do a forensic analysis of this notebook, I didn't want editorializing words complicating the narrative. Words like *compelling*, or god forbid, *sexy*. I set the notebook on my nightstand, and switched back off the lamp.

TWO

I WAS AWOKEN THE next morning by my phone's ringtone, which started off as a mild robotic beep and ascended to something closer to a nuclear attack warning. It took me a few seconds to register that my screen was a mess of spiderweb lines, took me more to remember the events of the night before. I spent so long blearily staring at my phone, one eye still closed, that I missed the call.

It was impossible to tell who it even was, given the strategic placement of the largest fracture. But then there came a knock at the front door, a cheeky *shave-and-a-haircut* pattern, and I groaned. Conner. It had to be.

Still, I grabbed my old electric guitar from the closet just in case. If it turned out to be an intruder at the door, I could always clobber them with the instrument . . . or at least play an out-of-tune riff from "When I Come Around" until they left.

When I flung open the door, Conner was standing on the

front step, wearing these ridiculously oversized sunglasses and a doofish grin. "Hey!" he said, with way too much enthusiasm. "What's with the guitar?"

I leaned the instrument against the back of the couch. "Nothing," I said, opening the door wider to let him in. "I got in late, so everything's still a mess."

"Well, Phoebe, I didn't expect you to work miracles overnight," Conner said. "And what's with the desk?"

I looked over Conner's shoulder to my car, which should've had eight carved wooden legs jutting out from the top of the roof, four for each side, with a set of drawers and shelf. The desk wasn't there.

Instead, it had been moved next to the house, tucked under the eave hanging over the garage. And unless somehow my Victorian writing desk had gained the ability to shimmy its way off my car and walk itself over here, that could only mean one thing. The Nighttime Wanderer.

(The Sidewalk Stalker? The Moving Man? The Barefoot Butcher? Let's hope that last one never had any reason to stick.)

"This neighborhood is weird," I said. "Get in."

I locked the door behind Conner, taking a moment just to observe him as he looked around the living room. He was broader than I remembered—had he been working out? The idea of my little brother being enough of an adult to have a gym membership felt weird. But then I clocked the tattoo on his calf—Crash Bandicoot, doing his classic pose he'd do if you let the controller sit idle for too long, where he snapped his head back to look over his shoulder. Okay, that was more like the Conner I remembered.

There was a moment when we could've hugged. It would've

been most natural right at the beginning, when there was still the expectant pause before anything real had been said. Conner turned and smiled at me, and I reached for one of my dad's magazines from the box by the door.

"What's with all these?" I asked. "Did he get scammed into signing up for every subscription?"

Conner shrugged. "He got a lot of 'em from the free table at the library," he said. "He liked to clip out the articles he found interesting."

I flipped through the pages. Sure enough, there were several neatly cut rectangles sliced out, a ragged ridge in the spine where whole pages had been torn. I tossed it back on top of the box.

"I've been emailing with that real estate woman," I said. "She recommended we try to get the house ready to list by mid-July, for people who might be looking in time for their kids to start school." That gave us about a month and a half to get the house prepped.

Conner glanced around the mess, his gaze tracking from the old dishes left on a side table to the piles of laundry in the middle of the room to the flattened cardboard boxes that were wedged between the couch and the wall. I didn't even know why my dad had so much stuff, so much useless junk and trash, and I felt myself start to get angry at Conner for not doing more to take care of this place earlier. To take care of our dad, who'd always felt like more his than mine anyway.

Then Conner finally faced me again, pulling a comically exaggerated *yikes* face that almost made me crack a smile. Almost. I hadn't had any coffee yet.

"Tell you what," I said. "Give me fifteen minutes to take a

quick shower and get dressed, and then we can grab some breakfast and come up with a plan. Sound good?"

WE ENDED UP at the nearby Waffle House. There was something so comforting, so consistent about the place. I immediately
felt ten times more at ease freezing my ass off in a booth across
from my brother, both of us peering at the greasy place-mat
menus as though we wouldn't choose the same thing we always
had, than I had in that old house.

"So," I said after we'd ordered. "How's Shani?"

Conner's face lit up. It really was sickening, how much he
loved his girlfriend. I wasn't proud of it, but I'd even muted Conner on social media for their anniversary month, because he was
posting every day about one more thing he loved about her. The
cute scrunch she got in her nose when she laughed. The way she
cooked her Indian mother's masala dosa recipe. How she'd always
been there for him. The list went on and on.

He'd come up with a hashtag and everything. Not that
#ShaniLove was that creative, but still. The picture that had
really sent me over the edge was one where he'd written the
hashtag in mustard on a hot dog to commemorate their fifth date
at a baseball game. Who even remembered where they went on a
fifth date?

"She's great," he said. "She's got one more year left of nursing
school and then she'll be done. She said she's really liked working
on the neurology floor, but there aren't as many jobs in that department so she'll just take what she can get and go from there."

His leg was bouncing a mile a minute under the table. I recognized the habit from when he was a kid and he was excited about something. There was more he wanted to say, I could feel it.

"Okay . . ." I said, feeling him out. Maybe he and Shani were thinking about moving after she graduated? But then I didn't know why he wouldn't just tell me that. I was only planning to stay in Florida long enough to get Dad's house cleaned and sold, so it didn't matter to me if Conner moved away, too.

Shit, was Shani *pregnant*? But then he wouldn't be talking about her school and job prospects like they wouldn't be affected, right?

"I'm going to propose!" Conner blurted, reaching into his pocket to take out a midnight blue velvet box, which he opened and presented to me. In my peripheral vision, I could see the only other guest in the dining area look up from his newspaper, and my hand shot out to quickly close the box.

"Jesus," I said, "put that away before everyone thinks you're proposing to *me*."

"Sorry," he said, but opened the box to glance at the ring inside one more time before sliding it back into his pocket. "I sold my virtual reality system to buy it. It was four hundred bucks but I got it for three fifty, and they upgraded me to the nicer box for free."

"That's great," I said. My voice came out sounding weaker than I wanted it to. It wasn't that I wasn't happy for my brother, but the news was hitting me all at once. It seemed so fast. "You don't think you should wait? Until you're . . . older?"

I winced even as I said it, but Conner didn't seem to take offense. "Nope," he said. "That girl has my whole heart. Why wait to let her know?"

The waitress came then with our food, and Conner went into a whole routine about how the bacon was so overcooked it could stand up by itself. The waitress went from stiffly asking him if he wanted it remade to laughing with him as he pretended to march the bacon across his plate. That was my brother.

His words shook me, though, and I didn't know why. Was it just because I worried about him, hoped he wasn't acting impulsively? I didn't think so. He was barely out of college, which felt so young to me, but he and Shani had also been dating since their senior year of high school, so it wasn't like their relationship was brand-new. My knee-jerk reaction aside, I liked Shani a lot from the couple times I'd met her, and she and my brother seemed really happy together.

Was it because I was jealous? My last relationship couldn't even really be called one. I'd hooked up with a guy I'd had a crush on since our first-year bibliography class, a truly beautiful blond-haired Adonis who'd been a *Beowulf* scholar (my first fucking sign), who'd given me a few nights of lackluster booty calls (another sign, I supposed) before ghosting me entirely.

But that had hurt my pride, not my heart. And I think it was that phrase that had burrowed deep, like a splinter—*my whole heart*. Had I ever given anyone or anything that much of myself? Did I even want to?

"Are you going to eat the egg whites?" Conner asked, his fork already poised over my plate.

A petty part of me wanted to say *yes*, but he knew I ordered eggs sunny side up only to dip my toast in the yolks and then ignore the rest. He used to call it the Eye Gouge Special.

I pushed my plate toward him. "You could at least wait until

I'm done eating," I said as he started cutting the whites away from the yolks and sliding them over to his plate.

"But then they wouldn't be as hot, Pheebs," he said, his eyebrows wagging.

"So," I said, "when are you going to propose?"

"It's not about *when* so much as *how*," Conner said around a bite of egg.

I waited for him to finish, then twirled my hand in a circle to prompt him when he didn't. "Okay . . . so *how* are you planning to propose?"

"I don't know!" Conner said. "That's why I haven't figured out when. It has to be epic, like, viral-video, clickbait-headlines-about-how-you-won't-believe-what-happened-next type of epic."

It seemed to me that the fastest way to guarantee that kind of response was to have something go epically *wrong*, but I didn't say that.

"A rose petal path leading her to some significant location," I suggested.

"Amateur hour."

"Get one of the divers at the aquarium to hold a sign."

Conner gave me a rueful smile. "Shani hates turtles."

"Skywriting."

"I looked into it," he said. "Too expensive."

Obviously, this was not my forte. I'd never proposed to anyone, much less been proposed to. I'd never even come close. And the idea of putting yourself out there that publicly, or having someone else put you on the spot for that public of a response . . . I'd rather watch the absolute darkest episode of *48 Hours* than that kind of horror. The "Nightmare in Napa" one, where the killer turned out to be the now-husband of the victims' room-mate, the very same guy who'd given a sympathetic interview to *48 Hours* before they knew it was him.

"Wait." I finally caught up to what Conner had said. "Shani hates turtles? Not sharks or jellyfish or eels, but *turtles?*"

"They don't have bodies inside their shells," he said, "their bodies *are* their shells. Freaks her out."

"Got it." I blinked away that information before moving on to the actual topic we were supposed to be discussing. "Anyway, like I said, I've been in contact with the real estate agent. She said there's no way we can get the house perfect in time, so we should just clean it, spruce it up as much as we can, and prepare to sell for under market. We have to be careful not to sink too much money into it, too, because there won't be a lot left over after Dad's other debts are paid off."

Conner's brows knitted together. "What other debts?"

"A credit card that seemed to be mostly for Home Shopping Network purchases." I paused. "Your student loans."

"Ah," Conner said. "Right."

It killed me a little that he registered no guilt or chagrin over that at all. When our parents divorced, it turned out that their deal with each other was to take over all finances for the child in their full-time custody. So while our mom had refused to pay a cent toward my education, telling me I was eighteen and should start thinking of my own self-sufficiency, our dad had cosigned for Conner's undergraduate studies.

"Which reminds me," I said, "I have to finish my dissertation this summer so I can defend in the fall. I won't have funding if I push it any further than that. I know you have your new job, so

I'm not expecting you to come over every day or anything . . . but I really need you to carve out time on your weekends to help out. Okay?"

"Of course, Dr. Walsh," Conner said. "What's your dissertation about?"

I took a big gulp of my coffee, which had gone cold. "Not a doctor yet. And it's about true crime as a genre," I said, my pat explanation for when I didn't really want to get into it more specifically. "The relationship between author and subject, our fascination with serial killers as a culture. That kind of thing."

"Cheerful," Conner said. "You gonna finish that waffle?"

I forked another bite into my mouth. "Back off, bro. The rest of this is mine."

THE QUESTION OF what to do about that behemoth of a writing desk reared its ugly head again once we got home. It was still sitting there, next to the front door. I guessed I should be relieved that the Midnight Mover didn't extend his services to breaking and entering.

There was a nook in the living room, the perfect size for putting a piano if we'd been that kind of family, but instead my dad had thrown an old leather chair there and piled it high with stuff. I convinced Conner to help me move the chair to the middle of the living room and then shove the writing desk into the nook.

"Aren't we"—Conner huffed as he struggled to get the desk through the door—"supposed to be taking things *out*?"

"This hunk of wood is the only thing I love in the entire world," I said, before pinching my finger between the desk and the wall and letting out a violent curse. I examined my reddened joint and started thinking about how hard it would be to type with a fractured finger before the pain dulled and went away. "Besides, I need it to work."

I went to close the front door, but then I caught sight of a guy coming down the sidewalk. Not a guy. *The* guy. The Midnight Mover.

Just as I was standing in the doorway, my heart beating out of my chest, he glanced up. He looked a bit more presentable in the daylight—khaki pants, white button-up shirt, brown hair brushed maybe, definitely wearing shoes at least. As I continued to stare, he lifted his hand in a wave.

I shut the door so fast it made my old guitar vibrate with a low, toneless buzz.

"What's wrong?" Conner asked.

"It's him," I said, crossing over to the window to tweak the blinds and look out. "The guy who moved my desk for me last night."

"Uh," Conner said, "isn't that what we just did? Or do you have two of these things?"

"No," I said impatiently, not really wanting to get into the whole encounter. "It was strapped to the top of my car. He must've taken it down and brought it to the house."

"That was nice," Conner said. "Very neighborly."

"He's not a—" I started to say, then paused when I saw him getting into a truck in the driveway next door and backing out onto the street. Huh. He was a neighbor.

Well, I knew one thing. If the local news ever came to interview me after he'd been caught for some massive spree, I wasn't about to be one of those shocked innocents who was all, Who, *that* guy? He was so nice and neighborly! He moved a piece of heavy furniture for me once. Kept to himself. Polite as could be. Would wave when he saw me outside.

Was he nice, or performing niceness? Had moving the desk been a way to make me feel subtly indebted to him? Secrecy was a practical necessity if you had something to hide; politeness was social chloroform.

They say all serial killers on some level *want* to be caught, and that was the only way to explain the wave.

"'. . . Old neighbors viewed each other strangely, and as strangers,'" I said softly to myself.

From behind me, Conner laughed. "If anyone is acting strangely here, it's you. This is a real '""Tis," replied Aunt Helga' moment you're in."

I'd been quoting Truman Capote's classic *In Cold Blood*; trust my brother to answer with a reference to one of our favorite *Simpsons* episodes when we were kids.

"We may as well start with this room," I said, letting the blinds drop again. "I'll grab the garbage bags."

THREE

———

B Y THE TIME Conner left, we'd made pretty good progress in the living room. It was still filled with junk, but at least the stuff was stacked somewhat neatly and organized by what could be donated and what probably just needed to be thrown away.

After that, it was off to the grocery store to stock up on some food. I drove a few miles away to a store where my father *hadn't* collapsed, and then took longer to unload everything into the house than I'd thought, so I was wiped when I finished. My best-laid plans to start working on my dissertation flew out the window, when all I wanted to do was nap.

Except that just as I was drifting off into sleep, a sharp rap came at the door, jerking me back awake. It couldn't be Conner this time—no way would he come back to do *more* work today, and he'd ended up taking the case of Mountain Dew with him, so even the promise of that neon green liquid wasn't a lure.

I opened the door just in time to see a delivery truck pull away, and glanced down to see a package at my feet. My dad had ordered a lot of shit—was it possible he had some kind of automatic subscription that needed to be canceled now that he was gone?

But no. The label on the box clearly read *Samuel Dennings*, with an address two digits off mine.

The Midnight Mover.

The navy blue truck was back in his driveway, so before I could think twice, I marched over there and knocked on his door. I could've just left the box, but that wouldn't be quite as satisfying. Now that I had a name for this dude, I wanted to get a better look close-up.

I was about to knock again when he finally opened the door. I wasn't prepared for how small the distance between us would be, and I took an automatic step back, holding the box between us like a barrier.

He was still wearing the khaki pants, his more formal shirt now unbuttoned and a little askew, the sleeves rolled up just past his elbows. His dark hair hung over one eye, but I could see his gaze sweeping over me, taking me in. At least this time I wasn't wearing coffee-stained pajama pants. I'd put on what was essentially my uniform that morning—black leggings, black T-shirt, my long hair in a messy bun, and winged eyeliner because fuck it why not. Still, I resisted the urge to tug my shirt down, make sure it wasn't showing a flash of belly.

Not that I cared what he thought.

"I believe this is yours, Samuel," I said, holding out the box.

He paused for a moment before taking it. I couldn't help notice that behind him, his house was the same layout as my dad's but flipped, and a hell of a lot cleaner. There didn't seem to be any need to say anything else, so I turned to go. Then, from behind me, I heard a clearing of his throat, and a single word.

"What?" I asked, turning back.

"Sam," he said. "My name is just Sam."

"Well, *just Sam*," I said. "If you *just put* your house number on your mailbox, the mix-up probably wouldn't have happened."

That sounded really bitchy, the way it came out. I hadn't meant it to. But then again, how had I *thought* it would land, a criticism of this guy's mailbox, of all things? It had just been so unsettling, being back in my dad's house, and I felt on edge all the time. Still, there was no reason to take it out on this guy. If anything, it was a good idea to stay on your neighbors' good side. I'd read that story about the New Jersey family who received all those cryptic notes from "the Watcher" until eventually they had to move out.

I took a breath, and tried to start again.

"Thank you, by the way," I said. Even that came out grudging and a little churlish. I gestured vaguely toward my car, and his brows knitted together as he stared at me. "For helping with the desk."

He leaned against the doorway, and I tried to ignore that he was actually kind of hot. He was turning the box over and over in his hands, and the movement made the muscles of his forearms flex under the light dusting of dark hair. Maybe it was my recent celibacy talking, but I felt my palms going clammy.

"You're Phoebe," he said finally.

Okay, maybe he needed a new nickname. The Sidewalk Snoop. The Psychic Stalker. You'd have to say that one aloud to really get the alliterative effect, though.

He must've seen my confused expression, because he blew his hair out of his eyes, giving a self-deprecating shake of his head. Turned out his eyes were blue. "I was at the funeral," he said. "Back in January. I'm sorry about your dad."

Oh. I guessed that made sense—he would've been my dad's neighbor, after all. Still, the thought that he'd been there, that he'd had all that time to observe me and my family, before I even knew that he existed . . . it made me feel prickly and self-conscious. And sure, he had no reason to pay any particular attention to *me*. But I couldn't help but see myself as I'd been that day through a stranger's eyes, and I didn't like what I saw.

I'd looked like shit, for one thing. Conner and I, in a rare moment of sibling bonding, had decided to get drunk together the night before. We'd both rolled into the funeral hungover, but while Conner still looked like a human being, I looked like I was wearing Halloween makeup, I was so pale with purple circles under my eyes.

I'd also forgotten to pack the right shoes to go with my black dress, so I'd ended up wearing these gold sparkly pointy-toed flats that had been like a flashing neon sign in the midst of all the somber clothes. This, from a woman who dressed in black ninety-five percent of the time. I shouldn't have been able to fuck *that* part up, of all things.

The dress itself had been made of this draped, diaphanous gauze that looked ethereal on the size 2 model in the sponsored post. On me, it looked like I was carrying an entire dance troupe's costumes around my body. When I sat down, I worried people would throw dirty laundry on me.

But worse, perhaps, I didn't know if I'd looked . . . grief-stricken. The entire funeral had been a blur. My dad's death had come as a shock—he was still in his fifties, he was supposed to have plenty of time left. But the whole day had felt surreal, like I was in a dream, or in someone else's life. I hadn't known what to say or how to act, and so I'd just kind of shut down, retreated inside myself to the place I could always go as a kid when I needed some quiet.

And now people were always saying this kind of thing to me. My dissertation advisor, when she heard why I'd need to push our meeting back. A couple people in my program, when I let it slip at a board game night hosted by a professor and his partner. My landlord, when I'd told him why I was leaving for Florida.

This time it was Sam, saying the words he'd probably said to me at the funeral, too, although I didn't remember. I didn't know what to say now any more than I had then. *We weren't that close? Actually, he hadn't been a part of my life since I was a teenager? He wasn't that nice to me?*

"Thanks," I said instead, because it was the safest response, the one that most people wanted so we could move on to the next topic.

But Sam was looking at me, and for a minute I worried that it all showed on my face—my ambivalence, my guilt, my anger. I did a finger-gun gesture toward the box in his hands that would haunt me for the rest of my life.

"If that's a severed head, I'm going to be very upset," I said, and then, at his confused expression, I added, "That's a *Wayne's World* reference. Never mind."

He started to say something, but I was suddenly desperate to get out of there. So, before I could make the exchange any weirder, I turned on my heel and headed back.

OVER THE REST of the week, I didn't have much other opportunity to observe Sam further. His comings and goings were still baffling to me. He'd leave the house dressed in that same bland business casual attire—sometimes he was gone only for an hour or so, while other times he could be out half the day. On Wednesday a nondescript sedan parked in front of his house, but I missed seeing the person it belonged to either entering or exiting his house, so no leads there.

He was also up late most nights, almost as late as I was, if the lights in his windows were anything to go by. I knew it was none of my business, but that didn't stop me from becoming obsessed with figuring out the answers to things like *What does he do for his job?* or *What Myers-Briggs type is he?* I almost wished another package for him would be mistakenly delivered, just so I would have the opportunity to go over there again. But wonder of wonders, he'd actually taken my advice and stuck vinyl numbers to the side of his mailbox.

Regardless, I needed to buckle down and focus on my dissertation rather than the psychological profile of my neighbor. I owed another chapter to my advisor by the end of next week.

It hadn't been easy to convince the English department to let me study true crime in the first place. I still remembered the first time I'd ever stepped onto campus, for an interview and informational tour before I was technically accepted into the program.

The grad student showing me around had explained the course-work for the first few years, the way you branched out depending on if you were on a literature, rhetoric, or technical communication track, then the terror that was comps exams. After that, she said, her eyes lighting up, you could basically "study whatever you want."

What they'd really meant was you could study the emasculation of Hemingway's wounded characters or Faust allusions in *Lolita* or the intersection of composition and creative writing pedagogy.

But true crime was a genre like anything else, with conventions and expectations. It was nonfiction but never wholly objective, always instead reflecting trends or cultural reactions or public desires. I'd been fascinated with it since I was thirteen and had read *Helter Skelter* for the first time.

Which, incidentally, was the book at the heart of the chapter I was working on. I'd decided to focus on the relationship between author and subject in true crime, with sections on professional, personal, and familial relationships. When I'd first read *Helter Skelter*, a book subtitled *The True Story of the Manson Murders*, it hadn't even occurred to me to doubt any of its information or second-guess the author's motive in writing it. As the lead prosecutor, Bugliosi had practically *been there*, after all. It was still an amazing book, but you gotta think about the inherent bias of a dude writing a book literally defending the job he did in putting the criminals away.

My current problem was that I absolutely could not find my flagged, underlined copy I'd been working from. I tore through every box I'd brought from my apartment, double-checked that

I hadn't put it in my backpack to keep it that much closer to my heart, but came up empty.

There was a chance I still had my childhood copy in my room somewhere. I'd brought a lot of that stuff with me when my mom and I moved out, of course, but I'd kept enough stuff at my dad's to keep me entertained when I'd had to spend weekends there. A quick search of my bookshelves showed that I'd left all three books in the *Emily of New Moon* series and a giant tome on Rasputin I'd loved to lug around but never read, but no dice on the only book I needed.

I knew I could order another copy through some fast-delivering capitalist website, but something in me balked at spending another fifteen dollars on a book I'd already owned multiple copies of in my lifetime. I brought up the county library's online catalog and confirmed that they had the book sitting at my local branch. If I was going to be stuck here all summer, it would make sense to apply for a library card anyway. I went ahead and filled out all the information, using my dad's address as my own.

I'd just submitted the form when I heard a loud clatter outside. If this was the start of some Golden State Killer shit, it was probably not a great idea to go to the window to check out what it could be. But then again, presumably a serial killer would be a little more slick than going around neighborhoods dropping suitcases of wrenches or whatever that sound had been.

I tweaked the blinds to see Sam, emerging from his open garage. He was barefoot again, and holding his arms awkwardly out from his body. They appeared to be covered in . . . what *was* that? It was liquid, but in the darkness it was impossible to tell color. Could it be red? Could it be *blood*?

He went to open the door of his truck, then stopped when he realized his hands were covered in the liquid, too. He just stood there for a moment, the set of his shoulders expressively conveying the curses he was probably muttering under his breath, before turning to head back to the garage.

It was eleven o'clock at night. What the hell was he *doing*?

He emerged again, seeming cleaner this time, and using a rag to open his truck door. No fingerprints. Savvy.

(Although if the handle was *too* clean, wouldn't that look more suspicious? Since it was his own truck?)

When he pulled a roll of plastic dropcloth from his truck, I let the blinds fall closed and stepped away from the window. This was too weird. I knew I was a little jumpy, given how marinated I'd been in matter-of-fact descriptions of brutal crimes over the last year, but all I could think was how this scene would play out in the *Forensic Files* reenactment and it wasn't good. I hoped at least they cast a fat actress to play me. Representation was important.

Before I could think too hard about it, I dialed Conner's number, breathing a sigh of relief when he picked up with his usual cheerful hello.

"What do you know about this neighbor," I said, not really a question, as I tweaked the blinds again. Sam was nowhere in sight, but the light from his garage still spilled over his driveway. That had to be a good sign. He wouldn't be working in his *Dexter* room of plastic for the whole street to see, right?

"Pheebs," Conner said, "this again? Dude, chill."

I'd never been chill in my entire life. "His name is Sam Dennings," I said, then corrected myself, as though this were an official

background check and I needed to use his legal name. "*Samuel.*
Around my age, give or take a few years. Occupation unknown
but dresses like he works at a Verizon kiosk."

Conner sighed. "He just moved in around a year ago," he said.
"The whole time I lived there, the neighbors on that side were
that older couple who would groom their dogs in the driveway.
What were their names? They didn't like us, you could tell."

Randy and Viv. I remembered them now. They had two
bark-y Collies, and you knew when they'd recently been groomed
because tufts of their hair would float in the air for weeks afterward. And yeah, they'd low-key hated us. Probably because when
my parents were married there was a lot of yelling and not a lot of
landscaping going on.

"I didn't even know his name until you said it," Conner said.
"But he seems fine. You should be nice to him. We may need his
help moving stuff."

Even now that my dad was gone, I still had a visceral reaction
to the idea that anyone who wasn't family or an emergency HVAC
technician would ever set foot inside this house. Growing up, that
was always the way it had been. The only friend I'd ever been allowed to have over had been Alison, and that was only after I'd
cleaned half the house and promised we'd stay confined to my
room.

Given the way our friendship had ended, though, it was better
not to think about just how small my trusted circle had gotten
after my parents' divorce.

Over the line, I heard some muffled talking, and then Conner
was back. "Shani says hi," he said, and then apparently held the

phone up for her to speak, because I heard a distant, tinny "Hi, Phoebe!" and then some rustling and Shani's voice up close.

"I came across a book the other day and grabbed it for you," she said. "You don't have to read it, but I thought it might be helpful."

"Tell me it's *Helter Skelter* and I'll name my firstborn after you," I said.

She laughed, but I could tell it was more out of confusion than humor. "No, it's called"—more rustling, before she read out the title in a semitriumphant voice—"*Life after Loss: Teens Talk about Grief.* I know you're not a teen, obviously. But since I know that's also around the age you were when you and your dad were estranged . . ."

She trailed off, perhaps recognizing that she might've overstepped a boundary. I liked Shani. She was one of those people you described as *sweet* and meant it. But yeah, I didn't particularly want to talk about my dead father or the nonrelationship we'd had.

"Thanks," I said. That one word was doing a lot of heavy lifting lately.

"Well," she said. "I'll bring it when we come on Saturday. If you'd find it helpful."

Never in a million years would I read that book, and definitely not right now, when I only had time to read works I could lovingly format into MLA style. "Sure," I said. "Maybe Conner would want to borrow it first."

Shani hadn't been around me long enough to recognize when I was being tongue-in-cheek, but my brother definitely clocked it.

Apparently they were on speakerphone together. "*Conner* already has a reading list from his therapist," he put in.

"You're seeing a therapist?"

"Yeah, dude," he said. "You probably should be, too. It'd be a perfect place to talk shit about our parents and explore why you're so obsessed with this neighbor."

That made me flush, which I was grateful Conner couldn't see over the phone. "Not obsessed," I said. "Curious. Suspicious, even."

"Tomato, potato," Conner said. "If you'd really been worried you would've called nine-one-one instead of me."

Well. He had a point there. "There are other community numbers you can call before resorting to the police," I said stiffly. "I just wanted to ask you to pick up some boxes."

"Sure."

"I swear, that's the reason I called!"

"If you say so. I can get some."

"And not ones that say Smirnoff all over them, please," I said. "Real moving boxes, in a few different sizes."

My brother's pause was long enough that I knew absolutely he'd been planning to raid a liquor store dumpster. "I'll buy some boxes," he said. "But Phoebe?"

"Yeah?"

"*Chill.*"

And I would've had a snappy comeback to that, only he laughed and hung up. Apparently obnoxiousness aged in little brothers like a fine wine.

I glanced out the blinds one more time, but the street was dark. Even my mysterious neighbor had gone to bed.

FOUR

——————

PULLING UP TO the library the next day was an immediate kick to my nostalgic solar plexus. I'd gone there almost every Saturday when I was a kid, just to check out the Fear Street books again or see how much of a large-print Harlequin I could read before my mom caught me and yanked me out of the section. She should've been relieved that I was getting my sex education that way instead of porn.

It was a tall building, with all the kids' books, media, and fiction on the first floor, and all the nonfiction and computers on the second. By this point, I could zero in on true crime by Dewey Decimal or Library of Congress classification in five seconds flat. It wasn't long before I had *Helter Skelter* and was browsing the rest of the section, seeing if there was anything else that might be interesting. There was one book with the greasy plastic cover of a Waffle House place mat, the red font large and garish, that promised to be a tell-all from the daughter of a serial killer who'd been local to Central Florida in the 1980s. I didn't remember putting it on my bibliography for my section on familial relationships between author and subject, but it could be helpful.

In the end, I checked out three books, including those two and one on getting a house ready to sell that I'd probably flip through while eating dinner. I brought them to the front counter and started scrolling through my phone, looking for the email with the temporary number I was supposed to provide to get my library card.

"Oh my god," I heard. *"Phoebe Walsh?"*

I glanced up. The librarian was a pretty South Korean woman, her black hair cut into a chic chin-length bob, her red-framed glasses just this side of nerdy to make her look hip instead. Maybe it was how much more sophisticated she looked than when we'd been fifteen, or maybe it was the unexpectedness of how happy she seemed to be to see me, but it took me a second to place her.

"Alison," I said. "Wow. You work here?"

The fact that she was behind the counter was a dead giveaway, but I couldn't think of anything else to say.

"I got my master's in library science last year," she said. "Remember how we said we wanted to be librarians because we'd be so good at book recommendations?" She spread her hands wide, like all this could've been mine except for the elephant graveyard. "Well, now that's what I do. I love it."

Alison had always been one of the most organized people I knew, so I could totally see her as a librarian. But I couldn't tell if she remembered why we'd stopped being friends. She had to. It had been a pretty big deal at the time, at least to me. But the way she was acting now, it seemed like everything was fine, we were just two acquaintances catching up.

"Yeah," I said. "Cool."

To be fair, I was pretty sure I'd said I wanted to work at our local Barnes & Noble instead, because for some reason I had it in my head then that all librarians were unpaid volunteers. If I was going to recommend books to people, I wanted at least minimum wage. But then the bookstore conglomerate made me take a one-hundred-question personality quiz as part of the application process, and they never called me for an interview. The books I could've moved in the true crime section alone.

"What about you?" she said. "I didn't know you'd moved back. Or are you just visiting your dad?"

It was probably weird of me *not* to mention that he'd died. This was a girl I'd known for the formative years when I'd crushed on Joseph Gordon-Levitt so hard my stomach hurt. She'd known my dad, too, had eaten his signature Southern goulash and heard him yell at me for leaving the bread bag open.

But that was exactly why I didn't feel like getting into it. I couldn't put her off with a simple "Thanks."

"I'm just here for the summer," I said. "I applied for a library card online, actually. Do you need the code?"

A flicker of hurt crossed her face. "I can look it up by your last name," she said. "W-a-l-s-h?"

Okay, I guessed I deserved that. "Yup, that's it."

She was silent as she typed a few more things into the computer, then waited for my card. I was going to make some comment about how cool it was that they could print those on the spot, but it would either look like I was fishing for conversation because I felt bad about being short with her (which was true) or like I was easily impressed (also maybe true in this case).

Once the card was ready, she scanned it and then my three books, making no comment as to the subject matter. The consummate professional. "Here you go," she said. "You saved forty-nine dollars, eighty-nine cents by using the public library today."

I took the books and card and tried to give her a little, cautiously friendly smile. But she was already looking down at another stack she was sorting into piles. I thought we were done, that she was letting me know she could dismiss me as hard as I had her, but then I heard her voice again as I started to go.

"I was just worried about you, Phoebe," she said. Her hands rested on top of the books now, paused. She wore a wedding ring. At one point this girl had been my best friend and she'd gotten *married* at some point in the probably recent past and I hadn't even known. "I didn't mean to . . . well. You scared me."

The sudden lump in my throat made it hard to swallow. I wanted to say something, but my mind was a blank, the words physically stuck somewhere that I couldn't reach.

"You seem to be doing okay now," she said, looking up and giving me a small smile. I heard it for the question it was, and I could answer that at least, could get out a simple *Yes.*

But I couldn't. I gave her a jerky nod of my head, and left the library.

SEVERAL TIMES ON the drive home, I almost turned around and went back. I thought up a million different things I could've said. I could've told her about my dad. It felt weird that I hadn't. I could've told her that I wasn't mad at her, not anymore, that I understood why she'd done what she did. I could've apologized for letting us drift apart. I could've asked her about her wedding.

But instead my mind went around and around in circles, until the idea of going back seemed so pointless. I pulled into my driveway and shut off my car, leaning my forehead on the steering wheel while I thought about how I'd only been in town for a few days and already everything seemed so fucked up.

There was a guttural sound of a motor outside, loud and getting louder, and I lifted my head just in time to see Sam come around the corner on a ride-on lawn mower, wearing these giant goofy headphones. He made a path up to the edge of the backyard, then came back, passing by me just as I got out of the car. I stood there, my hands on my hips, while he did another complete strip of grass, up and back. Finally he must've seen the look on my face, because he brought the mower to a stop, the engine still idling, and slid the headphones off one ear.

"That's my yard!" I yelled over the rumble.

He tilted his head, squinting into the sun. "I know," he said.

"So why are you—" I gestured toward the grass. "Are you one of those guys who thinks women are incapable of using power tools? Or pushing a lawn mower? Or moving a desk? I didn't ask for your help, and at some point, it starts to feel kind of—"

He killed the engine, leaving enough silence for my last word to carry down the street and resonate through the neighborhood.

"Sexist!" I finished, then repeated under my breath, "I didn't *ask* for your help."

He brought the headphones down around his neck, leaning against the steering wheel of the mower. He really looked better than he had any right to. I reminded myself that the last time I'd seen him, he'd been covered in some mysterious substance that could've been blood and had been carrying plastic sheeting into his garage.

"I'm sorry," he said. "I used to mow for your dad, when I did my yard. And then after he . . . well, I've kept doing it. But I should've asked you. I'm sorry."

Lately it felt like my entire life was one big AITA thread and the answer was always yes, it's me, I'm the asshole.

"No, it's not—" I rubbed my forehead. "You used to mow my dad's yard for him?"

"He got tired easily," Sam said. "This was a few months before the heart attack, and I don't know if it was connected or not. But he was having a little more trouble getting around."

I hadn't known that.

"You can borrow the lawn mower, if you'd rather do it yourself," he said.

"Not me," I said. "I'd just as soon let the whole yard become Area X. But if mowing makes you happy, go for it. I'll stay out of your way."

There was an opening, maybe, where I could've asked what he was up to the night before. I could've worked it in real casual, like, *By the way, I heard a crash last night from your garage . . . everything okay? Is there a tip line I should call?* But then he was putting his headphones back on and giving me a little salute, and all I could do was disappear into the house.

NOW THAT I had the book I'd been looking for the night before, I should've probably sat my ass at my writing desk and typed out

another three thousand words of analysis on Bugliosi's role as prosecutor and truth teller in the Manson case. But instead, I tossed
the books on the kitchen table and headed back to my bedroom.

I opened my closet doors and stood on tiptoe until I saw it.
The Converse All Stars shoebox I kept with a bunch of notes
from Alison we'd exchanged in eighth grade, all folded in intricate little rectangles with a pull tab to unfurl them for reading.
Her bubbly handwriting, almost always in pink or purple or teal
gel pen, was immediately familiar.

The first one I grabbed featured a doodle of the lasagna they'd
served at lunch that day. I'd been weirdly obsessed with that lasagna, I remembered now. I used to pay extra to get a second one
and take it home to reheat for dinner. That year, I'd been making
a lot of Easy Mac and tuna sandwiches for me and Conner. It was
funny how you forgot all about that kind of thing, until you saw a
sparkly pink doodle of a steaming square of lasagna, and it all
came flooding back.

*You HAVE TO ask your mom if you can come to the movies Friday
night. Stephen is going to be there. I know you said you didn't like
him anymore, but...*

I unfolded another one, which featured large bubble letters
taking up six whole lines, colored in rainbow stripes. *I'M BORED!!!!*

Another one: *You ask the most morbid would you rather questions
lol. I guess I'd pick drowning, too. I think it's faster than fire?*

And another: *Sorry I didn't call you back. My mom wanted to watch
Friends together again. You ever seen the one where Joey puts on all
Chandler's clothes? So funny!*

I shoved the notes back in the box without bothering to fold them all back up. Alison and I had the same science class, which was where we'd done most of our clandestine correspondence. Just handling the paper pulled me back to that classroom—the black Formica tables where we sat in groups of four, the chemical smell that never went away, the glare from the fluorescent lights on Mr. Ford's bald head.

For the first few years after my mom and I moved out, we hadn't gone too far. We'd stayed in the county, just in an apartment farther east. When I went back to my dad's every other weekend, it took us only twenty-five minutes to get there.

Still, twenty-five minutes could be the difference between best friends forever and barely acquaintances when you didn't drive yet. Alison and I had done our best to stay in touch, mostly by texting or through the phone, and I tried to see her in person when I could. But it wasn't the same.

I also always had the feeling that her parents didn't like her hanging out with me as much once my parents got divorced. Alison's parents had doted on her—I don't know if it was an only-child thing, or an adopted-child thing, or simply the right combination of neurotic parents with a child who never gave them any actual trouble. But they were very protective. They didn't like Alison watching Disney Channel shows because they said that there weren't strong enough parental figures in them.

And then there had been the Incident.

I'd been spending the weekend at my dad's. Pretty much that meant I was holed up in my room, switching between fan fiction and Murderpedia tabs while I messaged back and forth with Alison. I didn't even know how it had come up, but I'd made some joke about how I was going to swallow a bottle of pills.

Obviously, I know now that it's really insensitive and shitty to joke about something like that. But at the time, I'd meant it as a dramatic way to say I was bored, or restless, or sick of something. It definitely hadn't been an actual *plan*.

But I guessed something made Alison take it that way. She called my mom, my mom called my dad, and not long after that I'd convinced my mom that maybe I didn't need to go over to my dad's twice a month, or even at all.

I shouldn't have made the joke. I knew that. And Alison had been trying to be a good friend. But I couldn't help but be angry at the way she'd reacted—the way she'd *over*reacted, in my mind—and the sequence of events it had set in motion. Maybe that wasn't fair. It didn't change the way I'd felt then.

I closed the box and put it back up on the closet shelf. I'd look through it later, when I went through the room to clean it out. For now, I didn't have the energy to excavate any more of the past.

FIVE

M Y ADVISOR HAD wanted to have a call before I turned in my next chapter, so after I'd worked on weaving a few more quotes and examples throughout, I emailed her to set up a time. To my surprise, she got back to me right away with Now works for me.

Dr. Nilsson was intimidating as hell. She'd taught that first-year bibliography class we all had to take, and had a reputation for taking absolutely no shit. I'd seen her glance at her watch while you were rambling around a point. I'd seen some of the most articulate scholars I knew—people who made me feel like an imposter, like there'd been some mix-up in the mail system and someone had sent Billy Madison to grad school—start stammering and going red in the face as they lost the thread of their argument under her withering stare. Her expertise was in Virginia Woolf, and our final project had been a scavenger hunt around the university library to find answers to all these esoteric questions about Woolf texts, like how many copies of this were in existence or what edition contained this annotation or where were the original letters she wrote to this person housed.

I'd barely eked out the B-minus I needed in the class to keep my GPA up, but she had once written on a response paper of mine that it was *freewheeling* in a way that seemed like a compliment. So when I was searching the department for someone— *anyone*—who might be willing to let me study true crime for my dissertation, she'd come to mind.

"Dr. Nilsson, hi," I said, adjusting my earbuds to make sure the mic part was close enough to my mouth. The longer I'd known Dr. Nilsson, the more I suspected that some of her *what are you talking about* faces in class were due to hearing difficulties rather than just her being difficult. "It's Phoebe Walsh."

"Phoebe," she said in her cool, cutting voice. "I understand you have another chapter for me. What did you want to discuss?"

This was what she did every time, without fail. She asked me for a call, and then immediately put me on the spot, as though I'd asked for it. This set me up beautifully for inevitably disappointing her with my inarticulate and ill-thought-out questions. I could almost hear her thinking, *Why did she call for a meeting if she wasn't prepared?*

"Well," I said, searching for something that hopefully sounded reasonably intelligent. "I really focus on Bugliosi's book in this one—remember, he was the prosecutor in the Manson trial. But I didn't know if I should weave in my analysis of the Gacy book, the one written by his defense lawyer, to contrast their approaches. Or if I should include more from the book by the prosecutor in the Avery case. That one editorializes so much more, it's wild, but I guess that's what happens when Nancy Grace writes your foreword—"

"I'll have to read it," Dr. Nilsson said, cutting me off. "And then I can give you more feedback on your approach."

It took all my strength not to say *That's exactly why I didn't need this call in the first place.* Instead, I just clicked "send" on the email with the draft attached. "Okay," I said. "Sounds good. You should have the draft in your inbox."

"Excellent," she said, but she already sounded distracted. "Now let's talk about your job application materials. What do you have ready—your CV, your teaching philosophy, sample student syllabi and assignments . . . ?"

How much did I have *ready*? None of it. I had a Russian nesting doll of folders on my computer for classes I'd taught, and could dig through those for my best syllabi and assignments, hopefully the ones that were the least plagiarized from other people who'd taught the course before me. I had a CV that I used when submitting to conferences, but it needed some work to get it ready for the job market. I didn't even want to think about writing a teaching philosophy. Those scared the hell out of me.

Outside, I heard the rumble of Sam's truck. I'd only been here a few days, but already the sound of his comings and goings felt familiar, if unpredictable. I looked through the blinds to see him hauling a truly unnecessary amount of bagged ice into his house. Interesting.

I must've been silent for too long, because Dr. Nilsson cut in impatiently. "You *are* planning to go on the market for next year?"

"Yeah," I said, letting the blinds drop. "I mean, yes. I hope to. A job's always good, right?"

I'd forgotten for a moment that of all Dr. Nilsson's truly brilliant qualities, a sense of humor wasn't one of them. "Do you have geographic limitations?"

These were all the questions I knew were coming at the end of my six-year time in the academic cocoon. I'd had that entire time to think about them, I supposed. But now my mind went blank— my only brother was in Florida, my mother and her new husband had moved to Georgia, I'd been living in North Carolina for the last five years to go to grad school. Did I feel an attachment to any of those places?

"Not really," I said. "No."

Something about Dr. Nilsson's questioning made me feel restless, and I went to check the mail just for something to do while we talked. The oppressive humidity assaulted me the minute I stepped outside. Sam was already back in his house, presumably dumping all that ice into coolers. I tried not to think of Jeffrey Dahmer, but at this point it was a reflex.

My other neighbor's cat—or what I assumed was her cat, since it had been in her driveway the night I'd arrived—was now lying across the Spanish tile of my front step, as if trying to keep cool. I almost stopped to say hello before remembering I was still on the phone, and would probably sound insane. Still, I tried to give her a little nod of acknowledgment, stepping over the cat and shutting the door behind me so it didn't go inside.

"Remind me," Dr. Nilsson continued, "whether you have anyone in your life?"

Considering that a cat was the first strange creature who'd inspired true friendliness since I got here, I was inclined to say *no*. And then I realized Dr. Nilsson meant whether I had anyone *romantically* in my life, which was more a *hell no*.

"Not right now."

"Good." It was the first time I heard her sound truly pleased the entire call. "Keep your options open. It's the best way to ensure you have a high chance of landing somewhere."

"Definitely," I said absently. Everything in my dad's mailbox was junk. Coupons, an urgent notice about his car insurance that I could tell was just an ad, and a local circular that featured a front-page story about a kid who'd won a statewide songwriting contest.

"So you're moving on to the next section?" Dr. Nilsson prompted. "This is where you'll discuss Capote more, if I remember your proposal."

The cat was still stretched across the front step. She tilted her head back and squinted up at me as I approached the door, almost as if she wanted some attention.

"That's right," I said, kneeling down to give her a tentative scratch under her chin. I had no way of knowing how feral this cat was—whether she was a stray or a domesticated outside cat or a neighborhood mascot. She was small, not quite a kitten but maybe an adolescent cat, and black with white paws and a white underside, like a little tuxedo. "There will be a whole chapter focusing more on *In Cold Blood* and how close Capote got to Perry and Dick, how that relationship influenced his narrative and the true crime genre as a whole. Then I'm going to have a chapter about Ann Rule's book about Ted Bundy, *The Stranger Beside Me*, where she describes the time she worked with Bundy at a Seattle crisis clinic. It's interesting actually, because—"

"I'm glad to hear you have a plan," Dr. Nilsson said. "I received your latest chapter in my inbox, and you can expect my notes in the next week. And if you wanted to send me your draft application materials, I'd be happy to take a look."

"Oh," I said. "Okay."

It was a generous offer. I had several friends whose advisors were looking over their job stuff for them, but in most cases it was because they'd worked together for years. In many cases, it was because their research was tied together—they'd coauthored a paper, or presented at a conference, or the professor had introduced them to some professional contact or another.

In my case, despite working with Dr. Nilsson on what was arguably the biggest project of my life to date, we didn't really *know* each other that well. I didn't think Dr. Nilsson considered me a protégé or anything.

"Talk later," she said, and then she hung up.

The cat was still letting me pet her, purring slightly. She didn't have a collar, but she definitely wasn't wild. "*You* were interested in hearing more about Ted Bundy," I murmured to the cat. "After Ann visited him in prison for the first time, she had this dream where she had to save a baby, only the baby turned out to be a demon that bit her hand. Very *Rosemary's Baby*, if you ask me. Which connects back to Roman Polanski, then to Sharon Tate, and back to Manson . . ."

The cat gave a skeptical twitch of her whiskers.

"I know," I said. "I'm reaching."

CONNER AND SHANI surprised me that night by showing up with burritos for dinner. I would never admit it, but I was beyond grateful not only for the food but also for the company. Already a few days in this house was inching me dangerously close to REDRUM territory.

The only problem with hanging out with them as a couple (besides the sometimes sickening levels of PDA) was that I was scared to death I'd blurt out something about the marriage proposal. I wished Conner had never even told me, because now I kept thinking about it at all these different junctions in the conversation. They were talking about going to another baseball game, and I almost made a remark like, *Please tell me you're not going to propose over the jumbotron.* Shani made a comment about not looking forward to some assignment she had to finish up, and I thought about telling her at least she had *something* to look forward to, with a wink. I never winked. This secret was eating me alive.

"Pheebs?" Clearly, Conner had been trying to get my attention for a while.

"Hmm?"

"I asked if you thought we should get a dumpster," he said. "You know, to help get rid of a lot of this . . ." He glanced around, as though no word in the English language could quite encompass what he was looking at. Finally, he settled on an anticlimactic ". . . stuff."

"How much do those cost?" One effect of talking to Dr. Nilsson earlier had been that it had sent me on another spiral about my finances, thinking about how much the process of even *applying* to jobs was going to cost me. The document sites for me to upload my materials, the cost of any interviews that didn't pay to fly you out, I'd probably need a nice blazer . . .

"I should get my first paycheck this Friday," Conner said. "I can pay for it."

"We'll split it at least," I said. There was some big-sister part of me that still found it hard to let my little brother take that on all by himself, even though it would've been a relief not to worry about it.

He shrugged.

"He's doing so great at his job," Shani said to me, as though this were a parent-teacher conference. "You got your calls to what, eight minutes?"

"Seven and a half," he said around a bite of burrito, "and that's not *good*. I've still got a long way to go."

"Can't you make a little more small talk," I said, "pad the numbers a little? You've always been good at that, just talking to strangers."

Conner swallowed, rolling his eyes at both of us. "The calls are supposed to be *shorter*," he said. "You're ranked on efficiency, and every hour they want you to do nine calls averaging six minutes and fifteen seconds apiece. That leaves almost four minutes an hour for a break, but you just save them all up at once and then you can take a fifteen-minute break every four hours."

I glanced at Shani, who was smiling encouragingly at Conner.

"That's . . . a lot of numbers," I said.

Conner shrugged. "They gave me a laminated printout to keep at my station," he said. "So I don't have to do the math myself."

"How do you like it?"

"It's great," he said. "They gave me a water bottle with the company logo on it. If you work there for a year you get a T-shirt."

"Well," I said. "Keep grinding."

"It's what I do best," Conner said. "Remember how we played Heavy Machinery over and over, just to get enough lives to tackle the harder levels toward the end?"

It took me a second to track what he was talking about. Then he pointed down to the Crash Bandicoot tattoo on his calf, a goofy grin on his face, and I closed my eyes. Of course.

"It was mostly Slippery Climb," I said. "It was about a billion years before they gave you a checkpoint."

"But there was High Road, too," Conner said. "That level was a bitch."

Shani glanced between the two of us. "I'm assuming this is a video game."

"This is *the* video game," Conner said, "that started it all."

From Shani's nonplussed expression, I wasn't sure that was the endorsement Conner seemed to think it was.

"Oh," she said, springing up from her seat on the couch. "I brought that book I was telling you about."

She rummaged through her oversized purse, coming up with a slim book with a black-and-white cover and the font choice of a church brochure. It was also obviously meant for an even younger audience than I had imagined, more preteen than teen. It seemed inappropriate to my situation for a number of reasons, and I had a visceral negative reaction to what on closer inspection was definitely Brush Script MT with a shadow effect. But Shani had been sweet to think of me, and she was about to be family soon. I accepted it with a smile.

"I read a few pages on the way over and it's really powerful,"

Shani said, glancing over at Conner as if for encouragement. "I think you'll find a lot to identify with."

That glance told me a lot. It told me that they'd discussed this, that they'd discussed *me*, and I could only imagine what conclusions they'd drawn. Conner had been only six when our parents divorced, only eight when I'd stopped coming back to my dad's house every other weekend. So if he thought he had some insight into how I might feel about losing my father, who'd already been lost to me for years before, I'd love to hear it.

Shani gave me a sad smile, and all the energy fizzled out of my anger. It really had been thoughtful of her to think of me, even if I didn't like the idea that she and Conner were somehow conspiring to get me "help." I flipped through the pages as if I was semi-interested in what they might have to say.

"I'll put it on my reading pile," I said. "Right after the memoir by the Sunrise Slayer's daughter. You remember that one, Conner? He was linked to at least eight murders around Central Florida in the eighties."

Conner shook his head. "That was before my time," he said. "And I don't watch black-and-white television."

I rolled my eyes. "It was before my time, too, jackass," I said. "But it happened close to here—just over an hour north. You could've still heard about the guy."

"I just collected Pokémon cards like a normal person," Conner said. "Speaking of normal people, is the neighbor having a party or something? There were a bunch of cars out front."

I jumped up to check the window. Sure enough, there were three new cars packed onto his driveway, and several more lining the street halfway around the circle. All my vigilance, and I'd completely missed this whole development.

"Well, that explains the ice," I murmured.

I turned just in time to see Conner giving Shani a *speaking* look. First they'd had their little exchange over the book, and now this. I couldn't let it go. "What?"

"Nothing," he said, his eyes wide.

"Conner thinks you're fixating on the neighbor as a way to deal with all the change in your life," Shani said at the same time.

Conner gave her a *thanks a lot* look that would've been more effective if he hadn't still had taco sauce smeared around his mouth. "I never said that. I said my therapist *suggested* that might be one explanation for Phoebe's focus, but—"

I held my hands up, as if warding off the whole conversation. Now he was discussing me with his *therapist?* Jesus.

"Both you and Dr. Freud are making a much bigger deal out of this than it is," I said. "We had a couple weird interactions, okay? It's natural that I would want to look out for myself. I'm a single female, living alone."

"Okay, but . . ." Conner wrinkled his nose in a supremely annoying look of little-brotherly doubt. "Weird because *he* was weird, or because you were?"

"Hey, he's the one who—" I realized that I had no way to finish that sentence that helped my cause. He'd moved my desk for me, politely accepted a misdelivered package, mowed the lawn. It was hardly the Macdonald triad.

There was still that night he'd been doing something in his garage. A mysterious liquid on his hands. The plastic dropcloth from his car. None of that would make him the most careful killer ever, but there had been blood all over the Ford Bronco and O.J. still got off.

"It doesn't matter," I said. "I won't be needing to borrow a cup of sugar anytime soon, and if I do, there's always the cat lady on the other side."

"Pat's still there?" Conner said. "She always reminded me of the grandma in *Napoleon Dynamite*. She'd be out in her yard throwing bread to the birds, like, *I'm doing this for your own good! Eat up, you little shits!*"

"If you think about it," I said, "she has all those outside cats and still encourages the birds to come. Pretty dark."

"I hadn't thought of it that way," Conner said, making a face. "But listen. The point is, we know you're isolated out here. We hate the idea of you worrying or feeling unsafe."

He reached out to grasp Shani's hand, and that was honestly the first clue that the "we" in his sentence had been him and his girlfriend, rather than him and his therapist. It saved me from having to have a serious talk about boundaries, at least.

"And that's why we've decided," Shani said, glancing at him as if for support, "that we're going to move in here, too. That way you won't be so alone."

I had no idea what my face was doing. In my mind, my eyes were wide with disbelief, my mouth opening and closing like a fish, my nostrils flaring with a barely contained exasperation. But outwardly, I must have been maintaining some semblance of control, because my brother was grinning at me like they'd just presented me with the greatest gift.

And objectively, it was very well-meaning of them. Very kind. It was true that I'd moved back to a town where I didn't really know anyone—except Alison, which was a relationship best left buried under old issues of *Teen Beat*. And it was true that there was a lot of work ahead with the house, work that I'd sometimes wished Conner would be around more to help with.

But it was also true that if I had to live with Conner and Shani, I would go out of my fucking mind.

"Well," I said, choosing my words carefully. "I appreciate that offer, but—"

"It would be for a couple of months while we got the house ready to sell," Conner cut in to reassure me. "We only have a month left on our apartment lease, and we can put our stuff in storage before we sign a new one."

"Except for the bed, of course," Shani pointed out.

"Yeah, we're not sleeping on the *floor*," Conner said. "And we need the Xbox and PlayStation." He looked at me hopefully. "Unless you brought your own?"

I rubbed my temples, giving the slightest shake of my head.

"That's okay," he said. "Mine has all the cool stuff loaded on it. And Shani has this statue of a Buddha that's really personally meaningful to her—"

"I'm not Buddhist," Shani said sheepishly, "but my cross-country coach in high school gave it to me, and she said—"

"It's not *huge*," Conner put in, "like, it could easily fit in the corner of the living room if we moved those bins of Christmas stuff. Oh, and we'll also bring Hank, of course, but he takes up almost no room, just any flat surface that can handle ten pounds—"

"Ten *gallons*," Shani corrected, "which is closer to eighty pounds. But babe, we can always bring the table we have Hank on now . . ."

This was getting out of hand. "Who is Hank?"

The room fell silent as both Conner and Shani looked at me, the expression on their faces almost like . . . betrayal. Like they couldn't believe I would even ask that question and I had a lot to learn, honey.

"Hank is our goldfish," Conner said. "We won him at the county fair last year?"

"They say those ones never last," Shani said, "but Hank's hardy."

"Well, and we take care of him," Conner said. "Most people just feed their fish any old flakes, but we've been ordering—"

"Okay, stop," I said. "Hank is not moving in here."

That sounded harsh, and unfairly prejudiced against the fish. In fact, Hank had the best chance of moving in here of the three of them. I started over. "It's not that I don't appreciate the offer. I do. I'll need your help with the house for sure, and I'm really . . ." Ugh, the next part was as close to touchy-feely as I got, and I felt the words lodge in my throat. ". . . loving getting the chance to get to spend more time with both of you. But I have this dissertation to work on, and I really need a lot of peace and quiet for that, and—"

Conner frowned. "But that's what I'm talking about. You're holed up in here, reading about grisly murders and then getting paranoid about your neighbor . . ."

"I'm not paranoid!" I said. "And it's not about the neighbor. Whose name is Sam, by the way."

"I remember," Conner said. "I believe your exact words the other day were, 'Sam, comma, Son of.'"

"That was a *joke*," I said. "Obviously I don't think my neighbor is an actual serial killer. First of all, there aren't even any unsolved murders around here that appear connected. And second of all . . ."

Conner raised his eyebrows, waiting. I could tell he hadn't been impressed with my first piece of evidence, although he should be. That had taken some research to find out. So maybe I was still reaching, desperate for something convincing enough to get Conner and Shani to drop this whole idea of *living* here, because I said, "I mean, would I go to a serial killer's house party?"

SIX

FIVE MINUTES LATER, all three of us were standing on Sam's doorstep, me in front and Shani and Conner hanging behind me. We'd already rung the doorbell once, but from the faint strains of whatever luau music was playing inside, I figured Sam must not have heard the sound.

"Is this a themed party?" Conner asked from behind me. "Should we have dressed up?"

"I don't know," I said, shifting the bag of Kit Kats I was holding to my left hand so I could ring the bell again, really depressing the button for a few seconds before letting it go.

"Well, what did he say when he invited you?"

From inside, I could hear someone give a shout that someone was at the door. "Shhh," I hissed to Conner.

"Oh my god, we're party crashers," Conner said just as the door swung open.

Sam's eyes widened for a moment at the sight of the three of us, but I thrust the Kit Kats into his arms before he could say anything. "Hey," I said, feeling suddenly nervous. "We heard the music from next door and . . ."

I trailed off. It *was* a themed party. Everyone was dressed in loud-patterned shirts and drinking out of plastic pineapples. Sam's shirt was bright pink with white flowers on it. That coupled with the day's growth on his jaw gave him a bit of a *Miami Vice* look, but I didn't hate it.

"Did you need me to turn it down?" he asked.

"Oh," I said, "no. It's fine. We actually . . ."

To my surprise, Sam stepped onto the front porch, closing the door behind him. I had to back up to keep my personal space, which made me tread upon Conner's foot, which made Conner yelp in a tableau of melodrama. Without saying another word, Sam stalked over to my driveway, where he stood for a minute, his head tilted, as if listening.

"Ow," Conner said loudly, as if unsatisfied with my reaction to his plight.

"Oh, come on," I hissed back, still watching Sam. "I barely got you."

"You're wearing *combat boots*."

I glanced down at his feet. "And you're wearing *flip-flops*, which should teach you to cover your toes better. Nobody needs to see that."

"At least I'm on theme," he grumbled. "What is he doing?"

To be honest, I had no idea. Sam had moved closer to my house, standing just in front of the door while we continued to stand just in front of his. Finally he walked back over to us.

"You must have really good ears," he said, but he was frowning down at the Kit Kats, as if there was something troubling about the idea. Then he glanced up, taking in Conner and Shani before turning his attention back to me. "Sorry. I did a lot of soundproofing to the garage, so I thought it would dampen the music enough. Did you guys want to come in, have a drink?"

He went inside, leaving the door open for us to follow, but Conner stopped me with a hand on my arm. "Phoebe," he said. "Dude. *Soundproofing?*"

"Told you," I said, and then we went inside the house.

THE FIRST THING I noticed was that Sam did have a piano in the little nook in the living room that seemed perfect for one. I bet he didn't even *play* the piano, just liked the impression it gave that he was the kind of guy who would. But then there was a big banner hanging on the wall above it—WE'LL MISS YOU, BARBARA!—and that was a little harder for me to parse.

"Where do you think Barbara's going?" Shani asked.

"The crawlspace?" I suggested, and Conner and I both cracked up. We were still laughing when Sam appeared, juggling a few cans of LaCroix before handing them out.

"Sorry we don't have any soda," he said, "but—" He gestured vaguely at the tropical decorations, which upon closer inspection seemed to mostly be a corrugated cardboard border with little palm trees on it that had been hung up around the room. "The alcoholic stuff is in the kitchen. I figured you'd want to fix your own drink."

His gaze slid to me briefly when he said that, and then away. From across the room, someone called his name, and I waited until he was definitely out of earshot before I turned to Conner and winced.

"I think he may have heard us," I said.

"So?" Conner traded cans with Shani, so she had strawberry and he had orange, and then he opened his with a loud *pop*.

I chewed on my bottom lip while I watched Sam move through the crowd of people, stopping to talk to a couple before disappearing into the kitchen. Despite what Conner said, I felt a fluttery, anxious guilt low in my stomach at the idea that I was being an asshole yet again. This time, crashing his party and then immediately talking shit. I handed Conner my unopened LaCroix, because he could down two in the time it took me to even wrap my head around willingly drinking flavored hair spray, and headed to the kitchen.

Sam was reaching for a bowl in the top cabinet, the action revealing a strip of skin between his jeans and the bottom of his shirt, a fine line of hair leading to his navel. By the time he'd set the bowl on the counter and flicked his hair out of his eyes, startling a little when he saw me there, my entire face felt warm and I worried my pale skin was turning a betraying pink. I glanced over, and saw through the kitchen window to a swimming pool in the backyard. A few people were gathered around it, some sitting at the edge with their feet dangling in the water.

"You have a pool," I said stupidly. What I meant was, *Can I submerge myself and only come up when everyone has left, including you?*

He followed my gaze. "Yeah," he said. He tore open the bag of Kit Kats with his teeth and dumped the individually wrapped candy bars into the bowl. He gave the bowl a little shake, as if adjusting the presentation of the candy, and then set it on the counter next to some chips and dip.

"You really shouldn't do that," I said before I could stop myself, and his brows drew together, his hand remaining on the bowl as if waiting to commit to the placement. I shook my head, wondering for the eight millionth time what my specific problem was. "I mean opening stuff with your teeth—it's not good for your dental health. I'd tell you a harrowing story about a girl in second grade involving a fruit roll-up, but it's not really a good party anecdote."

He just stared at me, which was somehow my cue to keep going.

"To be fair, her tooth was loose anyway. So." I grabbed a Kit Kat from the bowl, just for something to do with my hands. After giving him such a hard time about the way he'd opened the bag, of course this one wrapper had to be made of Teflon. I twisted and pulled, but I couldn't get the stupid thing open. Finally, I gave up. "Actually, I guess that's the whole story. There's not much else to it."

His lips parted slightly, like he was going to say something. Instead, he grabbed a Kit Kat, opening it easily before popping one bite-size stick in his mouth. The bastard.

It turned out that it's almost uncomfortably intimate to just watch someone chew. And yet for some reason, I couldn't look away, and so we just stayed locked in that moment in the kitchen. His blue eyes swept my face from my too-high forehead to my pointed chin, lingering on my mouth for a beat so minuscule I wondered if I'd imagined it. In the background, "Don't Worry Baby" by the Beach Boys was playing, and I realized I was holding my breath.

He swallowed. "How's the desk?"

Now it was my turn to stare, his question rattling in my head but for some reason not able to land.

He raised an eyebrow. "Heavy? Wood? Very 'Tell-Tale Heart'?"

"Oh," I said. "That desk. It's . . . inert."

I hadn't realized he'd been opening another Kit Kat while we were talking, but he held it out to me, still in its wrapper but open at one end. I took it, feeling as inert as the furniture we were talking about, and his eyes crinkled around the edges.

"Good," he said. "Let's hope it stays that way."

I FOUND CONNER and Shani in a corner, talking with a bearded guy wearing a truly eye-watering shade of orange. Conner waved me over when he saw me.

"Pheebs!" he said. "It turns out I've played *League of Legends* with this dude for three years, isn't that wild? He's a friend of Dan's, who added me to his server, and then even after Dan left, I stuck around because those guys could *play*." Shani cleared her throat pointedly, and Conner rushed to add, "And girls! I mean, there were no girls on that team—*that I know of*, obviously—but girls can game, too, and I'm not looking to spread any toxic gamergate bullshit otherwise." Shani elbowed him, and he said, "Anyone can game, wherever they are on the gender spectrum! It doesn't have to be a binary thing, either."

The orange-shirt guy laughed and held out his hand. "Josue," he said. "Do you guys know Barbara?"

"Not exactly . . ." I said. I realized that my motivation in seeking out Sam earlier had been to apologize for crashing his party, and instead I'd only rambled about his pool and dental horror stories.

"Sam is her neighbor," Conner filled in.

"Well, kind of," I felt the need to clarify. "It's our dad's house. He died, and we're getting it ready to sell, so . . ." And yeah, I realized about three words in that there would be no reason for Josue to care about any of that.

"I'm sorry to hear about your dad," Josue said, managing to sound sincere while also segueing immediately to a more emotionally stabilizing topic. It was so well done I wanted to applaud. "When are you thinking of putting the house on the market?"

"Hopefully soon," I said, even while Conner said, "Within a month, if Phoebe will accept our help."

I rolled my eyes at that—I had no issue with accepting his *help*, if that meant he would show up this weekend with a go-getter attitude to recycle every magazine that predated the *CSI* franchise. I just didn't need him and Shani up in my space.

"Well, I'd love to take a look," Josue said. "Hit me up in the chat when it's ready."

"Really?" Conner said, looking at me with a triumphant expression, as if he'd just single-handedly sold the house right then and there.

"*Really?*" I said. "It's a fixer-upper, you know."

Josue shrugged. "Sam's a good dude, and I wouldn't mind living next door to him. Plus, he has it sweet, living so close to the school."

"The school?" Shani asked curiously. I'm glad she did, because I definitely would have framed the question in a way that made it seem more accusatory.

"Yeah," Josue said, taking a pull of his beer. "Sam teaches music at the elementary school down the road. I teach fourth-graders about math, science, and some basic hygiene when I'm brave enough to try. Most of us in this room teach there—we're all here for Barbara's retirement."

Okay. That explained so much, although I was still reeling a little at the idea that Sam was an elementary school teacher. I had not seen that coming. And just then, "Wouldn't It Be Nice" came on, and I realized it had been nothing but Beach Boys songs since we got there, and another piece clicked into place.

"Let me guess," I said. "Barbara Ann."

"Yes!" Josue said, genuinely delighted. "She'll love that you made that connection. Hang on, let me find her. Barb!"

Before I could protest, he was already halfway across the room, getting the attention of an older woman in a voluminous flowered muumuu that looked comfy as hell.

"Aw," Conner said. "You're making friends."

"At least this one's in her sixties," I muttered, "which is a lot more my speed."

"You were talking to Sam for a bit, too," Conner pointed out. "What did you talk about?"

I regretted not grabbing a replacement drink when I was in the kitchen. Even the LaCroix was starting to look good to me. "Teeth."

Shani's lip curled in what appeared to be an involuntary expression of *Girl, you're a lost cause.* Conner almost spit out his sparkling toilet water.

"Not Ted Bundy's teethmark evidence," he said. "Please for the love of Neo Cortex tell me you didn't whip out your phone to show him the trial pictures."

"I'm not completely feral," I said irritably. "I know how to behave at a party. In my next life I'm coming back as an expert witness, that's all I'm going to say. God knows I'd make more money."

Conner rolled his eyes at that. "So, Sam's a teacher, huh? What does that do to your serial killer theory?"

"Nothing," I said. "Equating an occupation's projected societal ethos with an individual's personal morality is one reason why our police force is so fucked in this country."

"So in other words, neighbor threat *not* neutralized."

I shrugged. Out of the corner of my eye, I was aware of Sam standing in another group, facing us, but I didn't dare turn my head. I didn't know why it even mattered to me, to know if he was paying attention, if he was as attuned to where I was in the room as I couldn't help but be of him.

"But okay," I said grudgingly. "Maybe he does actually play that piano."

———

BARBARA TURNED OUT to be the fifth grade language arts teacher I wished I'd had, and once Josue had introduced us, we spent an enjoyable twenty minutes talking about the Harry Potter books and what a shame it was that the author was such a

TERF. I congratulated Barbara on her retirement, and she showed me pictures of the grandkids she was moving to Indiana to be closer to.

We were in the middle of an energized conversation about the three-paragraph essay when suddenly the never-ending Beach Boys were turned way down. I glanced up to see Sam standing at the front of the room, tapping a plastic fork uselessly against the side of his beer bottle.

"Uh," he said, and someone in the crowd encouraged him to climb up on a chair to give a speech. To my surprise, he did. No way would you ever catch me trusting all my weight and balance to a regular old dining chair, much less in front of a roomful of people.

Now I had to crane my neck to see Sam, but I liked this arrangement—where I could feel free to observe as openly as I wanted, because everyone's attention was supposed to be focused on him. He shouldn't be that attractive, objectively speaking. His nose was crooked and a little too big for his face, his hair skated a fine line between bedhead and bedraggled, and the hot pink of his shirt gave me corneal flash burns.

And yet there was something about him that made me want to figure him out.

"Thank you all for coming," he said now. "And thank you, Terry, for tenting your house just in time to force the location change."

A few chuckles and titters from the crowd, and an older dude I assumed to be Terry raised his plastic pineapple cup in acknowledgment. Barbara leaned in toward me. "For the best," she said. "The only reason Terry hosts in the first place is to show off his latest renovation project. We're lucky this current undertaking precludes anyone from entering the house."

"Anyway," Sam continued, "we're all here of course to celebrate our favorite champion with a red pen, a gifted reader-alouder whose British accent is *almost* BBC ready, the only one of us who could get eighty fifth-graders to stand still for a group photo, the keeper of the teachers' lounge Diet Cokes"—here Sam pointed at someone in the audience—"abandon all faith, ye who drink what's clearly labeled in Sharpie. So give it up for a lovely person and colleague who will be missed . . . Barbara!"

And I hadn't thought this through, because I was standing right next to Barbara, which meant that Sam was now gesturing right at me. Not *me*, obviously, but I felt conspicuous as all eyes turned in my general direction. I tried to step subtly away from Barbara, out of the metaphorical spotlight, as I clapped along with everyone else.

Only when I glanced back at Sam, he'd jumped down off the chair, his chest rising and falling. He went to take a sip of his beer, before seeming to realize that it was empty. He had barely set it down before Barbara crossed over to him and enveloped him in a big hug.

"That was a wonderful tribute," she said. "I'm going to miss working with all of you."

From my vantage point, I could see his arms go around her, could see the way the tips of his ears went pink as she said more to him that I couldn't hear. He squeezed her shoulder, glancing around the room until his gaze landed on me. I startled, turning on my heel to find wherever Conner and Shani had gotten off to. Suddenly, I was desperate to leave.

SEVEN

CONNER CAME THROUGH on the dumpster and boxes that weekend, which was almost a shame. I'd half expected him to forget or order the wrong thing, and then I'd have an excuse to spend the whole time hunched over my Edgar Allan Poe desk, typing away on my analysis of *In Cold Blood*.

Which was basically all I'd done since Sam's party earlier in the week. Despite normally having a strong constitution for the stuff, I had to admit that it was hard to read Capote's true crime classic late at night when I was in a house all by myself. I'd shifted my work schedule to do more during the day, leaving my nights free to wander from room to room and think—arguably, a more frightening place to be than with Dick and Perry on their way to the Clutters' home in Holcomb, Kansas.

My dad had never been a super-demonstrative guy, and there hadn't been a lot of evidence around the house that he even had kids even when we were young. No school pictures hanging on

the wall, no artwork on the fridge, no pantry door marked with
our heights throughout the years. My mom was more sentimental, but appearances were also important to her, so she'd culti-
vated a very chic and sophisticated look to our living spaces after
the divorce that didn't allow for mismatched tchotchkes or DIY
decorations. Every Christmas now that she and my stepdad, Bill,
were together, she decorated her fake silver tree with only white
and silver ornaments, a Waterford crystal star at the top. I didn't
even know where stuff like Conner's clay handprint ornament
from kindergarten would be at this point.

I didn't consider myself a very sentimental or demonstrative
person, either. Like that one episode of *The Office*, where Jim
hosted a silly version of the Olympics and made everyone medals
out of yogurt lids? At the end, Ryan the Temp throws his away,
and gives a talking head about how he could either throw it away
then or wait two months, but either way what was he supposed to
do with a medal made from trash. Ryan the Temp is clearly the
worst, but in that moment, I felt seen.

Back in North Carolina, the small office in the English Department I shared with another graduate student for our teaching
assignments looked like a decorator's version of Dr. Jekyll and
Mr. Hyde, one where Jekyll loved *Stranger Things*, Funko Pops,
and artistically desaturated wedding photos, and Hyde loved
death row cinder block walls. I'd never bothered to put up anything, because I always thought the job was temporary, anyway,
over once I graduated. Except I'd been teaching there for the last
four years now, longer than I'd ever held down any other job.

So it wasn't necessarily a hardship for *me* to start tossing stuff
from the house. Conner, on the other hand, was struggling.

"Dude," he said, "check this out. My *sobresaliente* award from eighth grade Spanish. I have to keep this. It's so sick."

I hurled another box of old appliance parts, who knew what they belonged to, into the dumpster. We'd only been at it for an hour and already I was drenched with sweat. God, I hated Florida.

"Say *sick* in Spanish," I said.

"Uh." He turned over the trophy in his hand, as if the answer might be engraved somewhere on the bottom. "Well, in this case I mean *sick* like *excellent*, so . . . *excelente*."

"Put it in your car to take home if you want," I said. "It just can't go back in the house."

He bounced it in the air, letting it spin before catching it again. The corner of the statuette caught him on the palm. "Ow," he said and, as if mortally offended now by the trophy's very existence, threw it in the dumpster.

Next door, Sam emerged from his house dressed in his bland business casual again, looking like a stock photo from a credit union's website. Khakis, white button-up, sunglasses on top of his head. He gave Conner and me the briefest nod, sliding the sunglasses down over his eyes before climbing into his truck.

"Well, *that* was weird," Conner said.

I glanced down to see if I looked as sweaty and gross as I felt. My Torrid skinny jeans were black, thank god, so they didn't show any stains. It was probably one reason I was overheated, but I hadn't owned a pair of shorts in over a decade. As one concession to the sun beating down on us, my shirt was gray instead of black—DEATH + TEXAS written across my chest in cracked screen-printed letters. I'd gotten it while in Austin at the Pop Culture and Literature conference I attended each year, and it was one of my favorites. My messy bun was messier than usual, tendrils of hair falling out and sticking to my neck and face. I stopped to take my hair down and wind it back up again, looping the elastic around it tightly and hoping it would stay.

"I know, right," I said. "Don't try to figure out what he's up to. Maybe he gets discounts on the Dockers if he puts in an hour appearance at the store every now and then."

"No," Conner said, "I mean weird that you didn't even say hello. We were in that guy's *house* a few days ago."

And I'd forgotten to even try the garage door to see if it was locked. Truly a missed opportunity. "Uh-huh."

Conner gave me an exasperated look I couldn't read. He'd been a little taken aback when I'd wanted to leave so abruptly, but then Shani reminded him that they both had to wake up early for work, and he'd shrugged and gone along with it. We hadn't even said goodbye. Was that rude?

I had a feeling that was rude.

"Josue told me some very interesting things about your neighbor Sam," Conner said, waggling his eyebrows.

"Did he give you a handwriting sample?" I asked, starting to rifle through a box of old mail before tossing the whole thing in the dumpster. "Does Sam use an excessive amount of pen pressure and leave odd spacing between individual letters?"

"You act so cool," Conner said, "but I know when you bring up handwriting analysis it's because you're dying inside for answers."

"Only because of the lack of closure around the JonBenét ransom note," I said irritably. "Just tell me whatever you learned, Conner. You obviously won't leave it alone until you do."

"Well," Conner said. "For one thing. He's single."

A treacherous flutter, low in my belly. "So?"

"Apparently he did have a girlfriend," Conner said. "They were together a long time—Josue told me her name, something with an *A*? Anyway, she broke up with Sam right before Christmas. He was pretty wrecked by it."

We should really go back inside to load up more to sort through and toss. We'd run out of the load we'd brought out of the house already and were just standing in the driveway at this point, talking. But for some reason I didn't feel like breaking this up just yet.

"Why did Josue even tell you all this?"

"Oh," Conner said. "I asked."

I tried not to react to that. Knowing Conner, that meant that he'd come out and said something really embarrassing, like how his sister was paranoid or, worse, how his sister was single herself and increasingly thirsty.

"Amanda!" Conner said, like an exclamation of *Eureka!* "That was the girlfriend's name. Ex-girlfriend."

It was just too hot to have this conversation outside. I finally moved for the front door, already dreading the next time we'd have to lug more stuff out here.

"Let me guess," I said. "She's thin and sophisticated and parts her hair down the middle."

"See, that's the problem with you." Conner followed me into the house, giving a box by the door a kick to see if it was empty.

Of course it wasn't. "I can never tell if you're saying, like, typical jealous girl stuff, or more serial killer stuff."

"*I* am not jealous," I said emphatically. "First of all, I have no claim to Sam, nor do I want one. Second, you know that the greatest trick the patriarchy ever pulled was pitting women against each other."

I meant every word. At the same time, it did give me a funny feeling, learning more about Sam. I didn't know why. Maybe it just felt strange, having to acknowledge that he was a real person with a past and a present and a life beyond the little snippets I observed and pretended I could draw conclusions about.

It was the way I'd felt when I saw him hug Barbara at the party. It had been so clear in that moment, that these people all had relationships with each other, inside jokes and histories and real feelings. And if I normally felt like a fish out of water at most parties, suddenly I felt like the biggest bottom dweller who shriveled from any exposure to daylight. Sam looked like he gave great hugs, and I'd wanted one so bad.

Disgusting.

"Any ideas about the proposal?" I asked, because I'd take any subject change at this point. There was the most random stuff piled on a chair pushed over to one wall—clothes and a manila folder of warranties and wireless headphones still in their case. I separated the headphones out and started shoving the rest into a laundry basket.

His face brightened. "I was thinking graffiti?" he said. "A giant mural that asks her to marry me, and we can go on a walk and just, like, stumble on it. But you know my artistic skills tapped out by first grade, and I have no idea how you'd even go about hiring someone to do that or if it's even legal. So it's back to the drawing board."

"Pun intended," I said.

He blinked at me.

"Or not." I hefted the laundry basket up, propping it against my hip so I could carry it outside and upend its contents into the dumpster. Conner trailed unhelpfully behind me, empty-handed and oblivious to my struggle to open the door while carrying the basket.

"I thought of doing something at the hospital," he said. "During one of her shifts. Like seeing if they would let me say it over the intercom or something. But I don't know. That's probably against some rules, right? And would you be mad if someone proposed to you at your job?"

"Yes," I said. Then, seeing Conner's dejected expression and feeling somewhat guilty about my terseness, I sighed. "But Shani is also very different from me! You know her best. In general, though, I would make sure you propose at a time that wouldn't be massively inconvenient to her, or might make her uncomfortable. Like what if she just happens to be having a terrible day, and she's under a lot of stress, and she's still covered in the contents of a patient's bedpan or something. A marriage proposal might feel like just one more annoyance to deal with, when it should be the happiest moment of her life."

My gaze slid to Conner, who was looking at me with an uncharacteristic thoughtfulness on his face.

"Supposedly, anyway," I muttered. "You know what I mean."

"No, that's good advice," he said. "Thank you. I don't want to make an ass of myself."

"A creed to live by."

The neighbor's cat was back again, this time laid out on the driveway in a patch of sunlight shining through the oak trees overhead. She was exposing her belly to us, but I still didn't feel confident enough to assume that was an invitation to pet. For all I knew, she just wanted an even tan.

Conner had no such compunction, though. He crouched down, giving her a light scratch on her stomach. She tolerated it for a minute, her eyes in contented slits, until she reached out a paw to bat his hand away. She flipped over to her feet and stalked away, finding a shady spot under the car.

"How would you want to be proposed to?" Conner asked abruptly.

"You planning to whip that ring out again, tiger?"

He straightened again, rolling his eyes. "I'm serious. I know you're very different from Shani, and I know we live in a modern age and you could do the proposing, blah blah blah. But it might help me out, just to get your perspective on it."

I tried to picture being with someone for years, the way Conner and Shani had. Making all these joint decisions together like whether to spring for the Investigation Discovery channel and what excuse to use to get out of a coworker's baby shower. Tried to picture being so sure about that one person that I wanted to legally make a promise to love them forever. Tried to forget just how little *forever* really meant, how little it had meant for people like our parents who maybe should've never married at all.

But Conner was looking at me, his face a complete open book. How was he the product of the same history as I was, and yet managed to hold on to that earnest optimism?

I didn't know, but I wasn't about to be the one to shatter it.

"I guess I wouldn't care," I said. "As long as I could tell the person really loved me."

By the end of the day, Conner and I had cleared out the entire living room with the exception of my writing desk and a few boxes of stuff to keep we'd stacked in one corner. We'd only argued once—about whether to put the giant TV out on the side of the road or not. Conner said we should, because it was wasteful to throw it away when it still worked perfectly well. I said I had no intention of moving the damn thing twice, once to the curb and then a second time to the dumpster after it had sat out there overnight and gotten wet with dew. Conner promised me someone would take it. We went inside for five minutes to get some water and, to my intense irritation and relief, the TV was gone by the time we came back out.

"Don't worry," Conner said. "If Shani and I moved in now, we'd bring a TV."

"Not going to happen," I said.

Conner stopped to pick up the book on my desk, the memoir written by the daughter of the Sunrise Slayer. I'd been reading it instead of *In Cold Blood*, which was a travesty both because the latter was much better written but also because it was the one I needed to analyze in my next chapter. Even if I wanted to include the daughter's memoir—and I wasn't sure I did, in any more than a passing reference—no way would Dr. Nilsson let me. It was way too "sensationalistic" and "tabloid," two adjectives that were the equivalent of steaming piles of dog shit left on the porch the way she said them. I could discuss the cultural significance of the pulp true crime genre as a whole, and give a few examples, but anything more and some hack author would be spending the first chapter of their mass-market paperback describing how *my* body was found.

But for all that, there was something compelling about the daughter's memoir that held my attention. Maybe it was how compartmentalized she still seemed to be about her father, the murderer, and her father, the man she'd grown up with and loved. The disconnect was understandable, given the unfathomable darkness of living with the knowledge of what he'd done. But it also felt like the question it raised was the exact one you wanted an answer for, and you kept reading, hoping to find one.

Conner flipped to the glossy pages in the middle, going straight for the photos. From his next words, I knew the exact picture he'd stopped on—one of the author and her father in front of a spring, looking like any other family with their dumb bucket hats and tired smiles.

"Do you remember that camping trip?"

He didn't need to specify which one. We'd gone camping a few times as children, but the most memorable time had been the last one, the summer before the divorce. I'd been twelve; Conner, five.

"What set him off again?" I asked.

"Marshmallows," Conner said. "We'd been snacking on them, and there weren't enough to roast over the fire."

I closed my eyes. There had been other spats and skirmishes throughout the weekend, of course—nobody was helping him put up the tent, nobody knew how to put the tent up right, he was convinced the campground was trying to cheat him out of five dollars with a hidden charge, there were twenty minutes where he couldn't find the car keys. But the marshmallows had been the big one.

"There were still *some* left," Conner said now. "Mom said she was full from dinner, anyway, and I'd probably eaten my weight in sugar by that point. Dad could've just told me I didn't get dessert and roasted a few for himself and you and been done with it."

But then Conner would've been upset, and started crying, and Dad would've looked to Mom like it was her fault that her kid was so out of control, and it would've been the same problem with a different patina on it. As it was, he'd ended up angrily declaring he was going to the store to pick up more marshmallows, and then he just . . . hadn't come back. I could still remember the way we'd tried to gather all the stuff up at the campsite, the way we'd had to push it to one side and stand there awkwardly while a new couple came to set up for the next day. The way the couple kept glancing over at us, like *Why won't they leave?*, and my mom had held her phone to her ear and smiled as she tried to call my dad over and over.

Obviously he ended up coming, eventually. And we packed up the car and never said a word about it.

"You played Rock, Paper, Scissors with me," Conner said. "While we waited. I remember that because I didn't believe you that paper beat rock."

"You said that rock would rip paper to shreds."

"Was I wrong?" Conner asked. "Rock is overpowered. It can crush some scissors but it can't do shit to paper? Please."

He looked back down at the book in his hands. In a strange way, I was relieved that glancing at it had made him think about our childhood like that. It meant I wasn't alone.

I'd realized in reading it that one of the main reasons I found myself drawn to the narrative was because of all the ways it made me think about my own father. Not because I thought my dad could be the Sunrise Slayer, or whatever equivalent, but because there were parts of the author's childhood that felt too familiar to ignore. How they would walk on eggshells around her dad whenever he was in a "mood." How everyone knew not to touch his stuff or ask any questions. How there were these moments of real affection and happiness, but they would always feel distant and doubted later, under the weight of other memories.

"I don't know how you sleep, reading this kind of thing," Conner said.

"It's better than melatonin."

"Really?"

I gave a little laugh. "No," I said. "Not really. Currently, I don't sleep much. But that's to be expected with the dissertation and with—" I gestured around the living room.

"Your nighttime surveillance activities?"

I pulled a face, snatching the book from him. "Those have mostly stopped, thank you very much," I said. Or at least, Sam hadn't been up to anything interesting lately. No more suspicious sounds or mysterious items being moved from his truck to the garage late at night. In fact, it had been fairly quiet next door since the party, with the exception of a single splash I'd heard the other night around eleven, as though Sam were taking a late-night dip in his pool.

Conner gathered up a box he'd put together of stuff he wanted to take to his apartment, stopping briefly one more time at the door before heading out. "All I'm saying is, maybe it's time to call

Crime Stoppers if you think your neighbor's up to something so bad."

It was so tempting to hurl the book at Conner, but it was property of the library and I wanted to be able to return it in one piece. "I don't," I said. "I was just giving in momentarily to the paranoia that is my evolutionary birthright for survival. You can let it go now. I have."

"Mmm," Conner said. "That's a shame."

"Why's that?"

Conner gave me an infuriating smirk. "Because," he said. "I happen to know from Josue that Sam finds *you* very interesting, as well."

EIGHT

———

T HE SECOND TIME I went to the library, Alison was there again, working behind the counter. Luckily she was busy helping another patron, so I slid the serial killer's daughter's memoir in the book return slot and made my way upstairs before she saw me.

I wasn't looking for anything particular in the true crime section—just looking to be inspired. I should be writing about *In Cold Blood* right now, had no idea why I was putting it off. It was arguably the book that had gotten me the most excited to write about the genre, although maybe that was the problem. Maybe I was starting to feel the pressure.

There was another book on the shelf about the Sunrise Slayer. This one was more standard true crime fare, a black cover with the title written in matte red letters, a grid of eight pictures underneath. It looked like a cross between a 1980s Stephen King novel and a grisly yearbook. I grabbed it and started back downstairs, heading to one of the self-service kiosks in the middle of the main floor.

OUT OF ORDER

Please bring your items to the front desk for checkout.

I stood for a minute, just staring at the office paper taped to the front of each of the machines, the message typed out in efficient Times New Roman. I glanced over at the front counter to verify what I already knew with a sinking feeling in my stomach. Currently, Alison was the only staff member stationed behind the main computer, which meant that there would be no way for me to avoid her if I checked the book out.

I wanted to read the book. I didn't want to have to talk to Alison. It seemed like an impossible conundrum.

So naturally, I went back upstairs, plopped myself at a study table, and opened the book to begin reading.

It was weird that with all my interest in true crime I'd never really read much about this serial killer who'd struck so close to home. He'd earned his moniker by mostly attacking women on their morning jogs—*this*, of course, being the reason why you'd never catch me pounding pavement, my earbuds blasting Paramore so loud I couldn't hear the inevitable threat. Also, because jogging sucked.

The real surprise in the book was the way he'd been caught. They'd suspected him for a decade, all the way into the midnineties, because he lived nearby and had been stopped by a police officer once for peeping in windows. But it actually ended up being the daughter who inadvertently provided a crucial piece of evidence that allowed them to put everything together.

Her home had been burglarized, and she filled out a report listing all the items that had been stolen. Among them was an innocuous piece of jewelry—a thin gold chain with a bird pendant. She described the bird as more swallow than dove, its wings spread. There was a staff member who'd recently been recataloging cold case files, and the description struck a chord. A necklace with a similar description had been one of the items believed removed from a victim of the Sunrise Slayer's, almost fifteen years earlier.

I had to sit back after reading that whole passage. In her whole memoir about her father the serial killer, the daughter had never mentioned that detail. It seemed like a huge omission. She'd been given the most macabre gift possible, and then her description of that gift was what, in a roundabout way, landed her father in prison.

I'd already read the Wikipedia article on the Sunrise Slayer, and knew that he'd died there a few years ago, at the age of sixty-seven. But I wondered if the daughter still lived in the area.

I put the book back on the shelf when I was done with it, making sure to slide it in its correct alphabetical slot. Then I headed out into the sunshine, grateful again that I'd made it the whole time without having to interact with Alison. It wasn't that I was planning to avoid her for the entire rest of the summer . . . but also, that plan didn't sound too bad.

I climbed into my Camry and turned the key. Nothing. I wiggled the steering wheel, making sure it hadn't locked—the car was old, and sometimes had weird quirks like that. Turned the key again.

Still nothing.

"*Fuck,*" I said.

It had been raining on the way to the library. One of those quick Florida sun-showers that made you turn on your wipers and lights to drive a couple miles, and then disappeared just as quickly. Only I hadn't remembered to turn *off* the lights when I pulled into the library parking lot.

It was a Monday, which meant Conner would be at work. Not that I wanted to bother him. Shani was also probably working on one of her online classes or at the hospital, and I realized I'd never actually programmed her number into my phone.

I considered my options. I'd let my roadside assistance program lapse, so that was out. I could use my phone to search for a nearby auto shop, and hope that one was close enough for me to walk to. But then what was I supposed to do—buy a whole new battery and put it in myself? I'd need at least a half hour on You-Tube University to figure that one out, and then I'd probably kill my phone battery, too.

I thought of Sam suddenly, inexplicably. Ever since Conner had told me that Sam found me *interesting*, my mind couldn't stop circling back to my neighbor. And this time it was definitely less in a *should I be worried or nah* way and more in a *but what does he mean by "interesting"* way. If I had his number, I would be tempted to call him right now. Lucky for my dignity I didn't.

There was only one other thing I could think of, and I really, really didn't want to do it.

Alison wasn't behind the counter when I walked in, so I stood by the front, trying to look like I was engrossed by the colorful flyers and bookmarks advertising library services. Down in the slot for returns, I could still see my book. Now that I'd read more about the Sunrise Slayer—including the surprising reveal about his daughter's role in getting him caught—I actually wanted to revisit the greasy-covered grammatical nightmare. The slot was just big enough to fit my hand in up to my wrist, and I reached in, trying to see if I could flip the book up with my fingers enough to wedge it back out.

"That's supposed to be a one-way system," Alison said from above me, her voice amused.

I yanked my hand back so fast that I scraped the top of my wrist. "I dropped my book in there by accident," I said. "I was just trying to see if I could get it back out."

"We're really not supposed to do this," Alison said, but she reached in to retrieve my book and handed it to me. "I can see your reading tastes haven't changed."

She smiled at me, as though I hadn't been a complete weirdo the last time I was in here—and this time, too, although hopefully she hadn't clocked me coming in earlier. Her bright red lipstick and penguin-dotted button-up made her seem like a cross between Taylor Swift and a kindergarten teacher.

"Sorry," she said, pulling a face. "I normally try not to comment on patrons' items in a way that might come across as judgmental. I didn't mean it like that. Just that I remember you reading a lot of crime stuff back in high school."

"My dad died," I blurted.

I hadn't meant to say it like that, so baldly and out of nowhere. But even having it out in the open, not having to worry that she'd find out somehow and then wonder why I hadn't told her, was a relief. Her face crumpled into the expected expression of sympathy, and I rushed to provide more context.

"It was a heart attack," I said. "At the beginning of this year. So it was pretty sudden . . . I'm getting his house ready to sell and taking care of a few things."

"Oh my god," Alison said. "I'm so sorry. I had no idea."

"It's okay."

There was an awkward silence. I'd been trying to convey *It's okay that you didn't know*, but now I worried that it came across more like *It's okay that he died*. And that's not what I meant at all, but also I wanted to convey *I'm okay, I don't need pity or sympathy*, and in general it was exhausting, needing words to do more work than I was willing to put into them.

Alison glanced at her watch, a slim band that looked elegant until you saw the Mickey Mouse in the center of it, his gloved hands pointing to tell the time. "I can take a fifteen-minute break," she said. "If you wanted to catch up."

I already knew I wasn't going to ask her to help me with my car.

"Okay," I said. That word again.

THE LIBRARY OVERLOOKED a small, man-made lake with a bridge out to a small wooden gazebo. Alison and I ended up walking there on her break, since there wasn't enough time to go off-site.

"If I stay in the building, they'll loop me into something," she said. "So I often come out here when I need a breather."

"Was this here when we were kids?" If it was, I didn't remember it.

"I think they built the gazebo just after you moved. It used to be *the* place to go in high school to get high or make out." She gave me a rueful smile. "Not that I did much of either."

Neither had I. I'd spent my first two years of high school in a haze of not doing schoolwork and then lying about it, my sleep schedule so messed up that I'd tried to convince my mother to just let me nap right after school and then wake up at two a.m., like a vampire. *I'll never see you!* she'd said to me in the middle of a particularly fierce argument. *That's the point!* I'd yelled back.

Sometime around my junior year, after the Incident, I'd buckled down. I realized I was spending as much energy pretending to work or not working or putting off working as I would if I actually just, you know. Did the work. I turned my grades around, applied for scholarships, and went to a college several states away where I could start living my life on my own terms.

But right now, I was much more interested in Alison's life. "I see you got married," I said tentatively. "Congratulations."

She looked down at her ring and then back up at me, beaming. "Thanks," she said. "Our third anniversary is coming up in September, actually. We've planned a big weekend at Disney." She held up her watch now, rolling her eyes a little self-deprecatingly as Mickey's hands ticked around the face. "I know, I know. My wife Maritza's one of those Disney people, and she converted me."

Alison and I had spent a lot of real estate in our eighth grade notes making fun of those classmates who seemed to go to the amusement park every weekend, always coming back bragging about some new dessert at Epcot or comparing favorite rides. Every week there was a different one that was considered the "right" answer, and once a girl had plopped down at my lunch table and fired at me, staccato-fast: "Haunted Mansion or Space Mountain?"

"What," I'd said. My mouth had probably been filled with chicken sandwich with too much mayonnaise on it. Truly, eighth grade was a black hole.

The girl repeated her question faster, if possible, as though I were wasting precious time. I'd heard of both rides, obviously—I didn't live under a rock. The answer seemed like a no-brainer to me. "Haunted Mansion," I said.

She rolled her eyes. "Ugh," she said, and then moved on to the next table.

Looking back, at least some of those kids had to be lying, desperate to fit in with the popular annual-pass-holder crowd. But sometimes it felt like Alison and I were the only two people in the universe who hadn't been to Disney and, more importantly, the only two people who didn't care to pretend otherwise.

I knew Alison wouldn't be the same person I'd last known almost fifteen years ago. I wasn't the same person as I was then. But for some reason this one reminder of how much had changed, how different our lives were, depressed me.

"What about you?" Alison asked now. "Are you seeing anyone?"

"Not . . ." I trailed off, leaning forward a little on the railing of the gazebo to make sure my eyes were working right. Because unless I was hallucinating, it looked like Sam was walking through the library parking lot, a book tucked under his arm. He disappeared inside.

". . . exactly," I finished.

Alison waited, as though expecting me to say more, but I just couldn't believe this development. Had I conjured him somehow?

Or was he following me?

But no, that was insane. If anything, my brother would've pointed out, *I* was the one who should be singing "Creep" at the next karaoke night.

"Well," Alison said, glancing over her shoulder, as if trying to figure out where my attention had gone. "Listen. I know things didn't end on the best of terms all those years ago. But I'm really glad to see you, and I'd love to hang out if you have time while you're in town. What do you think?"

Even a few days ago, the very idea would've made my guts twist. But for some reason, now the idea almost seemed . . . nice. Doable, at least.

We got out our phones and exchanged contact info, made a few more minutes of banal small talk about changes to the area over the last decade, and said goodbye before Alison had to go back to work. For one horrifying second I thought she was going to hug me, but then instead she just lifted her hand in a little wave. A minute after she'd left, a text came in—**This is Alison!** it said.

What are the odds, I started to type across my cracked screen, then deleted it. For some reason, my normal sarcasm felt all wrong here, like I was making fun of a cute kitten picture on the internet. So instead I typed, **This is Phoebe!** and, at the last minute, a smiley face.

I glanced up to see Sam emerging from the library, and I slid my phone back in my pocket. Here went nothing.

NINE

I THOUGHT OF SIX different opening gambits in my twenty-yard walk to Sam, but ended up settling on the first one that popped into my brain once I was standing in front of him.

"Hi," I said.

He startled, dropping the two books he was holding, a piece of paper fluttering to the sidewalk. Not gonna lie, it was a little satisfying to do that to him after he'd scared the bejeezus out of me that first night. And *his* phone even made it through this encounter intact. I was bitter, but not vindictive.

I bent down to help him pick up the books. One was a novel I remembered getting quite a lot of buzz a few years back, about a brother and sister and their family home, spanning five decades of their lives as they navigated life and love and loss. Or whatever. Honestly, even if any story described as "epic" or "sweeping" didn't normally make my insides shrivel, the plot of that one seemed a little too close to home right now.

The second was just a heavy reference text with a garish grass-green cover, the word *Soldering* printed across the top in royal blue font.

There was a picture on the cover, too, that appeared at first glance to be some vaguely 1980s geometric pattern they loved to put on reference books, but on closer inspection turned out to be a pair of earrings.

"Making some jewelry?" I asked before I could stop myself. Alison said she tried not to comment on patrons' reading choices in a way that could come across as judgmental, but that's why I didn't work at the library.

"Not exactly," he said.

Well, *that* didn't make my brain jump to more nefarious activities at all. He was back to the white button-up and khakis again, as if he were aggressively cosplaying Normal Dude. I had a brief moment where I thought maybe I shouldn't ask him for help with my car, maybe Alison had been my best bet after all, or even Conner once he got off work. But I was tired of hanging around the library. If nothing else, I was starving.

"So," I said. "I have a bit of a problem. My car over there"—I gestured vaguely toward my poor, incapacitated Camry—"won't start. I think it's probably my battery, but I don't have any jumper cables. I was wondering if you maybe . . ."

I trailed off, as if not completing my sentence meant that I hadn't *actually* made the request. If he turned me down, or said he couldn't help, I'd left myself some wiggle room of plausible deniability. Like, calm down, psycho, I was just going to ask if you maybe agreed that it sounded like a battery problem! Obviously I can take care of it by myself!

But he only shook the hair out of his eyes and, without moving his attention from me to my car, said, "Sure."

THE ONLY SLIGHT wrinkle was that Sam hadn't parked at the library. He'd had another errand to do nearby, so he offered to go get his truck from that place and bring it back to hook up to my poor dead vehicle. The idea of walking even a quarter mile in the oppressive Florida heat wasn't appealing, but the idea of having another glimpse into whatever errand Sam might've been up to most definitely was, so I offered to walk back with him.

The sidewalk was narrow enough that it was hard to stay side by side without bumping each other occasionally, but I didn't want to lead because I didn't know where we were going, and I certainly wasn't about to trail behind like some puppy. I tried to make myself as small as possible, but these hips weren't going anywhere. Sam rubbed his palm on his pants before reaching up to grasp his books with both hands, as if they were so heavy he needed the extra support.

The silence between us grew as thick as the humidity, but Sam didn't seem in any hurry to break it. I wondered, not for the first time, if Conner had somehow gotten it wrong in the game of telephone through middleman Josue. Because if Sam supposedly found me interesting, why wouldn't he *say* anything?

It's not like we hadn't talked before. He'd strung whole sentences together about mowing the lawn. If that was such a scintillating topic, imagine how stimulating talking about car trouble could be.

"You don't talk much," I said finally. When in doubt, I liked to state the obvious.

"Whereas you talk to cats about serial killers," he said. It was delivered so deadpan that I had to turn my head to catch the slight smile tugging on the corner of his mouth.

"I was on the phone with my *dissertation advisor*," I said, although I believed she'd hung up by the time I was seeking a cat's opinion on Ann Rule. But Sam didn't need to know that. "Whose cat is that, anyway?"

"Not really anybody's, I don't think," Sam said. "We have a lot of outside cats in the neighborhood, if you hadn't noticed. The lady on the corner has a few, and they just keep having kittens."

"This one's been fixed," I said. "She has the ear-tip to prove it."

"She hangs out by Pat's because she feeds all the animals," Sam said. "You're lucky it's not springtime, because there's this one cardinal who hangs around Pat's bird feeder and then will launch himself at your windows, on the attack against the territorial threat of his own reflection."

That had been possibly the longest I'd ever heard Sam speak, and it was about a cardinal. He hadn't said anything to indicate he'd gone all Betty Draper on the bird with a rifle, so it looked like I could check *cruelty to animals* off the warning sign list.

Sam turned toward a parking lot, but I hadn't been paying attention, and so his shoulder bumped mine, sending me stumbling slightly into the brush by the sidewalk. He reached out a hand to steady me.

"I am so sorry," he said.

"Not your fault." I tried to give him a smile, because he looked truly upset that he might've hurt me, but I worried it came out more like Wednesday Addams' attempt to mollify the counselors at Camp Chippewa. I was very conscious of the warmth of his hand, which was still wrapped around my upper arm.

He sighed. "I'm not normally this clumsy," he said.

"Seriously. Not a problem. Nobody's phone got cracked, nobody dropped any books." Looking up, I realized that we were in front of a large building with a sign that said JOCELYN'S MUSIC, Sam's truck parked in the far corner of the lot. "This was your errand?"

Sam removed his hand from my arm to run it through his hair, and I was surprised at how bereft it made me, to lose even that brief contact.

"I teach lessons here," he said. "Over the summer. It's not much—maybe four or five hours a week, depending on who's signed up—but it's a good side job to make a little extra money."

A few things clicked into place—his seemingly random comings and goings in the middle of the day, those fucking *khakis*. I gestured to his outfit. "I guess this business casual look is your uniform?"

He glanced down at himself. "Technically, they call it *neutral professional*. It's supposed to be a solid light-colored shirt, no logos, and khaki pants. Navy or black are too harsh, apparently. I just bought a few sets of this exact outfit because it was easier that way."

"So if I opened your closet, it'd look like Doug Funnie's, a row of white shirts and khaki pants all lined up?" I shook my head, wanting to dispel any image of his closet or why I'd be in his bedroom in the first place. I started walking toward the music store.

"Let's go inside for a sec," I said. "I could use some . . . well, nothing from here, actually. But I'm hot and the air-conditioning sounds good."

Really, I just wanted to look around. Now that at least one of Sam's mysteries had been solved, I was curious about this place where he spent some of his time. I didn't remember it being there when I was a kid, but then again, I was never very musical. I'd tried to teach myself guitar in high school when it seemed like the cool thing to do, but I should've tapped out after mandatory recorder lessons in fourth grade.

Inside, the place was bright and filled with instruments of all types—violins and violas hanging in a glass case by the door, keyboards set up to form one walkway through the store, and a couple of drum sets that had to be the bane of every employee who had to hear small children banging on them every day. There was a kid in front of one set right now, happily pounding a loud, percussive beat while his mother talked with one of the clerks.

"So what lessons do you teach?" I leaned down to peer inside another glass case by the front counter, showing various expensive items that appeared to be replacement parts for instruments I'd barely be able to name. Another clerk appeared from behind the counter, greeting me with the sunny solicitousness of someone who thought she might be about to make a sale. I stood back up quickly.

"Oh, hi, Sam," she said, apparently spotting him behind me. Was it me, or did she sound a little breathless when she said his name? *You have no claim on him*, I reminded myself. *You're not jealous.*

"Hey, Jewel," he said. "We're just browsing."

Jewel? Now I was jealous, because that was a beautiful fucking name. I wished my name was Jewel.

She arched her eyebrows at us. I could tell she was curious about who I was, but I could also tell that she wasn't going to ask. She made some general noise about letting her know if we needed anything, and turned to help another customer who'd come up behind us.

Two more people stopped to say hello to Sam as we walked through the store, which was I guessed my fault for wanting to come inside a place where he spent four to five hours a week, depending on who was signed up. I realized he'd never answered my question about the lessons he taught, so I asked it again.

"Guitar, mostly," he said. "Some piano."

"How many instruments do you play?"

He seemed chagrined, as if he knew the number was a lot and he was pre-embarrassed to have to reveal it. "Proficiently?" he said. "Not that many. Wind instruments are not my specialty, for example, so I can only play the saxophone at the level of a mediocre high school student."

"So how many do you play proficiently?"

He ran his fingers over the ivory keys of a keyboard as we passed by, depressing one slightly with the dull *thud* of an electronic instrument that wasn't plugged in. "Maybe nine? I think I should be allowed to count the tambourine. I play a mean tambourine."

We'd ended up in a small room set off in the back, guitars double-stacked in rows hanging on the walls—acoustics all along one side and electrics on the other, with a few amps plugged in next to stools clearly designed for people wanting to sit down to try an instrument.

"Play something," I said.

"Come on," he said. "No."

"Why not? I already know you're good." I widened my eyes. "Or is that the problem? Is this like me casually asking . . . who's a great guitarist?"

"Which era? What style of—never mind. Off the top of my head, John Frusciante."

I made a face. "Red Hot Chili Peppers? Okay, we'll come back to that. So is this like me casually asking John Frusciante to just play me something, when it's like, he doesn't even touch a guitar pick for less than ten thousand dollars?"

Sam laughed, but I could tell he was embarrassed again. "No," he said. "Nothing like that."

"You're worried I'll be so impressed I'll, like, drop my pants," I said. "I won't be able to help myself, because your playing is so magnetic. It'll be like a John Mayer concert, or what I imagine a John Mayer concert would be like if I had the stomach for it."

I reached up for one of the electric guitars, even though there were multiple signs that specifically said to ask an associate for help. Sam was here, still dressed in his neutral professional. Close enough.

"Play me the dorkiest thing imaginable, then," I said. "And I promise I'll keep my pants on."

He took the guitar from me, giving me a dry tilt of his head like, *really?* To which I made an exaggerated gesture for him to take a seat on one of the stools like, *yes, really.* He reached down to plug a patch cord from the amp into the guitar, turning the volume knobs low before tuning the guitar up. Which of course he could do by ear, the bastard. One of the main reasons I'd stopped trying to learn to play was because I'd lost the digital tuner my mom had gotten for me one Christmas.

He stayed standing, having used the stool to set his library books on instead. Now he stared up at the ceiling, as if considering what to play, before he started picking out a slow, thoughtful melody on the strings. It sounded vaguely familiar, but I couldn't place what it was, until he played it faster and faster, watching my face for recognition. When it finally hit me, I broke out into a grin.

"'Farmer in the Dell'?" I said. "Joke's on you, dude. That song speaks to me on a cellular level. This cheese has always stood alone."

"It's big with the kindergarten set," Sam said.

"So how long have you taught elementary school music?"

"Five years."

"Do you enjoy it?"

"Yeah," he said without hesitating. "I know this sounds obvious, but kids just love music. And not for how cool it is, or how deep the lyrics are, or anything like that. They just like hitting a xylophone with a mallet and hearing whatever sound comes out."

He was still playing while we were talking, his fingers idly plucking out some random tune. It was the most at ease I'd ever seen him, and that included when he'd been standing in front of me barefoot or when he'd been wearing beach clothes. I hadn't even realized until now, but there was a tension around Sam, a keeping to himself, that seemed to go away when he picked up the guitar.

"I tried out for fifth grade chorus," I said. "Only because my friend Alison was going for it, and I thought, why not? I'd always heard that anyone could be in chorus in elementary school. If you didn't have a great voice, they'd just stick you in the back and tell you to mouth along. But you'll never guess what happened."

He smiled, his eyes crinkling in the nicest way. "You didn't make it."

"Is your school's chorus that cutthroat?"

"Not really," he said. "All the competition is in going out for hall patrol. It's a campus of narcs."

I snorted at that. "There was this music teacher in seventh grade, though," I said. "I never actually had any classes with her because—well, see Exhibit A, my choral rejection. But Alison . . ."

I trailed off as it hit me that all my childhood stories seemed to involve Alison, and also that this one wasn't exactly a banger. It was my first year going to a Real Junior High that had lockers like all the schools on TV, and I'd gotten it into my rebellious twelve-year-old brain that we needed more than seven minutes to pass between seven classes. I'd drawn up an impassioned petition, with diagrams of a sample route from class to locker to class and everything. I'd distributed it to my classmates and urged them to sign, and apparently even my general loserness could be overcome by a collective fight against the man, because they'd done it. Alison was passing it to another kid in her orchestra class when her teacher caught her, confiscated the petition, and told her I'd have to come collect it in person if I wanted it back.

I'd expected the teacher to be mad, but she wasn't. Instead, she seemed a little amused. She'd asked if I'd ever considered taking a music class, or joining the chorus. I knew there was no way she was impressed by my musical ability—first of all, since I didn't have any, and second of all, since she'd have no way of assessing that from a piece of paper with some kids' names on it, anyway. But she'd said she was impressed with my chutzpah. I'd trotted out my sad-sack story of being rejected in fifth grade, and she'd just laughed and said, "Anyone can be taught."

When it came to music, I emphatically did not believe this. My parents, brother, and I were all completely tone-deaf. It was practically on our family crest—an eighth note with a giant slash through it or something.

I'd never bothered following up. And the petition ended up being a nonstarter, because it turned out that things like bell schedules were heavily determined by the district and the teachers' union and there was only so much a budding activist could do.

But that teacher's words had stayed with me, for some reason. Middle school was a Venn diagram of all seven circles of hell, but that moment had been something to me. It was the feeling of being recognized, being seen as having potential. I hadn't realized how starved I'd been for it.

Now, Sam was watching me, as if he understood that I'd gone somewhere in the middle of telling that story and was patiently waiting for me to come back. I cleared my throat.

"Anyway," I said. "Sorry. Should we head out? You agreed to help me with my car and I'm just wasting all your time."

His gaze dropped to my mouth, and for one wild moment I thought he might kiss me. I blamed it on our close proximity in the small space, the fact that I could smell the detergent he used on those never-ending white shirts, probably something with *mountain* in the name. I swore I could still feel the imprint where he'd touched me earlier, a chalk outline of the ten seconds where electric current of desire had seemed to run through us before. Here it was again, a spark of awareness that made my breath hitch.

And okay, all jokes aside, there was a very real Guitar Effect that made him about ten times hotter. I swayed a little toward him.

Luckily, he pulled back in time to save me from myself. He unplugged the guitar, lifting it over his head and placing it carefully back in its place on the wall. He switched the amp back off, and if the anticlimactic *click* of it powering down wasn't a metaphor.

"Not a waste of time," he said. "But sure. Let's get going."

I BUCKLED MYSELF into the passenger seat of Sam's truck, stealing a glance at him as he turned his head to watch for traffic while backing out of the parking space. Already, I could see it again, that same strain in the line of his jaw that suggested he was holding something to himself.

Meanwhile, I'd officially lost it. Had I actually thought he'd just randomly *kiss me* in the middle of the music store? After we'd spent, like, half an hour together? What was wrong with me?

I had to remind myself of all the ways that he *might* be Buffalo Bill, and my erotically charged moment was his *puts the lotion on its skin*. He could take me anywhere. He looked like the kind of guy who'd be savvy about which highway exit had the best wooded area for dumping a body. Maybe that was why he drove a truck. Which I was currently sitting in.

Which of those options honestly scared me more—that he could be up to some dark shit, or just that I had a crush? Maybe my true crime reading had desensitized me after all, because I knew which of those made my heart speed up.

"We're here," Sam said. We could've been sitting in the library parking lot for the last five minutes, for all I'd noticed.

Luckily, Sam had been able to park right next to my car. I hopped down from his truck, opening my driver's-side door to pop the hood. I hoped Sam didn't need any more help from me, because that was about all I knew to do. But he'd already reached into a toolbox in the back of his truck, removing jumper cables, and was popping his own hood to hook them up.

"Why'd you leave so suddenly the other night?"

Sam's head was still bent over my engine when he asked the question, so I almost wasn't sure I'd heard him accurately. And then I wished there was some way to plausibly pretend I hadn't, because I couldn't think how to answer in a way that wouldn't make me seem like an asshole or a liar.

"I'm just . . ." I floundered, before deciding that something adjacent to the truth would work. ". . . not great at parties."

He wiggled one of the connections on the battery terminal before wiping his hands on his pants, black streaking the khaki. Jocelyn of Jocelyn's Music wasn't going to like that. He started his truck before coming to stand next to me on the grass next to the parking spaces.

"What do you mean, *not great at parties?*"

I rolled my eyes. "Listen, I'm sorry I crashed it. I didn't know it would be a work thing. Conner—my brother, you remember him, with his girlfriend, Shani—had the idea to bring a host gift at least, even if it was just some Kit Kats. Still, it was rude as hell. And if I'd stayed much longer, I probably would've ended up talking too much about the connection between Charles Manson and the Beach Boys or whatever, and that would've been a real downer."

"Not necessarily," he said.

He didn't even know. It had taken a lot of effort for me not to bring it up, and that was only because somehow I didn't think it was the vibe Barbara Ann was going for with her retirement send-off.

"I appreciated the Kit Kats," he said. "I was going to make some comment, about how backwards it was—me opening the door all dressed up and you there with a bag of candy."

I smiled. "You totally should've," I said. "It was Halloween in reverse."

He scratched at his forehead, and I noticed he'd left a smear of black there, too. "Well, I didn't think of it until later," he said. "And by then the moment had passed."

His gaze slid to me briefly, then away. "I'm also not great at parties," he said.

That made me think back to the speech he'd made for Barbara, how warm and insider-jokey it had been, how much she seemed to appreciate it. But then I also remembered the way he'd seemed after—flustered, his skin flushed. I'd been thrown off because *he'd* approached *me* first, that night by my car, and I knew how difficult it could be for me to make first contact. But now I'd unlocked at least one more mystery behind Sam.

He was shy.

I was still trying to figure out how to respond, when he nodded toward my car. "Try starting it now," he said. "We'll see if that was enough juice to get it going."

I slid in the driver's side, almost hoping I wouldn't hear the car turn over. Obviously I wanted it to work again, but there wouldn't be any harm if it took another five or ten minutes to charge up. Especially now that I felt like I was getting somewhere with Sam.

But of course, because I had the worst luck in the world, when I turned the key the engine sputtered and then roared to life. Through the front windshield, I saw Sam give me a thumbs-up.

"Sounds good," he said, already starting to unhook the jumper cables. "You're probably going to want to run your car for at least fifteen minutes before you turn it off again, to make sure the battery gets enough charge."

"It doesn't seem too busy here today. I'm sure they wouldn't care if we hung out a bit longer."

"Oh, you can drive it," Sam said. "I'm just saying, maybe take the long way home, do a few loops around the neighborhood."

It was enough to make me wonder if any connection we'd had was being transmitted through those cables, and now that our cars were apart again we were back to being separate, too. I'd had an idea to invite him to lunch, to offer to pay as a thank-you for helping with my car. But obviously that would be stupid, given that I'd run the risk of my car dying again at any new location, and he seemed anxious now to be rid of me.

This was why I preferred to keep people at arm's length. Things got so much more complicated when you actually cared if someone sent you a text, or accepted an invitation, or wanted to hang out.

I shut the driver's-side door, rolling down the window to give

Sam a jaunty wave. "Thanks for all your help," I said. "I guess . . .
see you around?"

"It'd be hard not to," he said.

I backed carefully out of the space, checking my rearview mir-
ror when I'd reached the exit of the library parking lot. Sam was
still standing there, the disconnected cables in his hands, the
hood of his truck still open. I almost thought about opening the
door and calling back to him, seeing if maybe he wanted to grab
that lunch after all, if we met back at our houses first. But then I
remembered that I was supposed to be working on my dissertation, that any invitation would lead to a bunch of annoying logistics about where should we go and whose car should we drive, and
god forbid he thought it was a date. God forbid *I* did.

I flicked my signal light on, and made the turn to leave.

TEN

THE PROBLEM WITH putting off writing was that the words didn't just magically appear the longer you left your computer to its own devices. If anything, the blinking cursor on my open dissertation document seemed more accusatory than ever, as if to say, *What's the holdup, bitch? If you love* In Cold Blood *so much, why don't you just write about it, then?*

The internal voice of my computer was quite rude, apparently.

When I was really trying to buckle down to work, I would switch my Wi-Fi off to remind myself to stop dicking around on the internet. Of course, the only thing stopping me from turning it back on was a double click and my own fragile willpower. So I told myself I was taking a quick break, and searched for the Sunrise Slayer's daughter's name.

Most of it was the expected stuff—reviews of her book, an interview she'd given for a local CBS affiliate. On the third page of results, I found a post she'd made a year ago on a quilting web-site, where she was asking if anyone had extra of some discontinued fabric she needed. In one of her follow-up comments, she mentioned her local fabric store, and I searched the name of that, too.

It was about an hour from my dad's house. So apparently she did still live in the area. And more power to her, too, because my dad didn't even murder a bunch of people and I still felt all antsy just being back in this place where I had a higher probability of running into people who might've known him.

My phone rang on the desk next to me, and I answered it without looking away from the search results. "Hello?"

"Phoebe. How are you?"

Of all the voices I'd thought I'd hear, I hadn't expected Dr. Nilsson. She never called me out of the blue without setting it up by email first. I closed out my boondoggle internet search and pulled my document back up, as though she could see my screen through the phone and knew I was fucking off.

"Great," I said, my voice pitched a little higher than was natural. "Just working on my Capote section."

I wondered if this was about the last chapter I'd turned in. Had it been so bad that she had to call to personally ream me out? Did I comma splice one too many times and cause her eyeballs to bleed, and she'd barked an order for Siri to call me as her one last action before she went under the deep sleep of anesthesia?

Shit, had I used *irregardless* again? I'd carelessly used the word once in a five-page response in her class, and she'd double-underlined it and written *NO* in the margin. The only things that could scare me were the brief shot of the girl in the closet in *The Ring* and those two letters written in her spidery script.

"I was talking to a colleague at Stiles College," she said. "I believe that's in your neck of the woods?"

I'd heard of the school. It was a small liberal arts college about forty-five minutes south in Sarasota, known mostly for being a little eccentric. The only kid I'd known from high school who'd gone there had been a state unicycling champion, for example. He'd wanted to show off his skills at the school talent show, but the vice principal vetoed it, citing liability issues. Meanwhile they let two girls do a very DIY gymnastics routine to Britney Spears' "Toxic," but okay.

"Yeah," I said. "I mean, yes. It's close by."

"Dr. Blake teaches African American literature," Dr. Nilsson said. "Their scholarship on Octavia Butler is impeccable. And they agreed to meet with you for a mock interview before school starts back up again, if you reach out with your availability."

Oh. I hadn't expected this development at all. So much so that I didn't even know how to feel about it. I was grateful that Dr. Nilsson had thought of me, that she was clearly still so committed to helping me with my future career prospects. At the same time, this all felt a little fast. I still hadn't written that teaching philosophy—I couldn't even finish this fucking *chapter*—and she wanted me doing mock interviews?

"You are available?" she asked, her inflection making it just enough of a question to be polite.

"Of course," I said. "Thank you."

"I think it will do you good to have someone outside the department assess your employability," Dr. Nilsson said. "Goodness knows we all have our biases toward our favorite students. But Dr. Blake will pull no punches, so I would advise you set up the interview for at least a month out. Give yourself some time to prepare. You should wear a blazer. Do you own a blazer?"

I didn't know how much I liked the sound of *pull no punches*. I preferred not to be punched, if possible. "No," I said, then hurried to add, "but I'll buy one. No problem."

"Good," Dr. Nilsson said. "A modicum of initiative would yield you Dr. Blake's email address on the internet, but just in case, I'll give it to you."

I dutifully wrote it down, knowing that Dr. Nilsson's comment was her way of reminding me that I should do my research on Dr. Blake before I met with them. Read a few papers on EBSCO, see if I could find a conference talk on YouTube, that kind of thing. If nothing else, it would be a healthier rabbit hole to go down than my current fixation on the Sunrise Slayer.

"I'll have my comments on your last chapter to you tomorrow," she said. "You may want to apply some of my more global suggestions on your current chapter, so shall we say beginning of next week for another check-in?"

Another question that wasn't really a question. "I can do that," I said with confidence I didn't wholly feel.

"Excellent. Talk later."

And then she hung up, leaving me so bemused that it took me a minute for one thing she'd said before to sink in. I was pretty sure she'd implied that I was one of her favorite students.

———

IDEALLY, MY CONVERSATION with Dr. Nilsson would've kick-started me into a new phase of my writing. But instead, I spent another hour typing paragraphs and then cutting and pasting them into a draft email I'd creatively titled notes, a graveyard of stuff I promised myself I'd incorporate at some point but never quite knew how.

In the past, my go-to procrastination technique had been to clean. My apartment was never as spotless as the year I was preparing for my comp exams. But lately it felt like all I'd been doing around my dad's house was gathering up stuff to pack up, throwing stuff away, wiping down surfaces. It was overwhelming and not that fun.

It felt like all the cool kids now were baking to procrastinate, but I was generally hopeless in the kitchen. The only thing I really knew how to make was a no-bake Nutella pie, which, come to think of it, actually sounded pretty fucking good right now.

Only somewhere between me driving out to the more distant grocery store—the one where my father *didn't* die—and me arriving home with an Oreo cookie crust, my plan changed. Sam's truck was in his driveway. I'd never actually thanked him for helping me out when my car died. I could make him a pie, right? That wasn't weird.

At times like this, I really wished I had a true best friend I could text about this sort of thing. I was friendly with several people in my grad program, but most of them were fifteen or twenty years older, some married with kids and mortgages and lives that felt way more adult than mine did even though I'd been able to vote for a decade now. I had no idea how any of them would respond if I texted out of the blue with something like, **Hey, long story but there's this guy next door, and is it a thirst move if I bring him some pie?**

Phrased like that, it made me emphatically *not* want to do it. But then that felt mean, like somehow the universe knew that I'd already committed to giving away pie and had now reneged on my promise.

Conner would tell me to go for it. He'd want me to make another one for him, too. Alison would say . . .

Well, who knew. We hadn't been that kind of friends for a long time.

After the pie was ready, I compromised by cutting it in two, putting half on a plate in the fridge with some cling wrap over it. The other half I would bring over to Sam's, but in a casual way. Like, I'm still wearing this old *Batman Forever* T-shirt and leggings with a hole at one knee, I haven't bothered to apply any makeup, this is *not* a thirst pie, that kind of casual.

Casual was not historically something I'd done well.

But I schooled my features into neutrality as I stood on his doorstep, waiting for him to answer the door. I wasn't going to ring the bell twice. That was beneath me.

When he finally answered, he looked bleary-eyed and more disheveled than usual, as though he'd been awoken from a nap. I thought he'd be happy to see the pie no matter what, but I hadn't counted on the formidable opponent that was midday sleep. Well played.

"Sorry to *Judgment Ridge* you," I said. "But I made this, and I thought . . . well, I really appreciate your help with the car. So."

I thrust it out to him, and he took it, still looking a little confused.

"Half of it is gone," he said.

"Well, yeah," I said. "I wanted some pie, too. But I used a knife to cut it in half—I didn't, like, rip into it with my lobster claws or anything. It was all very Solomon."

He leaned against the doorframe, looking like he was finally settling into the conversation. "So does that mean if I hadn't wanted the pie cut in two, I would've gotten the whole thing? Because it proved that I loved it best?"

"I can go get the rest out of my fridge and we can shimmy it back into the pan, if it means that much to you."

"No, no," he said, his forehead crinkled, as though he were genuinely afraid he'd offended me. "Thank you for making it for me. Nobody's ever made me a pie before, even half a pie. It was really sweet."

Ugh. No one, and I was pretty sure I could say this accurately even without telepathic powers, would ever describe me as *sweet*. *Prickly* was one I got a lot. *Aloof*. Maybe *intimidating*, which I wasn't mad at.

"It was a no-bake, my dude," I said. "This is checkers, not chess."

I turned to leave, but he called my name.

"Why don't you come in for a slice?" he asked. "You can share a slice of yours later if it means that much to you to keep it even."

Eating together with him now, with a rain check to eat together again, was a lot of commitment. But there was something about his open expression, something about the memory of him saying *I'm also not great at parties*. I shrugged, and followed him into the house.

"So what exactly does *Judgment Ridge* mean?" he asked as he grabbed two plates from a cabinet, two forks from a drawer.

Sometimes I didn't know half the shit that came out of my mouth. "It's this true crime book I read when I was a teenager," I said. "About the Dartmouth murders. Basically, these two kids pretended they were doing an environmental survey for class, and knocked on the door of these two professors. It just so happened that the guy taught geology and earth science, and he thought it would be a great opportunity to educate some teens, so he invited them in. And then . . . well, you know."

Sam paused in the middle of dishing out a piece of the Nutella pie. "Jesus," he said. "That's really sad."

"Yeah," I said. "And also the reason I jump a mile if someone's at my door unsolicited. That never ends well in these types of books."

"And yet you've come to my door three times now," Sam said. "Once, for the package, twice, for the party, thrice . . ."

"Okay, okay," I said, cutting off the rest of that little nursery rhyme. "No need to *thrice* me. Why don't you slice me instead?"

I held out my hand for the plate of pie he was holding, before realizing what that had sounded like. "Oh god," I said. "I meant *give me the pie*. Not attack me with the knife. It was supposed to be like when people say *beer me*, although come to think of it I've never said that in my life, and *slice* rhymed with *thrice*, so . . ."

I needed to stop talking. I took a quick, greedy bite, more as a way to shut myself up than anything else. But damn. I still got it. I didn't care if the pie was five ingredients and took as many brain cells to create, it was delicious.

"I can't believe I said that," I said. "I totally thought you were a serial killer when I moved in, you know."

Sam had been taking his first bite, but choked on it at my pronouncement. He kept coughing until he had to set the plate down, filling a glass with water from the fridge door dispenser. He sipped it for a long time, his Adam's apple bobbing.

"What," he said finally. Either his throat was still too raw to get the rest of his question out, or that *was* the question, because he just looked at me.

"Not *really*," I said. "Or not much more than the general way I believe everyone capable of the darkest shit. But that first night, you came out of nowhere!"

"I came from right here," he said. "My house. Where I live."

"Well, I didn't know that," I said. "And you were always doing mysterious stuff. Banging around in your soundproofed garage—you have to admit that sounds creepy—and coming and going at the most random times . . ."

I should really stop. I hadn't intended to ever tell Sam any of this, and certainly not in this stream-of-consciousness way that made me sound completely unhinged.

"So on a scale of one to ten," he said, "one being your grandmother and ten being H. H. Holmes, how much did you actually think I was a serial killer?"

I pointed my fork at him. "That is a bad example. My grandmother had it in her to be a black widow, for real. But that first night, I would say I was at a . . . six?"

"Holy shit." It was almost cute, how shocked he looked by my answer.

"The scale is broken," I said. "Being a serial murderer is a binary situation. Either you are or you aren't."

"When you came to my party."

I didn't pretend to misunderstand what he was asking. "Down to maybe a four?"

"When you asked for my help with your car?"

"Three point six."

He raised his eyebrows. "Living on the edge, accepting a ride from someone you thought was a three point six. Now?"

I looked at him. Really looked at him. Swept my gaze from the top of his messy hair—true bedhead this time, I suspected—to his blue eyes, sparked with amusement and something else. His T-shirt looked thin and soft and clung to his arms and chest in a way I didn't hate, and he was wearing actual jeans instead of that neutral-professional garb I'd seen him in so much lately. He was leaning back against the sink, holding his plate of pie, which was already half gone.

There was something intoxicating about being able to survey him so openly. What was it about his kitchen that seemed to bring out this heat?

"Two," I said finally, sliding another bite of pie in my mouth.

"What would get me to a one?" he asked. "This house doesn't have a crawlspace, you know."

"But you do have a garage," I pointed out.

"You think I'm hiding something in my garage?"

I shrugged. There was no way I was telling him about the one night I'd observed him, the suspicious liquid on his hands, the dropcloth, the paranoid call I'd immediately made to Conner. "It's another mystery," I said. "Solving it could bring down your number, I'm just saying."

He turned to rinse off his plate, placing it in the sink and then wiping his hands on a dish towel. "So let's go."

"I'm not even finished," I said around a mouthful of pie.

"Bring it with you," he said.

"If anything in there makes me lose my appetite, I'm going to be really pissed," I said, but followed him through the living room, past the piano. Now that the WE'LL MISS YOU, BARBARA sign was gone, I noticed there were some family photos hung up, showing Sam with a truly mind-boggling number of people. Did he belong to one of those families that had a group chat and wore matching shirts to family reunions? Because that wouldn't help my ability to trust him at all. I didn't have time to look any closer at the pictures, though, before we were at the garage door.

He'd stopped so suddenly I almost ran into him. He turned back, his hand on the doorknob. "Normally I make people sign an NDA first."

"The Corporate Killer," I said. *"He buries them under paperwork.* The *Dateline* episode writes itself."

He flung open the door and flicked on the light. Of course, at first glance everything looked normal. Disappointingly normal. There was a washer and dryer in one corner, a metal rack holding various toolboxes and old paint cans and other garage-y things. On the walls, I could see where he'd affixed several large panels of covered material, and I assumed those had something to do with the soundproofing he'd mentioned.

There was also a drum set, resting on top of old carpet remnants, and a guitar leaning against one wall. The guitar looked like it had seen better days, the paint faded, covered in stickers that were peeling off.

Toward the front of the garage, there was another guitar in pieces, laid out on some wooden boards balanced over a couple sawhorses. The boards had been covered in plastic dropcloth, which I guess explained at least one thing I'd seen. But there had been some liquid on his hands, too. I hadn't imagined that.

I looked at the concrete floor, trying to see any remnant of a suspicious stain. Sam stayed near the door, his hands shoved in his pockets, while I walked around the space as though conducting a forensic analysis.

"The other night," I said finally, not able to help myself, "I thought I heard a crash?"

I could've named the exact date and time, since I'd written it down in my notebook. But it was probably better if I didn't cross over from endearingly neurotic to obsessively weird (too late?).

"Hmm," he said. "Another mystery."

"I thought you were cooperating with the investigation."

He raised his eyebrows. "Is that what this is? It hardly seems fair, me giving up all my secrets and you giving up none."

I set my empty plate down on the top of the washer for now. I couldn't help but notice that I'd been right about the laundry detergent—*mountain fresh.*

"Okay," I said, my pulse quickening. "What do you want to know?"

He studied me, as though he were really considering his question. I hoped it was something easy, like *Why* Batman Forever?, at which point I could riff about how with villains named things like Penguin and Two-Face, it was better when adaptations of the comic leaned into the camp.

I hoped it wasn't anything about my dad.

"What are you writing your dissertation on?" he asked finally.

I wondered how he even knew I was working on that, until I

remembered that I'd told him about talking to my dissertation advisor the other day. "True crime," I said, pulling a face like I understood how on-the-nose that sounded at this point.

"Probably should've guessed," he said dryly. "What about it, specifically?"

I had quick, pithy answers for this inevitable question, since people's eyes tended to glaze over once I started saying *rhetoric* and *genre theory* instead of just talking about *The Ted Bundy Tapes* on Netflix like they really wanted to. But for some reason I wanted to explain it to Sam, wanted him to understand what I'd been doing with my life these last five years. Why that was important to me, I didn't care to analyze too hard.

"True crime is especially interesting," I said, "because it tends to reflect and shape our cultural attitudes toward crime in general. You look at how the genre has morphed in the last sixty years, even, from the way Truman Capote made it more literary in *In Cold Blood* to the more sensationalistic, hard-boiled accounts written in the eighties and nineties, to how personal and nuanced Michelle McNamara gets in *I'll Be Gone in the Dark*. And then it's like, who's writing these books? What relationship do they have to the subject going in, or what relationship do they form as they go down this dark rabbit hole? How do they choose to present the information, and how does that affect the way a reader might feel about it? Does that change how 'true' the books are, really? Or does—"

I cut myself off, realizing I was a little out of breath. "Sorry," I said. "I could keep going for about, oh, a hundred and eighty pages or so. But I'll stop."

"Give me an example," Sam said. "Like when you said something might change how 'true' the book is."

"Okay, well," I said, warming to my subject. This actually happened to be a major point of analysis in the chapter I should be at home writing at this very moment. Maybe I could even count this conversation as "brainstorming" time and not feel guilty that I was blowing off my work. "Have you read *In Cold Blood*?"

Sam shook his head. "I know you'll tease me for it," he said, "but I usually can't handle those books."

It caused a warmth to bloom in my chest, the idea that we had enough of a relationship at this point that I had things to tease him about, that he knew me well enough to know I might. And conversely, the fact that he assumed I'd tease him about not having the stomach for true crime made it that much less likely that I ever would.

I briefly explained the basic gist of the book, how Capote had gotten close with the two murderers and conducted many interviews with them in prison to form the narrative of the crime. "What was innovative about the way he wrote it," I said, "was that it was like you were reading a novel. He used all these fictional techniques of characterization, using juxtaposition in scene cutting to build suspense and drama . . . and he described all the scenes like he was there. It makes you feel like you're in that moment, like you're a voyeur looking in on what actually happened. And in a way he seems more credible for the fact that he never inserts himself in the narrative, like he's just this objective transcriber of all the action. But it's like . . . have you ever seen *America's Next Top Model*?"

"Uh," Sam said, blinking at the apparent change in subject, "not a full episode, I don't think."

"Okay, I *will* tease you about that later, but there was this one contestant who went to Yale, right? And in her talking heads, she was always like, *Yale this* and *Yale that*, and it made her sound like such a pretentious twat, like she couldn't help but mention her Ivy League education every fifteen seconds. But I read an interview with her later—don't look at me like that, it was Murderpedia or Television Without Pity in those days, so you should be grateful I was well-rounded—and she talked about how the producers would always *ask* her about Yale in the segments. And you were supposed to read the question back in your answer, so it made it sound like she was just blah blah blah about fucking Yale, when really it was the producers shaping the questions and then editing the footage in a way to make it seem like she was talking about Yale all the time."

Sam was looking at me as if he couldn't believe I was real. I couldn't tell if it was in a good way or a bad way, but it made me suddenly self-conscious.

"I can't put that bit about *ANTM* in an academic paper, obviously," I said. "But I'm just saying, it's the same idea with Capote. It's interesting to think about the questions he asked, the things he chose to emphasize, what parts of the narrative are factually true or emotionally true or whether it even matters."

"I think this round of Solved Mysteries goes to you," Sam said. "That was very thorough."

When it came to true crime, I knew I could get a little . . . passionate. But I resisted the urge to apologize again. For one thing, Sam didn't look like he needed it.

"So what was the crash?"

"Oh." He rubbed the back of his neck, gesturing toward the metal rack. "I was trying to get a screwdriver from the toolbox without putting down anything else I was carrying. I knocked that over, and spilled a bunch of stuff, including a can of paint all over myself . . . it was a mess. Not a very exciting mystery."

Paint. It had been paint.

We stared at each other. It had been ridiculous of me, really, to bring over the pie in the first place, much less stay to eat it with him, much less basically strong-arm him into showing me his very inoffensive garage.

"I think you get one more," I said. "You brought me here, and told me about the source of the mysterious late-night sounds. I only told you about my dissertation."

"To be fair, there were layers."

"Still."

Sometime in the last few minutes, Sam had moved closer to me, or I'd moved closer to him, because we were now both standing by the disassembled guitar parts. My fingers itched to touch something, and the guitar was right there, so I ran my finger along the smooth, unpainted wood of the body.

"One more mystery," Sam said, almost more to himself than to me. "I have a feeling you have a lot of them. You're a hard person to read, Phoebe Walsh."

I could say the same about him. I was the one word-vomiting in the most random ways every time we got together. He was the one who tended to keep his own counsel.

His gaze caught mine, before lifting to the top of my head. "How long is your hair?"

I blinked at him. That was what he wanted to know?

"Too long," I said. "I haven't gotten it cut since . . . I can't even remember. A trim six months ago, maybe."

"Can I see?"

Why did that feel like he was asking me to undress in front of him? And why did the idea of *that* feel . . . scary, sure, but also exciting?

"I haven't washed it for two days," I warned, because I was an idiot, and a queen of self-sabotage. Once, in sixth grade, a girl complimented the name necklace I was wearing, *Phoebe* in gold script on a thin gold chain. I'd told her it cost less than five dollars and snapped it in half, just to prove how cheap it was. This was the kind of shit I did when I felt backed into a corner, and compliments or kindness or attention was unfortunately what made me feel that way the most.

I reached up to remove the elastic hair-tie, unwinding my standard bun until my hair fell around my shoulders in dark waves. I scrunched my hands in it at my scalp, shaking it out to try to get it to lose the kinks from being wound up so long. I still had that funny, half-painful feeling around my temples of my hair being pulled back. Maybe I *should* wear it down more. I might be giving myself headaches with this style.

"So it's down to about . . ." I started to gesture, then realized I was about to point to just below my breasts. "Anyway. The more you know."

Sam was still looking at my hair, his gaze traveling to the ends before he, too, seemed to realize that he was basically also now staring at my breasts. He focused instead on some point at the crown of my head, clearing his throat. "It's pretty," he said. "You have very pretty hair."

Under my shirt, my nipples were tight and almost painful against the thin fabric of my bra. I'd never been more grateful for the thick screen-printed image of Jim Carrey's Riddler, because it hopefully did a good job of hiding this reaction.

"Thanks," I said, because what else could I say? I reached behind me to gather it up, starting to wind it back into its bun, when I heard a couple of loud bangs coming from somewhere outside the garage. I shared a look with Sam, where he seemed as confused as I was, until the sound came again. Knocking. Someone was knocking on the front door.

"*Judgment Ridge*," Sam whispered.

I smacked his arm. "Don't say that."

"You're the one who brought it into my life," Sam said. "Now I'll never be able to answer the door the same way again."

All joking aside, I did feel some trepidation as we both went together to the front door. My shoulders were somewhere around my ears as I hung behind Sam, trying to see around him as he opened the door to . . .

"*Conner?*"

ELEVEN

TEN MINUTES LATER I was in Conner's car, trying to kick the fast-food wrappers on his floorboard away from my feet as we sped off to some destination he hadn't yet revealed. He'd only said he "needed help" with something, which could mean anything from a legitimate emergency to trying to steal another Mountain Dew cutout from a gas station.

"You didn't have to come to his house," I grumbled. "I would've been home in five minutes."

"See it from my perspective," Conner said. "I tried texting you, you didn't answer. I even tried calling you, you didn't answer."

"That's because I—"

Conner shook his head, apparently not interested in hearing again that I'd left my cell phone back at the house.

"Then I come over, and the door is *unlocked*," he said. "Didn't you tell me that all *Dateline* episodes start with the door being *unlocked?*"

"No," I said. "Technically I told you that all *Dateline* episodes start with a family on the brink of achieving the American Dream. Anyway, I only ran over for a few minutes—"

It was only *supposed* to be a few minutes, anyway. I'd ended up spending half an hour at Sam's house, and who knew how long I would've stayed.

"I'm not mad," Conner said, grinning at me. "You're not under curfew or anything. In fact, it was good to see you let your hair down a little."

Ugh. I knew Conner would make a big deal of that the minute we'd opened the door, my hair still in disarray around my shoulders, the elastic hair-tie forgotten in my hand.

This was what made little brothers so annoying. If I told Conner that actually, *I* was mad, because he didn't need to insert himself into my personal life, he'd make some comment about how he didn't even know I *had* a personal life. If I told him I was frustrated he'd interrupted, he'd waggle his eyebrows, like he'd interrupted something particularly juicy, when in fact . . .

Well, I didn't know what that moment between me and Sam had been. Or what it could've been. But I knew I wouldn't be able to even dance around it without getting flustered and weird, and then it would be a case of *Phoebe doth protest too much*, and then he'd only tease me more. The best bet was just to let it go, and change the subject.

"So where are we going?" I asked. "I have a lot of writing to get done tonight."

"Maybe you should've been working on that instead of hanging out with neighbor boy," Conner said. We passed an old oil change place that looked familiar, then a sandwich shop that I was surprised was still around, a small law firm that always put encouraging messages for local sports teams on their marquee. I recognized this drive. Suddenly, I knew exactly where we were going.

"Tell me you're not bringing me to Skate Space," I said, sitting up so abruptly I crunched down on some empty soda cans on the floorboard.

But we'd already pulled into the parking lot of the garish hot pink warehouse building. "Here we are!" Conner announced. "The possible future site of my marriage proposal."

I had so many questions, but didn't get a chance to ask any of them until after we'd finished paying and were waiting at the back counter to pick up our rental skates.

"Why *here*?" I asked, looking around. The decor was space themed, naturally, which meant lots of black light and glowing paint. One mural—of a giant mouse in a space suit flying through the galaxy—was particularly disturbing given that I was pretty sure this place actually had real mice. The carpet was this multi-colored geometric pattern that was clearly designed to hide dirt but instead managed to just look dirty all the time. The whole place smelled like feet.

"This was where Shani and I had our first date," he said, having to shout to be heard above the Halsey song they were pumping through the speakers at truly brain-scrambling decibels.

"What were you, twelve?"

"Seventeen, and it was Rollerblade night! You know I kick ass on Rollerblades!"

I hadn't known that, actually, just like I hadn't appreciated how long he and Shani had been together.

He'd also apparently brought his own, because instead of waiting with me at the counter, he sat down on a nearby bench and took one Rollerblade with lime green wheels out of a bag I hadn't even noticed he was carrying. He strapped it onto his foot with so many buckles he looked like an Olympic snowboarder before removing the other one from the bag.

"What size?" the greasy-haired teenager behind the counter asked me, and I reluctantly slid over my shoes to accept a pair of dull tan skates. They had brown laces and orange wheels, brought to you directly from 1982.

"Why am *I* here?" I asked once I'd sat next to Conner to put my skates on. I hoped I remembered enough to not completely embarrass myself. If I went ass over teakettle wearing these throwbacks I'd be pretty pissed.

"You gave me such great advice before," he said. "I figured I could use my big sister's help in vetting the idea."

Well, that was impossible to refute. I let him help me to my feet, only because any loss of dignity from that move was mitigated by the much greater potential for lost dignity if I ate it on this dirty carpet. We made our way gingerly to the polished wood floor.

"So what exactly is the plan?" I asked. Everyone was going so fast.

"You have to skate clockwise around the floor," Conner said, pointing out a guy skating around in a black-and-white-striped referee shirt. "Otherwise they'll tell you to turn around. You can hug the wall if you need to, but I plan to pick up some speed."

"I meant the plan for your *proposal*."

Conner stepped out onto the floor, so I followed, but it really was slicker than I'd expected. My feet almost went out from beneath me, but I grasped the wall just in time.

"I'm thinking a meaningful song, then they can make a special announcement while I go down on one knee in the middle of the rink?"

That actually sounded cute. Cheesy as hell, but cute. "What song?" I asked. "Please don't make it one of those ones about how she doesn't know she's beautiful."

Conner had already started to skate a little, keeping it slow and easy for me, since I was still clinging to the wall. A four-year-old had lapped me twice and I officially left the last of my dignity back with my real shoes. I wasn't going to see it again as long as I was wearing these wheeled bad boys.

"What do you mean?"

"You know the ones," I said. "Like, you don't *know* you're beautiful, which is why you are. Because it's so ugly for a girl to have her own self-esteem, apparently. Or the ones where the guy is like, Girl, you don't know how beautiful you are, but *I* do. Like he's the keeper of her beauty or some shit."

"Shani loves that song!" Conner said.

"Well, sure, they make them catchy as hell!" I said. "You may hate yourself for humming 'Blurred Lines' but you'll do it anyway. That's the power of music."

"Maybe I'll use this song," Conner said, pointing up at the

ceiling as though to indicate the sound enveloping us. It took me a minute to place it, and once I did, I made a face at him.

"You are not going to use 'Whoomp! (There It Is)' as your proposal song," I said. "No matter how authentic it would be to the general skate rink experience."

"I'm pretty sure they played this on our first date."

"I'm pretty sure they've been playing it since the nineties," I said.

Conner only grinned at me, pushing out with one foot to pick up some speed, until he was way ahead of me around the floor. I had felt confident enough to let go of the wall, but was still half shuffling my way back to the other side. The four-year-old flew by me like Apolo Ohno, the wind coming off her so intense it made me wobble.

"Motherfucker," I muttered, stepping off onto a carpeted area on the other side of the rink, where there were benches I could sit on. This was Conner's plan. No need to torture myself for it.

My hair was already starting to droop from the activity, and I reached up to tighten the elastic around my bun. The truth was, I could make fun of those cheesy songs all I wanted, but I had been just as susceptible when Sam complimented me earlier. I prided myself on being able to appraise myself in a fairly straight-forward way—I knew I was fat, a word that didn't bother me as long as the person using it wasn't doing so pejoratively. My fore-head was too high but every single time I'd tried to hide it behind bangs it had been a mistake. My bottom teeth were crooked, which you only noticed if I smiled too big. Luckily, that wasn't an expression I was used to wearing too often.

But I knew my hair was healthy and a pretty color, dark brown shot with red in certain lights. I'd always liked my eyes, which were large and framed by naturally long lashes, and if I used to wish they were violet instead of brown, I was mostly over it now. That had been a side effect of reading too many romance novels, I knew, where the heroine's eyes were always sparkling emerald or velvety indigo.

I still hated that messaging of *she doesn't know she's beautiful and that's why she is*, but I couldn't deny that it had been nice to have someone else notice me, appreciate something about me. It gave me a hot, prickly sensation just thinking about it, that started in my toes and traveled up my spine.

Although maybe that was just these skates, which were too tight.

Conner skated by then, shouting out, "Watch this!"

I dutifully watched as he turned to skate backward, grinning at me as he skated through the corner before spinning to face forward again. It was so obnoxious, how much he was showing off, but I couldn't help but bite back a smile. He reminded me so much of the way he'd been as a kid, always desperate for attention, wanting me to watch him climb the highest tree or beat a level in a game or perform a card trick that he would inevitably mess up.

"You watching?" he called as he passed me.

"Yes!" I said, even though I doubted he heard me. He was already yards away, spinning to skate backward again.

I saw it coming about a split second before it happened, and I shot to my feet, as if I could do something to stop it. But of course he was on the other side of the rink, his momentum already too fast. He clipped another skater, who stumbled but was able to right himself, while Conner went flying on his butt, breaking his fall by putting both hands out.

"Conner!"

Skaters swerved around him, but he didn't immediately get up. He tried to push himself to his feet, but stayed on the floor as the guy in the referee shirt skated over to him.

I started to walk-run on the carpeted area to the other side of the rink, but that would take forever, so eventually I stepped back out onto the slippery floor, skating diagonally across the rink to reach him faster in a way that was definitely not sanctioned by the strict clockwise-only rules.

"Hey," I said once I reached him. "You okay?"

The referee guy had already helped Conner to his feet and skated away. I supposed Conner was an adult and clearly not unconscious or bleeding, and the demands on a single teenager policing the entire skating floor must be high, but I was still annoyed at the perfunctory treatment.

"Ah," Conner said, clutching his left wrist with his other hand. "I think I may have broken something."

I reached out, intending to help guide him off the rink, but stopped when I almost lost my own balance. The chance that I'd pull him down with me was greater than the chance that I'd actually help, especially since now that he was on his feet Conner seemed to be doing just fine getting back to the carpeted part. We finally made it to the benches and collapsed onto one, Conner still holding his wrist.

"Can you move your fingers?" I asked.

He started to waggle them, but winced. "It hurts," he said.

"Okay," I said, already unlacing my skates and sliding them

off my feet. "Can you get your Rollerblades off yourself, or do you need help?"

"I think I can get them."

I stood up in my socks, holding the skates by their laces so as to touch as little of them as possible. "I'm going to trade these ugly-ass bricks for my own shoes," I said. "And then we can head to the emergency room. Is Shani working, or do you want to give her a call?"

"She's out with friends tonight," Conner said. "I'd prefer not to bother her. And you think I make emergency room money? I'm an urgent care man."

I rolled my eyes. "Fine," I said. "If you can't get those stupid things off without hurting yourself more, just wait for me. I'll be right back."

"We didn't even get to have a slice of pizza!" Conner called after me as I headed toward the back counter.

I thought about the lukewarm, greasy food they tended to serve at places like this. Literally, that might be the only silver lining to my brother's dumb ass probably breaking his wrist.

"YUP," THE DOCTOR said once we were all gathered in the exam room, looking at an X-ray of Conner's bones. "That's a fracture right there."

"Can I keep these?" Conner asked, gesturing toward the negative images.

I turned away from him to the doctor, who was tapping the screen of a tablet with the energy of someone playing *Candy Crush*. We were fortunate to find an urgent care clinic that did

X-rays still open after six, although so far the bedside manner had left a bit to be desired.

"So what exactly do you do for a fractured wrist?" I asked. "Will he need a cast?"

The doctor glanced up. "Hmm?" he said. "Not today. We'll splint it while we wait for the swelling to go down. You can make an appointment a few days out and we'll take another look. Okay, buddy?"

The last question was directed at some point on the wallpaper instead of to one of us, and then the doctor tapped a few more things into his tablet before leaving the room.

It was a standard-issue urgent care room, which meant that it was bland and inoffensive and yet claustrophobic as hell. The wallpaper was off-white with even offer-white sprigs of baby's breath printed on it, a single picture of a faded seascape hanging up on the biggest stretch of wall. Otherwise, it was all medical equipment and signs advertising medications or warning you to call if you hadn't heard about your test results within three days. The sooner we got out of there, the better.

"So does that mean we wait here for someone to splint it?" I asked. "Or are we supposed to go back to the front desk?"

Conner reached over from the exam table to grab the X-rays of his wrist. "I'm paying for them, right? I should get to keep them."

"I hate doctors," I said. "If I'm like, my sinuses are congested, they're like, how many calories do you eat a day? If I say I have a UTI, they're like, you should take the stairs at work instead of the elevator."

"Gross," Conner said. "Don't mention UTIs."

"Are you sure you don't want to call Shani? She is studying to be a nurse, after all. She'd come out of professional curiosity if nothing else."

He sighed, looking down at his wrist. It really didn't look great. Not grisly or anything, thank god, but it was definitely all puffy and inflamed compared to his other hand.

"I texted her earlier," he said, "but she's probably in the movie by now. Shani is strict about no devices in the theater. She takes those *please do not disrupt the movie* commercials very seriously."

"A woman of sense and sensibility," I said. "Where do you land on the skate rink proposal now?"

"Ugh," he said. "Don't say *land*. Honestly, you're right. That place smelled like feet."

He looked so dejected, I took pity on him. "It was a nice idea, though. Going back to the scene of your first date. That was really thoughtful."

"I guess." He gave me a smirk that immediately made me want to take back any ounce of sympathy. "You want to talk about what you were doing over at Sam's house?"

It already felt like a lifetime ago that I'd been there, eating pie and rambling on and on about *In Cold Blood*. A lifetime ago that he'd turned the full attention of those blue eyes on me, that he'd seemed only a second away from reaching out and touching my hair, and then . . .

I didn't want to talk about what I was doing over at Sam's house. And more to the point, I definitely didn't want to talk about what I was *not* doing over at Sam's house, which was getting any action at all.

Not that I wanted any action. Gah.

"We're friends," I said, more as a douse of cold water on myself than as any response to Conner. But I realized when I said it that it felt true. We *were* starting to become friends. I felt like Sam was someone I could talk to. Even having him next door made me feel a little less alone. "I'm not comparing him to Most Wanted sketches anymore, if that's what you're asking."

"The start of every beautiful friendship."

"Shut up," I said. "You know I have a black, mistrustful pit where my heart is supposed to be."

"I know that's what you want people to think," Conner said.

That threw me. I hadn't expected him to go that hard. But before I could come up with a pithy comeback, there was a soft rap at the door and then a guy in scrubs entered, holding a thick gray tube with Velcro straps dangling off that must be the splint. It looked like part of Conner's Rollerblades, to be honest.

The nurse undid one of the Velcro pieces that had reattached itself, stretching the splint a bit to loosen it up. He started talking to Conner, explaining how to wear the splint and what to expect, but I tuned out their conversation.

I'd always been protective of my heart. Even as a kid, it had been important to me that people not know too much about the way I really felt. In eighth grade, a (very true) rumor had started going around that I had a crush on this boy who styled his hair like Gerard Way in the "Helena" video. Mortified, I'd denied it to anyone who would listen, until Mini Gerard himself came up to me one day in the cafeteria.

"I like you, too," he said.

My teen self short-circuited. I couldn't handle it; it was too much. What was I supposed to do with that information? Hold hands? *Make out?* I'd heard the phrase but barely knew what it meant.

"Cool," I said. "But for me it's like, more as a friend."

And then I'd dumped my lunch in the trash, tray and all, and walked away. I still felt terrible about that whole interaction. He didn't deserve the rejection when he'd been brave enough himself to say something, especially after he easily could've joined everyone else in making fun of me. Also, the tray was made from heavy plastic. You weren't supposed to throw them away.

"Phoebe!" Conner said now, ripping me out of my middle school reveries. The splint was on his arm now, and the nurse had already left. "Have you spotted the sailboat yet in that picture, or can we get out of here?"

Conner insisted he was fine to drive, and I wished I'd been paying attention a little more so I could remember if the doctor or nurse had explicitly forbidden him from doing that. Either way, I told him he wasn't going to be operating a motor vehicle on my watch.

It turned out that Shani's movie got out a little after we left the clinic. By the time we got to Conner's apartment, she was there, immediately falling on him with hugs and comfort and precise questions about what had happened and what the doctor said. Conner visibly perked up from the attention but answered her questions with varying versions of *I don't know* or *I think so?* Finally, he brandished the X-rays, but that was more because he wanted to know if she thought they'd clash with the shower curtain if they hung them in the bathroom than because he was looking for any medical feedback.

"What were you doing at the *skating rink*, anyway?" Shani said. "You haven't been there since . . ."

"Our first date," Conner said. He glanced at me with an exaggerated parody of *Don't say anything!* that was way more suspicious than anything I would've ever said. "I don't know. I just had the urge to get the Rollerblades out again."

"Well, hopefully this has cured you of it. That place smells like feet, anyway." She turned to me, giving me a quick hug before I could slip out of it. I'd never admit this out loud, but sometimes I was grateful to people who were automatic huggers. It took the pressure off me to initiate anything, and it felt nice, being embraced even for a few seconds by someone you cared about. The problem was that my list of people I wanted a hug from was pretty short.

I was pleasantly surprised that apparently Shani was on it. I gave her a quick pat on her back with one hand as she pulled away.

"Thank you so much for making him go to the clinic," she said. "On his own, he probably just would've come home, taken some ibuprofen, and then wondered why it still hurt days later."

"Oh, it was no problem."

"Do you want to stay, hang out? We're in the middle of watching *Selling Sunset* but we could go back to the first episode if you wanted."

All this time I'd been back in town, getting to know my brother and his almost-fiancée better, it hadn't fully hit me how they had a whole *life* here. That this was where they lived, and they had jobs and school and shows they watched and . . . each other.

Meanwhile, I'd be leaving in another month or so, and I didn't really have a place here. It was nice of them to try to include me, but I didn't want to intrude.

"Actually, I've already reserved a rideshare to get home," I lied. "But maybe another time."

I said my goodbyes and then headed down to the entrance to the apartment complex, opening up my rideshare app to see if there were any nearby cars. It wasn't my preferred way to travel for sure, but if the company's latest crime reports were to be believed it was relatively safe. I texted Conner a screenshot of my ride confirmation just in case.

Luckily, my driver had the attitude of someone begrudgingly picking up a coworker for a carpool she didn't want to be a part of in the first place. She barely spoke to me, which meant an automatic five-star review in my book. I had her drop me off a block away from my house, and walked the rest of the way home.

I had to pass Sam's house on the way, which hadn't been deliberate, but which did make me slow down. What if I went back, just for a minute? To apologize for leaving so abruptly (again), or to offer to take care of my dirty plate, which might still be sitting in the garage (probably not; I couldn't help but notice that his sink had been a lot clearer than mine)? But instead I just kept walking, stepping over the cat, who was back in my driveway again. She jumped to her feet as I passed, winding around my legs as I unlocked the front door, making a move as if she was going to dart inside.

"Sorry, little buddy," I said, blocking the entrance with a foot as I slid inside. "This isn't your home."

She gave a single, pathetic *meow*, and I shut the door.

TWELVE

HE CONVENIENT THING about Conner's broken wrist—
for him, anyway—was that it got him out of doing more
work around the house for a bit. I told myself that was why I put
off writing my dissertation chapter again in order to focus instead
on doing a deep clean of the kitchen. Now that most of the furniture and stuff was gone from the main common rooms in the
house, it was mostly elbow grease to finish the job—dusting
blinds, scrubbing baseboards, scraping at whatever had been
stuck to the stovetop since the early 2000s.

I was able to get the audiobook for *I'll Be Gone in the Dark*
through my library app, so I was kind of working. If not working,
then growing spiritually at least, which was what always seemed
to happen as I followed Michelle McNamara down her obsession
with the Golden State Killer. Some people had *Eat, Pray, Love*. I
had *I'll Be Gone in the Dark*.

I was right at the part where she revealed the origin of the title of the book—a bone-chillingly creepy moment, if ever there was one—and trying to carry two large garbage bags out of the house. I left the door open because my hands were occupied and why not? But then I glanced down right in time to see that fucking cat dart around my feet and into the house.

Shit.

This time I left the door open on purpose, hoping that maybe she'd exit as quickly as she'd entered. But instead she seemed to have already secreted herself somewhere deep in the house, because I went from room to room and didn't see her.

"Here, kitty," I said, feeling like an idiot. I made a *tch-tch-tch* sound with my tongue against my teeth, hoping she would respond to that. Those two techniques were the only ones I'd learned from watching TV, so if they didn't work, I was all out of ideas.

I'd never really had a pet before, other than a couple hamsters and a fish. We hadn't been allowed to, when we lived in this house as a family, because my dad said he was allergic. *Said*—I never saw any evidence of the allergy, even on the rare occasions when we were at someone else's house who had a dog or near someone whose clothes were covered in cat hair. For all I knew he *was* allergic, but I had my suspicions.

Once I'd moved out with my mom, I'd asked her to get a cat. The one I was interested in was a beautiful Russian blue who'd landed in a shelter because she had feline immunodeficiency virus, and I'd tried to sell my mom on how the shelter gave you everything you needed to take the cat home.

"Yes, because after that you'll be paying a fortune in vet bills and medication," she'd said.

"But doesn't this cat deserve someone who'll take care of him?"

"Phoebe," she'd said, in that voice that meant there would be no more discussion. "You are not going to bring home a dying cat."

Technically I could've pointed out that we were all dying, in an existential sense. That cat did end up finding a good home—it just wasn't us. And when I'd broached the idea of getting another cat, one who *didn't* come with a known diagnosis, my mom had shut that down, too.

Later, after I'd already moved out, she met my stepdad, who brought with him two Australian shepherds. Now she had a bumper sticker on her car that proclaimed her a "dog mom," which I guess meant I *still* didn't have a pet but rather two canine stepsiblings.

"Nice kitty," I said, and then, because I didn't feel comfortable saying something I didn't mean, "Sneaky kitty. Here, kitty, kitty."

My dad's bedroom door was closed and had been since I'd moved in, so I left that room alone. But I finally shut the front door and then did another sweep of the house, making as much noise as possible because I figured I wasn't going to out-stealth a cat, but maybe I could at least scare her out of a hiding place if she thought Godzilla might be coming.

In my room, I dropped to my knees, tilting my head to look under the bed. And of course, peering through the sliver of darkness were two glowing yellow eyes.

I sat cross-legged on the floor. No way was I reaching my hand in there. I remembered that shot in *The NeverEnding Story* where

Gmork comes out of the darkness to fight Atreyu, and this felt like a similar situation. I would wait her out.

"You'll have to come out of there eventually," I said, then made a face as a thought occurred to me. "Please don't go to the bathroom, dude. This is where I sleep."

I wondered if she'd ever been given a name. I glanced around my room for inspiration, the way a hacker in a movie might look around to discover a person's password that was always the name of their favorite book, helpfully left on their nightstand. My gaze immediately went to the Rasputin book, which seemed fittingly conniving right about now, but then I saw my huge Edgar Allan Poe collection and the perfect name just came to me.

"Lenore," I said softly, testing it out. "Come out, Lenore. You don't want to spend the day under a bed."

Except obviously that was exactly where she wanted to spend the day. I took out my phone, cursing the cracked screen that made a simple search of what Reddit thought I should do in this situation completely pointless. I could still read text on it, but scrolling through a bunch of repetitive answers and tangents and one helpful comment sounded like too big a headache.

I tried looking through my latest text messages instead, trying to remember if any of these people had a cat. Conner and Shani would probably give me advice based off their experiences as goldfish parents to Hank, which was exactly how Conner would phrase it, I could already tell. I'd texted a few times with another woman in my graduate program, but it had been more about the paperwork we needed to turn in if we planned to walk in December. It would feel awkward to break into that conversation now with a random question about a cat.

Then there was the recent text chain with Alison, from when we'd exchanged numbers at the library. My thumb lingered over her name for a moment, before I clicked to open the new message box. If I thought too hard about it I wouldn't do it, so instead I just typed my question fast and then clicked "send" before I could have second thoughts.

Hey do you happen to know anything about cats?

Her response came back almost instantaneously.

You think because I'm a lesbian librarian I must also be a cat lady? [cat emoji]

Then:

Yes, I have two cats. [two cat emojis] Why?

I explained the situation as briefly as I could.

She's probably hungry! Alison replied. **Do you have a can of tuna you could open? Don't let her eat out of the can. Put a couple spoonfuls on a plate and set it in the middle of the room to lure her out.**

When the Golden State Killer was breaking into people's homes, he didn't get this kind of hospitality, but okay. I guessed I could see how this situation was a little different. I leaned down to check if the cat was still there—yup, glowing yellow eyes—and then got up to check the pantry for any cans of tuna.

No luck.

I considered my options for a minute. I could try to She-Ra the bed up, but even then I wasn't confident in my ability to hold it up and somehow convince the cat to come out. I could get a broom and start swiping under there, but that seemed needlessly mean. I could just give up, lock the house and leave and let the cat have squatter's rights.

Finally, I headed next door to Sam's.

It was unfortunate that he only saw me at my very worst—coffee-stained pajama pants or *Batman Forever* T-shirt. Today, I'd dressed for cleaning, which meant I was wearing old ripped jeans and a Metric shirt from college that was just this side of too small. I'd even wrapped a bandana around my hair because that was what people who cleaned on TV always did.

"Hey," I said when he opened the door, barely taking a breath. "Can I borrow a can of tuna?"

He tilted his head. "I thought it was supposed to be a cup of sugar."

"Cats shouldn't eat sugar," I said, appalled. "That can't be good for their digestive tract."

"Wait," Sam said. "What are we talking about?"

"Just grab the tuna and come over," I said.

I didn't wait for him, but left the door ajar so he'd know it was okay to come in. I was worried Lenore would've moved already, making it that much harder to figure out where she was now, but when I peered under the bed, there she was.

In my pocket, my phone vibrated with another message. **Well???** Alison had typed. **Did you get her to come out? And if so, when are you sending a pic???**

I didn't bother replying yet. Better to wait when I actually had an update to share.

Sam appeared in the doorway of my room, hesitating at the threshold like he was a vampire who needed to be invited in. "I brought the tuna," he said, holding up a can, and then another implement in his other hand. "And a can opener. Just in case."

I gestured him in, and he joined me down on the floor. I'd already brought a fork and plate from the kitchen, and I opened the can of tuna and scooped a little bit out onto the plate, hoping it looked appetizing enough for Lenore to venture out. It certainly smelled strong enough.

"Is this a satanic ritual?" Sam asked. "Because I like to be asked for affirmative consent before I participate in one of those."

"Shh," I said. "Maybe we should back up, give her some space."

I withdrew, sliding back on the carpet until my back was against the closet. Sam joined me, angling his head to try to see under the bed. I could've reached out and tousled his hair—he was so close. It took massive self-control—and me sitting on my hands—but I managed to resist the temptation.

"How'd she get under there?" Sam asked.

"She's been trying to come in the house lately," I said. "Today I left the door open and she just darted in. Now she won't come out from under the bed, and I don't want to *hurt* her, but you know . . . what if she takes a dump under there or something? I don't want to have to deal with that."

"You should hope for poop," Sam said. "The alternative might be harder to get the smell out."

"Gee, thanks," I said. "Real helpful."

He glanced around, as if taking in the surroundings for the first time. "Is this your childhood room?" he asked. "There's a lot of black."

"Well, I didn't paint it that way until I was fourteen and capable of making cryptic comments about how I wanted my room to match my soul. When this was truly my *childhood* bedroom, it was perfectly normal, thank you very much. I had a wallpaper border with roses on it and an American Girl doll on the dresser and everything."

"Let me guess." He narrowed his eyes at me. "Samantha."

"Not all brunette girls needed to own a Samantha doll," I said, affronted. "But yes, it was Samantha. She had a really cool tartan cape and a valise and she stood up against child labor, so don't think she was just some prissy rich girl."

Sam held his hands up in surrender. "I would never."

"How do you have a handle on the Pleasant Company catalog, anyway? Not that dudes can't play with dolls, et cetera, but you said *Samantha* with the air of a man who knew about Molly and Felicity and Addy and Kirsten and Josefina and Kit . . ."

"You lost me at Kit," he said. "But I have sisters. I know stuff."

I remembered the pictures hanging in his house, the masses of people, all smiling as though they were actually happy to spend time together. "How many siblings do you have?"

"Five," he said, and that number shocked me even though I'd been preparing myself for it to be high.

"You come from a family of *six* kids?" I asked.

He started counting off on his fingers. "Tara is the oldest, then Jack, Megan, me, Erin, and Dylan."

"Are you all close?"

He shrugged. "Pretty close, I think," he said. "Obviously we're kind of spread out now. We grew up in Chicago, and Tara and Megan stayed near there, and Dylan still lives at home. Jack is stationed overseas, and Erin is in grad school in Seattle. We have a group chat, though."

I knew it.

"You and Conner must be close," Sam said. "What did he end up needing the other night?"

I waved my hand. "It's a long story," I said, not wanting to get into the proposal scheme and the broken wrist and all that. "Conner and I actually don't know each other that well. There's a seven-year age gap, and since I moved out with our mom when he was only six and he stayed here with our dad, we didn't grow up in the same house for most of our childhood."

"Oh." Sam had brought his knees up, linking his arms loosely around them, and he seemed to be thinking about what I'd said. We were the living embodiment of a Tolstoy quote—him with his happy family and me with my unhappy one. Or maybe that wasn't fair.

"I know that sounds like some awful *Parent Trap* shit," I said. "Like they separated us or something. But we each chose the parent we wanted to go with. My dad always let Conner get away with anything—I think it was because he was a boy and the baby—whereas with me . . . well, I never felt like my dad *got* me, I guess, or cared to try. It was an easy choice for both of us."

That had been more than I'd said aloud to a stranger about my family for a long time. Weirdly, it felt a lot like how it felt to have Sam in this house at all, which I still had conditioning from my childhood to believe was a place where you did *not* have people inside. The experience was a little surreal, but not unpleasant.

"It sounds like a hard choice," Sam said. "You were just kids."

His face was too close to mine, his expression too sympathetic, his eyes too blue. I was saved from having to make any response by the cat, who finally crept out from under the bed on her belly, eyeing us warily as she approached the tuna.

I put my hand on Sam's arm before I could think about it. His skin was still warm from even the brief walk over here, the lean muscles of his forearm hard beneath my fingertips. I wanted to leave my hand there forever. I wanted to give a squeeze.

"Shh," I said unnecessarily. "It's working."

We watched Lenore lick the plate, as if she wanted to experience the taste of the treat without fully committing to it. I could relate.

"So what now?" Sam whispered.

Alison hadn't gotten me that far. I snapped a quick picture of Lenore, shooting it off in a text with Sam's question below it.

Once she's settled in a bit, you should be able to pick her up with the plate and transfer both outside. Then just let her finish up her snack and voila, she's out of the house.

Three dots blinked, then another message: That is, assuming you don't want to keep her?? [gif of cat waving butt, then Shaq shimmying shoulders]

"I can't have a *cat*," I said aloud.

"Why not?" Sam asked. "She seems pretty sweet."

"For one thing, she doesn't belong to me."

"The neighbor feeds all the outside cats," Sam said. "Just like she feeds the birds and the squirrels. I don't think she has any particular claim over this particular cat. But you could always ask her, or put up a Found Cat poster around the neighborhood if it would make you feel better."

Pat did appear to like animals way more than people. I had no doubt that she'd dangle a small toddler in front of an alligator if one came up the street. The idea of asking her anything scared me a little, but the Found Cat poster wasn't a bad idea.

But I was only going to be here another month or so, and then after that I'd need to look for another apartment in North Carolina, which meant I'd need to put down a pet deposit if I had a cat, only to move again after I graduated in December. No. It would be impossible.

I started to reach for her, but then realized I had no idea how best to pick her up. Should I stand first, so I didn't have to try to get to my feet holding a ball of fur and claws? But if I made any sudden movement, did I risk spooking her back under the bed? Everything I knew about cats suggested that there were very *right* ways to handle them, and very *wrong* ways, and if you stumbled into the latter you risked becoming a human scratching post.

"You grab the cat," I whispered, as though she could process our speech, "and I'll grab the tuna. On the count of three. One, two, three . . ."

I let Sam move first, to ensure the animal was restrained before I made a move on her food. He made it look easy, scooping her into his arms, giving her a little scratch on the top of her head as he got to his feet. She stretched her body once, as if trying to escape, but seemed to settle down as he started walking with her toward the front door.

I followed close behind, setting down the plate of tuna next to the garage before the cat leapt out of Sam's arms and down to the pavement to continue her meal. I swear she gave both of us one withering look before resuming her laser focus on the food, as if to say, *Was* that *necessary?*

"Thanks for your help," I said. "If you hang on for just a minute, I can grab your can opener while Lenore's distracted."

I ran back to retrieve the can opener from my room, sliding back out of the door like the cat was going to try to battering-ram her way inside it any minute. "Here you go."

He took the can opener from me without really looking at it. "Lenore?"

The bandana around my hair had gotten knocked askew in the whole ordeal, and I gave it a self-conscious tug to fix it. "I had to call her *something*," I said. "And 'The Raven' is a banger."

I glanced down, and somehow in the time I'd disappeared back inside she'd eaten the entire plate of tuna. It hadn't been that much, but still—one minute she was demurely licking around the edge, and then the next minute she'd inhaled the rest of it. She lay out on her stomach next to the plate, giving a big yawn.

My phone buzzed, and I took it out of my pocket. **So are you keeping her?? [gif of cat hugging teddy bear]**

Alison was exacting with her capitalization and punctuation, which wasn't surprising given her profession, but she was also a much more prolific gif- and emoji-er than I would've expected.

"Sorry," I said to Sam as I typed out my response. **I wouldn't** even know where to begin. "My friend is very pro me keeping this cat. Which is hilarious, given that the whole reason I texted her in the first place was to ask how to get the cat *out*."

It surprised me, how easily that description of Alison had tripped off my tongue. *My friend.* Technically, she was the oldest friend I had, and exchanging a few texts did go a long way toward making it feel like we might have a place in each other's lives after all.

Hmm, if only there were a place where one could go for information . . . a place that had free books on every topic you could think of . . . [book stack emoji]

Smiling, I typed back the interwebs? just to be a shit.

I slid my phone into my back pocket, taking a deep breath as I considered the absolute folly of every single part of what I was about to do. "Any chance you're up for a library visit?"

THIRTEEN

S AM AND I agreed to meet back up in front of my house in half an hour to head out together. He said he needed to gather his books and finish a few things, and I desperately needed a shower and a change of clothes if I was going to reenter the world of other people.

I told myself that getting a book or two on how to care for a cat wouldn't be out of the question. It wasn't like I was knitting Lenore a sweater. Reading up on cat ownership would just give me an idea of what to expect, if I ever did decide to get a pet down the road.

Plus, I really needed to get out of the house.

There was also no particular reason for me to dress a little nicer than I normally would, in a black V-neck shirt, with nothing screen-printed on it, that hinted at my cleavage. I applied some winged eyeliner and red lipstick before I decided that both together were too much and wiped the lipstick off.

I was tired of my own usual updo but also self-conscious about the idea of wearing my hair down in front of Sam, lest it feel like I was trying too hard or purposely referencing back to our conversation in his garage. So instead I braided it in a loose, over-the-shoulder style.

Sam was already waiting for me by the time I headed outside. If I wasn't mistaken, it looked like he'd put in a little effort, too. He'd done something with his hair, at least, so that it was still shaggy but not as disorderly as it usually was. I'd never tell him this, but I kinda liked the disorder.

"Ready?" I asked brusquely.

He held up his books, the same ones I'd seen him with that day my battery had died. "As I'll ever be."

I unlocked the Camry and pulled open the driver's-side door, waiting until he'd settled into the passenger seat before saying, "What does *that* mean? If you need more time before we head out, just say so. Or I can make the trip myself—it's not like I *need* you to come."

He laughed a little. "It's something my dad says. If you ask if he's ready, no matter what, he'll answer, *As I'll ever be*. I didn't even realize it came out of my mouth."

"Oh."

My dad had had those, too. Little sayings or punch lines he used in certain situations—I guessed there was a reason dad jokes were a thing. Like if you said you were hungry, he'd say, "Hi, Hungry, I'm John," or if you said you were going to jump on the computer he'd say, "Please, don't jump." When I thought of my dad, it was as a quiet, serious man, prone to bouts of rage, but he'd actually had a pretty dry sense of humor. He could be silly, too. If he found a frog in the house—and it was Florida, frogs were always getting into the house somehow—he'd capture it in a glass and release it outside. "If you love something, let it go," he'd say with exaggerated somberness. "Only I hope you don't come back to us, my frog friend, because all that's here for you is toilet water."

"I'm glad you asked me to come with you to the library," Sam said now. "I'll return these early for once."

"Yeah, I need to renew mine." Which I could've easily done online, but I hoped he wouldn't point that out.

"Do you mind?" Sam asked instead, his hand hovering over my tote bag, and I shook my head. He pulled out the Sunrise Slayer's daughter's book, flipping it over to read the back.

I braced myself for the inevitable comment on how dark the subject matter was, how fucked up it would be to find out your dad was a serial killer. But Sam just made an ambiguous sound in the back of his throat, leaving the book on his lap as he looked out the window.

"Your dissertation is about the relationship between author and subject in true crime," Sam said finally. "Is that right?"

"In a nutshell."

"So why this subject for you? What's your relationship to it?" His voice was curious, not accusatory, but I still felt an immediate resistance to the questions. It was a knee-jerk reaction after a lifetime of being an incredibly private person. Sam must've seen some of that cross my face, because he hastened to add, "Sorry. If that's something you don't want to talk about, you don't have to."

"No," I said, the word coming out slow, like I was still considering it. "It's okay. It's a fair question. They'll probably ask it at my defense."

"That's where you present your work in front of your professors?"

"My committee, yeah," I said. This had been my entire world for so long, sometimes it was hard to remember what parts of it would be known by people outside of academia, and which esoteric details would be lost without explanation. "Basically, that's my main advisor and three other professors. I present all my research in front of them and anyone else who wants to attend, and anyone in the audience can ask me questions. Then the audience leaves and it's just me and the committee, and they can ask me anything they want—not just about my dissertation, but about anything I've studied the last five and a half years."

"Whoa. That sounds intense."

"A couple years ago, a guy started crying because they asked him all this stuff about the French Revolution and he'd taken one class on French literature his second year. I think that professor was being a dick, though—usually they're not trying to trick you. At least, I hope not."

Sam was running one finger along the pages of the book, the soft rustling sound oddly soothing. "So then after that you're a doctor?"

"Technically, not until after graduation," I said. "But the defense is a bigger milestone for sure. Once you pass it, you mostly only have logistical stuff to worry about like the final formatting and making sure you're all paid up on any parking fines."

Last year, I'd attended as many defenses as I could, trying to get an idea of what mine might look like. I'd been intimidated by the comprehensive exams I had to take a couple years ago, but I was actually looking forward to my defense. It was nerve-wracking, the idea of all this time and effort and work culminating in two hours of sink or swim, but I loved talking about true crime and how its genre conventions had shifted over the last century. I felt ready.

In fact, if I could skip to that part without having to actually finish the dissertation itself . . .

I realized I'd never answered Sam's original question about why I was drawn to the subject, but I also didn't have a satisfying hard-boiled answer. I switched on the radio to the local alternative station, turning the volume down so we could still easily talk. "What made you become a music teacher?"

"My grandmother taught piano," Sam said. "She gave all us kids lessons, but I was the only one who stuck with it. And then I did orchestra in middle school, playing the violin, before switching to band in high school as a drummer. Music was the most constant thing in my life, you know? Grades were good, grades were bad, I had friends, I didn't have friends, it didn't matter. I always had music."

I snuck a glance at him. He'd stopped ruffling the book's pages but was gripping it so tight his knuckles were white. I liked the way he got when he talked about music, how much he obviously cared.

"Hard to believe you ever lacked for friends," I said. If Sam the kid was anything like Sam the adult, it was difficult to imagine anyone not getting along with him.

"In sixth grade, I still wore *very* short shorts," he said. "My mom set out all my outfits for me on my bed every morning. I was oblivious. My favorite T-shirt was from the *Titanic* museum."

I bit back a smile. "In third grade, I told the whole class I was dead."

"So you were a ghost? Or was it more a *Weekend at Bernie's* situation?"

"I don't even remember. I just wanted kids to leave me alone."

The spot I'd parked in last time I came to the library was open, but I parked a few spaces down, because I had random bursts of superstition that made me believe in bad luck. Once I'd been wearing a new skirt on the day I got into a minor fender bender, and I'd never worn the skirt again.

"Your lights are off?" Sam said, apparently thinking about the last time we'd been here, too.

"Ha ha," I said, but I checked, just to make sure.

This time, when I walked in and saw Alison shelving DVDs in the media section, I immediately went over to say hi.

"I knew it," she said as soon as she saw me. "Section six hundred thirty-six upstairs, animal husbandry. We definitely have books on cats. Unless you want one from the juvenile section? I'm not making fun—some of them are better because they boil it down to just the basics. And they have lots of pictures."

"I think I can handle a grown-up book," I said dryly. I could see Alison peering curiously behind me, so I gestured to Sam. "This is my neighbor, Sam. Sam, this is my friend, Alison."

If I hesitated slightly over the word *friend*, I hoped neither noticed.

Sam lifted his hand in a wave, but Alison was already holding hers out to shake. "Hi, Sam," she said. "I've seen you around.

How's the—" She stopped herself, making a gesture like she was zipping her lips. "Sorry. Don't talk about patrons' checkout history in front of other patrons! I swear, it's like Library Science 101."

"It's okay," he said, then turned to me. "Your friend helped me find that soldering book from before."

"Wow," I said. "I've been mispronouncing that word in my head this whole time. It really doesn't rhyme with *smoldering*, are you sure?"

The corner of his mouth twitched in a smile. "Pretty sure."

"I was writing you a sonnet, but that's really going to throw the whole rhyme scheme off."

It was just a joke—obviously, I wasn't writing anyone a *sonnet*, I hadn't written a poem since my sophomore year of high school, when my poem "Indiffernce," typo and all, had been selected to be published in a Poetry.com anthology available to me and my loved ones for the low, low price of sixty bucks. I almost wished I had ordered a copy after all. The poem had featured a lot of winter imagery and had included the last lines: *And as I sink down to my knees / I feel only indifference.* I'd been very proud of them at the time.

But I realized after I said it what the whole joke had implied—that I was writing a poem for Sam, that I'd intended to use the word *smoldering*, presumably to describe him . . .

It was no wonder his cheeks looked a little pink.

Alison was giving me a knowing look of her own, and I knew trying to explain myself would only make things worse, so I tried to change the subject.

"So, cat books, upstairs?"

"Yup," she said, giving me and Sam a wide smile. "And for a

vet, I recommend the Care Clinic on the corner of Preston and Crosby. If you let them know that she's a stray or rescue, they'll give you a discount on the standard initial shots."

"I'm probably not going to take her in," I said. "I just figured I'd read up on the subject."

"Mm-hmm."

"I like to be informed."

Alison made eye contact with Sam, standing behind me, and rolled her eyes a little. I turned around to see him grinning, and when I shot him a look of betrayal, he just shrugged. "She named the cat Lenore," he said to Alison.

"Oh my god," Alison said, "remember that diorama you made for 'The Tell-Tale Heart'? You found a way to get the ticking noise and everything."

"It was just an old kitchen timer," I muttered.

"How long have you guys been friends?" Sam asked, glancing between the two of us.

That felt like a complicated question. Alison and I had met in fifth grade and become besties almost immediately, which led to three more years of trying to be in the same classes as much as possible, passing notes back and forth, and sleeping over at each other's houses. Even after I'd moved with my mom and gone to a different high school, we'd stayed in touch for a couple years, until the Incident. So I guessed we were friends for about five years or so, and then maybe again now for a couple weeks, so how did you add *that* up accurately? It was like a math word problem where any answer was wrong.

"Almost twenty years," Alison said easily. "We met at the end of elementary school. I'd just moved here and all the other kids made fun of me because . . . well, a mix of things, including racism and a lack of appreciation for my taste in eyewear. Phoebe saw me sitting alone at lunch, and sat down next to me."

"My old table was all Backstreet Boys fans," I said. "I got tired of arguing that *NSYNC was better. It's exhausting being so right all the time."

"Uh-huh. Meanwhile, I didn't listen to either band."

"'Being ignorant is not so much a shame,'" I quoted, "'as being unwilling to learn.' You let me play the *No Strings Attached* album for you."

"Whatever," Alison said, directing the conversation back to Sam again. "The point is, Phoebe was kind to me at a time when no one else was."

My skin felt all prickly, and I could feel Sam's attention on me. I hadn't introduced him to Alison so she could serve as a character witness for me, but I was afraid that was what it looked like now.

"Okay, well," I said, "you guys can keep going down memory lane if you want to. Meanwhile, if anyone needs me, I'll be upstairs in animal husbandry."

I headed for the giant ramp leading to the second floor without waiting for a response, although I heard Alison call after me, "Care Clinic!" and then heard her say a quieter *Sorry*, presumably to nearby patrons who were disturbed by a librarian breaking the number one rule of libraries everywhere in raising her voice. Sam caught up with me easily, falling into step beside me as we headed upstairs.

"Your friend Alison's great," he said. "I see her all the time when I come here, but I'd never spoken to her outside of general library-related stuff."

"We were actually friends when we were kids," I said. "But we haven't kept in touch since high school. We only started talking again because I'm in town and I texted her a few questions about the cat."

I didn't know why it was so important for me to clarify any of those points to Sam. I worried that maybe he'd gotten one impression from talking with her, that I was this loyal, good-hearted friend who'd stuck by her side since fifth grade, and I'd feel guilty if I didn't correct the record on that point. We may have had a *Baby-Sitters Club*—worthy friendship when we were kids, but the more recent history was a lot rockier.

I wandered down the aisle for 636, stopping when I saw all the books about pets. There were at least eighteen all helpfully named *Cats*, so I just went with my gut and pulled out the thickest one, figuring it'd be the most comprehensive.

"It seems like you have some roots here," Sam said. "Between Alison and your brother . . . do you ever think about moving back permanently?"

"No." I flipped through the book, my eyes glazing over as it covered various breeds in detail and described famous cats throughout history. Maybe an encyclopedic approach was overkill here. I put the book back and selected the one next to it instead.

"What if you found a job?" he asked. "Or met someone?"

"Jobs and people exist all over the world," I said, only half paying attention, "without me having to resort to Florida. Hey, did you know that cats' noses are as unique as human fingerprints? Lenore won't be getting away with breaking and entering on my watch."

"If first offense gets tuna, what does the second offense get? Catnip?"

I started to laugh, only to realize that Sam's expression looked closed off and not as jokey as I would've imagined given his comment. His hands were in his pockets and he was frowning down at the dog books. Either he felt *Marley & Me* was as emotionally manipulative as I did or I'd fucked up somewhere.

"Sorry," I said. "That came out really shitty. I know you live here by choice. I just . . . don't have super-happy memories of my time here, I guess."

It would be so easy to get lost in his eyes. It was probably for public health that he let his hair fall over them half the time, like wearing eclipse glasses to protect your retinas from burning. Except this would be like the sun wearing the glasses? I lost myself in my own simile. He withdrew his hand from his pocket, reaching—for my hand? I hadn't been fishing for sympathy, but I also couldn't deny the way my breath caught in my throat, while I waited for him to make contact.

A book. He was reaching for a thin, green-spined book, a fluffy orange-and-white cat staring directly out from the cover with amber eyes. It promised to be a complete pet owner's manual and had been, rather surprisingly, translated from German.

"Published almost ten years ago," I said, opening up to the front pages. "What if this doesn't have anything about the latest updates in kitten technology? Lenore might want the high-tech laser pointer all the other cats have and I'll have no idea."

"The basics stay the same," Sam said. "Food, water, litter box, veterinary care. Love. That's it."

Love. The way he said the word made my stomach flip. The

pause before it, like it was the most important one of them all. Which was stupid, because obviously you could die from lack of food or water, or lack of access to veterinary care. No litter box would doubtless mean some toxic shit I'd rather not think about. But no one ever died from a lack of *love*.

"All this," I said, "and I probably won't even see her again. She'll find another house to sneak into. She's a wild thing, roaming the streets."

"She'll be back."

"It's fine if she's not," I said. "I don't even know if I want a cat."

"Phoebe," Sam said. "I promise you. Lenore will be back."

BUT SHE DIDN'T come back, not that night at least. I gave the cat an entire canful of my tuna—okay, *Sam's* tuna—and the ungrateful brat hadn't even hung around to see if there'd be seconds.

After the library, I said goodbye to Sam and headed back into the house. Not even necessarily because I wanted to, but because I knew that I'd never get any work done if I kept hanging out with him. Now that I'd gotten over the *maybe he's a serial killer* hump, he was fast becoming my favorite person to hang out with. He was less annoying than Conner, less guilt-inducing than Alison, and generally easy on the eyes.

I was starting to wonder what it would be like to have a fling with the neighbor for my remaining time here, which was a bad idea on several levels.

For one, I had more than enough on my plate. I still hadn't finished the fucking Capote chapter, which Dr. Nilsson had started emailing about in messages that contained nothing but question marks. I still had a lot of work to do on my dad's house, including some harebrained scheme I'd cooked up to paint the entire common area this weekend to freshen up the place. In defense of Past Me, that had been when I thought I'd have help from Conner. Now that he was dealing with a fractured wrist, it seemed cruel to ask him to try to wield a paint roller in his remaining uninjured hand. Cruel and, more importantly, not conducive toward getting an HGTV-worthy finish on the walls.

For another, I'd tried "flings" in the past, and had always been left unsatisfied. In relationships, I tended to feel trapped and resentful. I didn't express my feelings in the way the other person wanted, or at all. "Sometimes it feels like you don't need me," a boyfriend I'd dated for six months after college had complained once. *That's because I don't,* I'd wanted to say, and had been pretty proud of my emotional maturity at the time in realizing I shouldn't actually say it out loud. Still, we'd broken up a few weeks later.

Flings were better in that I didn't have to pretend I was someone I wasn't. But they often left me feeling nothing at all—just empty and vaguely sad, like when you spend the night letting bad reality television wash over your eyeballs and it feels good at the time but then later it's like, fuck, what a waste of a night.

It was hard to imagine feeling that way with Sam.

Still, why risk it. And this was all if he'd even be into the idea, which seemed like a big *if* at this point. Sometimes I was sure the sparks were firing off him, too. You couldn't *accidentally* eat a Kit Kat suggestively, could you? And you didn't compliment near-strangers' hair for no reason, surely?

But then Sam complicated it by just being a *nice guy*. He'd mowed the lawn for my dad, so I couldn't take him doing it now as anything more than a neighborly gesture. I'd crashed his party. I'd asked for his help with the car. I'd made him come over to help me lure out a cat.

When I put it all together, it was like I was throwing myself at him. Disgusting.

I didn't want to have a fling with my neighbor. Just like I didn't want a cat, I didn't want to be friends with Alison again, I didn't want to stay here any longer than I had to.

It was exhausting, not wanting things.

FOURTEEN

T HE REAL ESTATE agent had recommended we repaint the walls an inoffensive off-white, just shaded enough to look like a deliberate design choice but not so shaded that anyone would have a visceral negative reaction. That way, she said, people could project whatever color they wanted on the walls.

"But if they're going to repaint anyway," I'd said, "why bother?"

"You're going to need all the help you can get," she'd said in a voice tinged with mild annoyance. Sometimes she made it hard to forget that she'd only agreed to take the house on as a favor because she'd known my dad. As far as I knew, she'd take her six percent no matter what, so "favor" seemed to be stretching it.

"I mean, I planned to *clean* the walls—"

"Unless you're planning to do something about the tile in the guest bathroom and the kitchen cabinets," she said, "I'd recommend painting at the very least."

There was clearly no point in arguing. After we hung up, I stood in the bathroom, trying to figure out what was wrong with the tile. It was old, sure, but I'd cleaned the grout with a toothbrush and thought it looked pretty good.

The kitchen cabinets were another story. They were a horrible fake wood laminate that may have been original to the 1978 build. Nobody would want to Instagram themselves cooking in front of those bad boys.

And once I was actually buying the paint, there were so many *choices*. Polished Pearl and Pale Palomino and Smooth Silk and other alliterative options. I thought about choosing one called Shoelace, just to be passive-aggressive, but went with Linen White. At least it sounded classy.

I was carrying in my second round of bags from the hardware store when Sam pulled up in his truck. Neutral professional was back, which meant he must be coming from teaching another lesson. If I wasn't careful, I'd start to develop a khaki pants fetish.

"You painting?" he called from his driveway.

Apparently the roller extension under my arm was a dead giveaway. "Yup."

"Are Conner and Shani coming by to help?"

"Shani has a shift at the hospital," I said, "and Conner offered, but he's still laid up with his fractured wrist. Painting doesn't seem like the best idea—for him or the walls."

He stood there for a moment, bouncing his keys in his hand. "Cool," he said finally. "I'll be over in a sec."

"No," I said, "you don't have to—"

But he had already disappeared inside his house. Fuck. This was the *opposite* of what I'd resolved to do. At least I hadn't explicitly asked him for his assistance. So it shouldn't really count, right?

I'd only gotten the baseboards around one wall lined with bright blue tape when I heard the knock at the door, and yelled for Sam to come on in.

"Why," I said without bothering to look up, "does nobody tell you how *long* the prep work takes? This is like a math problem from hell. *What is the perimeter of this room and how many times can you tape the perimeter before you want to die?* And the answer, apparently, is zero point two times."

"Tell you what." Sam started yanking up the tape I'd already laid down, and I gave an involuntary yelp of indignation. "Let me handle the trim. You can work on the rest with the roller. Sound good?"

I glanced up, intending to give him a piece of my mind for the way he'd taken over, the way he'd undone the little bit of work I'd managed to do so far. But instead I was shocked into silence. I'd seen him barefoot in the middle of the night; I'd seen him wearing his bland uniform to go teach kids how to play "Come as You Are" or whatever the equivalent was in this century.

I hadn't expected *this*.

"Are you wearing coveralls?"

He looked down at himself. "Yeah."

"With your name on them?"

He tapped the patch on his chest, embroidered with a red cursive *Sam*. "You're just jealous you don't have personalized painting clothes."

A little bit. I was in a *Pet Sematary* tank top, the armholes cut wide enough that you could see the sides of my bra underneath, and jean shorts. I had not expected anyone else to come by, much less *Sam*, so I hadn't cared how I looked. Now the outfit felt skimpy. I checked which bra I was wearing under the guise of wiping my arm across my forehead. At least it was one of my good ones—neon purple and trimmed with lace.

Sam poured the paint into a tray for me, and a Solo cup, for him, and immediately got to work. It didn't take me long to realize why Sam had taken off the tape. He was *good*. Like, perfectly straight line, no drips, every movement methodical, *good*.

I should've started painting myself, but I couldn't look away. It was mesmerizing, watching him work. He had one knee propped up, his arm holding the cup of paint draped across it, while he angled himself to paint a stripe of Linen White at the bottom of the wall.

"You're a ringer," I said.

"Sorry?"

I gestured toward the job he was doing, even though he was looking at the wall and not at me. "You're really good at that. Is this something else you do on the side?"

Finally, he seemed to make a mistake, a single drip of paint sliding down onto the baseboard. He wiped it away with his thumb, then wiped his thumb on the leg of his coveralls. "I used to," he said. "A-Plus Painters, the summer after high school and then on weekends and breaks my first two years of college."

"And they let you keep your coveralls?" There were a few smears of color here and there on the navy fabric, I noticed, but not as much as I might've expected from a professional painter. Or maybe that was all the paint-splattered pandas on Lisa Frank stationery giving me the wrong idea.

"I actually bought these for myself," he said. "For when I . . ."

He trailed off, frowning down at the corner he'd been wedging the paintbrush into. From my angle, the paint looked fine, so I couldn't figure out why he'd stopped.

Or maybe he was waiting for me to actually do some work on my own house. I grabbed a roller and loaded it up with paint, starting to press streaks of Linen White onto the wall.

"If you don't finish that sentence," I said, "you know I'll do it in my head with something like *for when I'm dropping a human body into the acid bath.*"

He gave a soft laugh. "I don't think this fabric is manufactured to withstand acid baths," he said. "No, I had this idea a year or so ago that I'd start making my own guitars. So I bought these for that project, because I thought it'd be cool, having this dedicated uniform I could work in, and that I wouldn't worry about getting paint or varnish or glue on."

"You make your own guitars?"

"Not really," he said. "It didn't work out."

I thought back to his garage, those parts that had been left, as if in the middle of being put back together.

"You're a giant nerd," I said, like it was a revelation. It kind of was. Anyone who'd even attempted to *make* his own instrument, even going so far as to buy his own work uniform to do so, definitely qualified as a nerd in my book.

"Yeah," he said, "I've been told that."

Something about the way he said it, something about the resigned set of his shoulders, told me maybe he hadn't taken that comment as the joke I'd meant it. "That's not a bad thing," I clarified. "I have a whole spreadsheet dedicated to episodes of *Disappeared*, where I Google the cases every few months to see if they solved what happened to the people yet. Music sounds like a much healthier obsession."

"Speaking of," he said, "we could put on some music while we worked. If you wanted."

Never let it be said I couldn't take a hint to shut up. I only had my phone, and I tried to put that in an empty Solo cup to amplify the sound, but only two songs into my playlist he said he couldn't take it and ran to his house to get a Bluetooth speaker. While he was gone, I checked my phone, and saw that Conner had texted a few times.

I can head over to help if you need me, the first one read, and then, **Happy to hold a ladder for moral support.**

Then, several minutes later, **That probably doesn't sound very secure, huh?**

Half an hour ago, I totally would've taken Conner up on his offer. If for no other reason than I had an older sister's distaste for seeing him get out of doing something that I still had to do. But then Sam was back, his hair already sticking to his forehead slightly with sweat, his smile genuine as he set the speaker up on my desk. And so I texted, **Nah it's fine. I've got this. You can bring me lunch tomorrow if you're feeling really guilty. And best believe I'll expect you to help repaint my room.** Then I added a line of skull emojis. That black was going to take a lot to cover.

Sam and I got into a rhythm with our painting, working on opposite walls so we wouldn't run into each other. I felt bad for him—while I was rolling on the paint willy-nilly, overlapping lines and hoping it would all dry as one cohesive color, he had to be down on the ground hunched over the trim, keeping his hand steady and neat.

He must've felt the opposite, though, because he looked up, giving me a sympathetic grimace. "Want me to roll some on for a bit? You're doing all the muscle."

Which made my gaze go to his arms, naturally. Even with the occasional smear of Linen White, they still looked delicious. I could sink my teeth into the wiry tendon above his wrist, not to draw blood but just to exert a soft pressure . . .

Jesus. I was scaring even myself. My own self-judgment made my voice sharper than intended when I said, "Why are you being so nice to me?"

Sam stopped painting, his brush suspended in midair. "What?"

"You don't *have* to be here," I said. "Painting sucks. If I could get out of doing this, believe me, I would."

"I actually like painting."

"I know, you're reliving your A-Plus glory days," I said. "But seriously, I'm not that nice to *you*. I don't understand why you would be nice to *me*."

Sam stared up at me, his brush still in his hand, as though forgotten.

"Drip!" I said, just in time for him to stick the brush back in his cup of paint. His gaze didn't move from the cup for a moment, as though he'd just had a near miss with death and was contemplating the meaning of his life so far.

"I think I need a break," he said. "Any chance you have more of that pie?"

I didn't, but we shared the last packet of cinnamon brown sugar Pop-Tarts, eating them untoasted directly from the foil. Thanks to the lack of furniture in the common areas aside from my writing desk, there weren't many seating options, but Sam said he wanted to stretch his legs anyway. Meanwhile, I'd take any excuse to get off my feet, so I settled into my desk chair and hoped I could find the energy to get back out in a few minutes.

"What makes you think you're not nice to me?" he asked finally, his voice so casual that I almost didn't connect his words back to our previous conversation.

I shrugged. I didn't want to enumerate all the ways I was probably a bitch, to remind him of the few he may have already forgotten about.

"*Nice* is a bullshit word, anyway," he said. "*Nice* is just surface politeness. Screw being nice."

I blinked a little at how emphatic he was. I didn't disagree—far from it—but it was surprising to hear him of all people express that sentiment. "Okay," I said, "but literally you came over here to help me paint, and I called you a nerd. There has to be a happy medium somewhere between surface politeness and insulting someone to their face, and I've never been able to find it."

"I *am* a nerd," he said. "I'm not insulted by that at all. If I seemed sensitive about it . . . well, it was basically why my last relationship ended. But you wouldn't have known that. It's not your fault."

"Your ex dumped you for being a *nerd?*" I could've phrased my question more diplomatically, but I'd been too shocked to put any filter on. This must be the ex-girlfriend Conner had mentioned, the one who'd broken up with Sam right before Christmas. "Honest question, but is it even possible to be a true nerd anymore, now that Disney owns *Star Wars*?"

He smiled at that. *"Deeply uncool* were the words she used," he said. "To be fair."

"Did she see you in those coveralls?" I asked. I'd meant it as a joke, a little sarcasm to lighten the mood, but it came out more sincere. His words had wrenched something deep in my chest. I hated the idea that someone would say anything like that to Sam, especially someone he'd trusted and cared about. Probably even loved.

I got up to grab the roller and start painting again, hoping my sudden panic didn't show all over my face. I'd always known I was protective of my own heart. It was unthinkable that I'd be so protective of his, too.

"Tell me more about this arbiter of cool," I said, pleased that my voice sounded so steady. "Did she have a tongue ring or something?"

"A nose ring, actually," Sam said. "How did you know that?"

I'd just been going back to high school and trying to think what could make someone seem intimidatingly badass. For me, a lip or tongue piercing always signaled *I don't give a fuck* and *The music I listen to would make your eardrums bleed*. But maybe I should update my rubric.

"How long were you together?"

"Two years," Sam said. "We met at a bar—I was playing guitar in my friend's band, and Amanda heckled us from the front row. I think that was part of the problem. She had this image of me as some kind of rock star wannabe, but I'd only been filling in while their usual guitarist spent time with her new baby."

Images of Sam from the past few weeks flickered through my mind—standing barefoot and disheveled in front of me at two in the morning. Holding a bag of Kit Kats in his doorway wearing a ridiculous tropical shirt. Plucking out "Farmer in the Dell" at the music store. Wearing those stupid fucking khakis.

I could see how the reality of him didn't quite fit a rock star stereotype, despite his love of music. But the reality of him was also a lot better than that.

"Did you play the tambourine up there, too?" I asked. "Because you gotta see how that would give a girl the wrong idea."

Sam had returned to painting, too, which was a relief. He was on the stepladder, focusing on edging around the ceiling, which gave me the perfect excuse to check out his butt. Briefly. Tastefully.

It was a very nice butt.

"Do you think you would've married her?" The question was out of my mouth before I could think about it, and *wow*. One hundred percent not my business, and since when had I cared about anyone's potential marital status, anyway?

Sam didn't answer right away. He was looking down at the cup of paint while he dipped his brush back in it, and I stared at the exposed skin of his neck, trying to glean what he wasn't saying. *Yes, I was madly in love with her?*

"I don't know," he said finally. "I'd never really considered it, and then we broke up, so I guess I'll never know for sure. Either way, it's obvious that we weren't meant for each other."

"Is anyone?"

It was taking him a long time to reload that brush with paint. "Do you really believe that?"

"I've read *The Phantom Prince*," I said. "The updated version with the foreword where she completely disavows her relationship with Ted Bundy. If that doesn't convince you that romance is dead, nothing will."

Sam stepped down from the ladder, as if he needed to be more grounded to have this conversation. "You do that a lot. Bring up serial killer stuff when the topic turns more serious."

"What could be more serious than mass murder?"

He gave me a look that immediately made me feel all prickly inside, all *you don't know me*, but then also a little *fuck, you really know me*. I blew my hair out of my eyes. The bandana wasn't doing its only job.

"My parents divorced when I was thirteen," I said. "And okay, I know as far as original wounds go, it's pretty banal. Most people I know have parents who aren't together anymore, or were never together in the first place. I remember talking to some kid in my class a year before they split, some guy with greasy hair I had a crush on, and he said his parents were divorced. 'I wish mine would be,' I said, half because, I don't know, I wanted to impress him. Like I didn't buy into the picket fence bullshit everyone else did. And half of me meant it, too. They fought all the time, and if they weren't fighting it felt like we were walking on eggshells, trying to avoid doing anything that might cause a fight."

Sam and I weren't even trying to pretend we were painting anymore. I'd set the roller back in the tray, to avoid splattering paint drops everywhere while I gestured with my hands, and he'd taken a seat on the stepladder, his elbows leaned on his knees as he listened.

"Like one time, Conner wanted Jell-O. I don't know why, but kid got it into his head that he really wanted to eat his weight in Jell-O as a fun Saturday activity. Our mom promised to make him some, but she was always tired from work. At that time, I think she was still the office manager for this law firm where the head partner was this complete jackass, like seriously, once he threatened to fire her because we had a trip planned for Memorial Day and she said she wanted to take the three-day weekend."

I was getting off topic, and saying more than I'd meant to, but now that I'd started I couldn't stop. "Anyway, so I figured I'd make him the Jell-O. No big deal, right? You throw some colored sugar in a bowl and mix it with water and put it in the fridge. It takes five minutes. But my dad took it out before it had completely set, because he couldn't get to something in the back of the fridge, and then he was angry that my mom had blocked up the fridge with this giant bowl, and my mom got defensive and upset that I'd made the Jell-O when she *said* she was going to, and then Conner was crying because he wanted to eat Jell-O and it wasn't ready . . ."

I didn't tell Sam how the story had ended, with my dad throwing the bowl across the kitchen, splattering red everywhere like a crime scene. I bet when we pulled the fridge out to sell the place, some of it would still be on the tile underneath.

"Sorry," I said. "I don't know why I told you all that."

"I can see why you'd doubt relationships, and family, and love," Sam said. "It sounds like a tense way to grow up, and I'm really sorry you had to go through it. But, Phoebe, your parents were just two people. Ted Bundy and whatever his girlfriend's name was were two people. Hell, Bonnie and Clyde stayed together until the bitter end, and even *they* were only two people. You can't extrapolate your worldview from such a small data set."

"I mean, I *can*."

He rubbed the back of his neck. Either he had a crick from all the painting we'd been doing or this conversation was wearing him out. Probably both.

"What about Conner and Shani?" he asked. "They've been together a while, right? And Conner is planning to propose?"

"How'd you know about the proposal?"

"Conner cornered me at the party and showed me the ring. I thought he was going to get down on one knee for *me* for a minute."

That made me laugh. Sounded like Conner.

"So do you think they're doomed?" Sam asked.

An unfair question. I wasn't going to be the asshole who actually *said* that I thought my brother's relationship was doomed. Inasmuch as I thought all human connection was a setup for disappointment, sure, I guessed I had a hard time seeing two people able to stay together for the long haul.

But I realized that when I actually thought about my brother—how earnest he was, how good-natured, how openhearted—I found it hard to imagine him betraying Shani or treating her badly. And when I thought about Shani—how dedicated and thoughtful she was, how much she seemed to love my brother—it was hard to imagine *her* doing anything to tank the relationship, either.

"I plead the Fifth," I said, but my final verdict must've shown on my face, because Sam's mouth curved in a half smile.

"Maybe we should put the music back on," I suggested.

"Fine by me."

This time, I selected Chvrches' album *Love Is Dead*, grinning at my own joke.

FIFTEEN

———

WE DIDN'T FINISH painting until almost one in the morning, and that was only doing a single coat. I was glad I'd paid a little extra for the paint-primer combination that was supposed to cover better, even though Sam had been going around and touching up little places where he swore the color was patchy. I blamed it all on the dim lighting and said it looked fine.

"Think of us as C-Plus Painters," I said. "Maybe B-Minus if you don't look too close."

At some point during the night, Sam had unzipped the top half of his coveralls and let them fall around his waist, so he was only wearing a white ribbed tank undershirt on his upper body. It made me want to do ridiculous, wild things, like lick his exposed collarbones or unzip him the rest of the way.

He totally caught me looking, too. My cheeks felt like they were on fire, and I knew I was probably all pink from the exertion of painting and embarrassment.

"God, it's hot," I said, fanning my shirt collar against my skin, hoping he'd accept that as the reason for my flush. "Even central air can't keep up with summer in this swamp."

"I have a pool," he said. "Want to go for a swim?"

I shouldn't. It was already late, and I needed to be up early the next day so I could try to finish my chapter to send to Dr. Nilsson before five o'clock. I'd be better off taking a cold shower and falling into bed.

Then again, a swim sounded amazing right now. And a swim with Sam . . .

"Sure."

I couldn't remember the last time I'd actually swum. I didn't even own a bathing suit, because buying one was such a nightmare and always made me feel like Cathy from the Sunday morning comics when I was a kid, which was just about the last thing I ever wanted to feel like. I figured the underwear I was wearing would work just fine, even though it didn't match—black on the bottom and purple on the top. Who cared, right?

Sam said he didn't, and promised not to look as I stripped down. I made no such promises, so I caught a glimpse of his boxer briefs, the lean muscles in his back as he pulled his undershirt off, the ridges of his spine as he bent over to kick the coveralls off his feet. And then he surprised me by diving right into the deep end, submerging underwater until he came up for air a few moments later.

"The water's warm," he said. "But it still feels great. Come on in."

He drifted over to the side of the pool, resting his arms on the concrete deck, and I knew that was his way of giving me privacy while I undressed. A part of me wanted to say, *Go ahead and watch me*, because I was an adult and it seemed silly to be shy about this kind of thing, but also because I wanted to see if his eyes could turn that darker shade of blue or if I'd imagined it. But I stepped out of my shorts and yanked my tank top over my head, and then I was in the water.

It *did* feel great. I floated weightless, the glow from the underwater light turning my skin a pale bluish color. I felt like an alien. I felt *happy*.

"I could get used to this," I said, referring to more than the pool.

Sam treaded water, watching me. Just when I thought he might say something, or when I thought maybe *I* should, he ducked back under the water. Bubbles on the surface traced his path, showing that he was moving closer, until he emerged again in the shallow end with me. He was only in up to his waist, droplets of water sliding down his chest and over his flat stomach as he slicked his hair back and ran a hand over his face.

"You have paint in your hair," I said.

"You have paint on your—" His gaze dipped to my breasts before coming back up to meet mine. Maybe it was the otherworldly lighting or the fact that his eyelashes were dark and spiky with water, but his eyes looked electric blue.

I glanced down at my cleavage, which, sure enough, had a smear of paint right across the top of my left breast. "Huh," I said. "How did that get there?"

You could also totally see my nipples through this bra. Whoops.

The tips of his ears were so pink by now that if it had been daytime, I would've thought he was getting sunburned.

"It's too easy," I said, moving closer to him in the water.

"What is?"

"Making you blush . . ."

I stood on my tiptoes, curling my hand around the back of his neck. His skin was warm and slick with water, and I grabbed the hair at the nape to pull him toward me. I hadn't known I was going to kiss him until a split second before I did it. I felt like I'd known the minute I'd seen that he'd moved the stupid desk outside my front door.

If I had control at first, I didn't for long. His hands came up to my cheeks, his mouth insistent on mine as he deepened the kiss. He had my lower lip between his teeth, giving a soft nibble while a whimper came from the back of my throat that didn't even sound like me. My nipples were tight and aching, rubbing his chest through the thin fabric of my bra. His hand slid under the fabric to cup my goosefleshed skin, his fingers rolling my nipple in a sensation so exquisite it almost hurt.

"You have great boobs," he murmured against my neck. "Can I say that?"

My bra was half-askew by now, one strap falling down my arm. "If my boobs are out, you're contractually obligated to say that." I reached down to grab his ass, pushing his hips toward me until I could feel the hard length of him against my thigh. "You have a great ass. It even looks good in coveralls."

"I was hoping those would drive you crazy."

"It was the name patch that really did it. Wear those the next time you jump my battery and I can live out the sexy mechanic fantasy I didn't even know I had."

I could feel his smile against my mouth. "Phoebe?"

"Mmm?"

"I'm trying to jump something else right now," he said, "if that's okay by you."

"My bones?"

He kissed me again, and I swallowed his response, feeling it as a vibration somewhere in my gut. And then all conscious thought flew out of my head as his hands cupped my ass, lifting me as I wrapped my legs around his waist, feeling him against the core of me in a way that immediately made a shiver run up my spine.

"Cold?" he asked.

I shook my head. "Just keep kissing me."

He sucked on my lower lip, my neck, his tongue circling my earlobe before returning to my mouth. I couldn't get enough of Sam, wanted to feel his bare skin against mine. Making out in a pool was hot, don't get me wrong, but I wanted to be with him without the water between us.

"Do you have," I said, coming up for air before kissing him again, "condoms inside?"

His eyebrows rose in an expression that was either incredulity that I had to ask, or incredulity that this was happening so fast. Maybe both.

"Yeah," he said. "Are you—"

I slid down his body, giving his collarbone a little swipe with my tongue, because I'd promised myself I would. It tasted like chlorine and salt and Sam. "I'm sure," I said, because I had a feeling about what he was going to ask. "Let's go to your room. Please?"

We wrapped ourselves quickly in the towels Sam had left on the back porch and came in through the sliding glass door, him leading me through the house, holding my hand. I couldn't remember ever feeling this way before, this total *need* to be connected to another person. It probably had a lot to do with how long it had been since I last had sex, I figured, and how much anticipation I'd built up the last few weeks just in watching Sam, thinking about him, spending time together. Once we actually had sex, I'd get it out of my system. A fling, like I'd wanted.

Except then we got to his room, and suddenly it didn't feel like only a summer fling. His room immediately felt like *him*, somehow exactly as I might've imagined it, with a tall shelf stacked haphazardly with books and a guitar case leaning against one wall and dark blue blanket mussed at the end of the bed, as if he'd gotten up in a hurry. Only how could a room feel like Sam to me, when I barely knew him in the first place?

He closed the door behind him, leaning against it as if giving me some space. I tried to keep my gaze on him from the neck up, because the rest of him was too distracting.

"It's late," he said. "We can just sleep, if you'd rather. Or we can get your clothes and I'll walk you back next door."

"Is that what you want?"

The problem with my neck-up strategy was that I'd underestimated those eyes, which bore into me now as he watched the emotions play across my face.

"I don't think *my* wants are in question here."

"Hey, I kissed you first," I said. "I think I made a pretty clear declaration of my intent."

He came toward me, one hand hooked in the top of the towel that rode low on his hips, as if making sure it didn't fall. Meanwhile I just watched it as he moved, half hoping it would.

"And now?" he said.

I didn't know how to put all the ways I was feeling into words. I didn't know that I wanted to. I'd anticipated this moment for a while—not just hooking up with someone, but *him* specifically. And now that it was happening, it was scary and exciting and a little weird, knowing that this guy who'd become an important part of my life in the last few weeks was about to become important in a different way.

I slid my hands up his chest, pressing my thumbs into the notches of his shoulders. "I want this," I said. It seemed safer than saying my first thought, which had been *I want you.*

I let my towel drop to the floor, until I was standing in front of him topless, the greenish light from the pool outside still coming through the window. We must've forgotten to turn it off, but I couldn't bring myself to care about it now. I hooked my fingers in my underwear, and pulled them down.

I heard Sam's sharp intake of breath, the hitch in his throat as he looked down at me. He reached up to gently pull the elastic from my hair, combing his fingers through the waves as they splayed over my shoulders. Even that massage on my scalp felt good, and I closed my eyes, swaying into him.

"You're so beautiful," he murmured against my mouth, his hands still in my hair as he kissed me. This kiss was different from the ones in the pool, somehow—slower, more exploratory, as though he had all the time in the world and he wanted to spend it with me.

Meanwhile, I felt restless and pent-up and like if I didn't have him inside me right then I would explode.

My insistent hands on his towel and underwear must've given him the hint, because within five seconds we were both naked and twined together on the bed, kissing and touching everywhere we could. I took the hard length of him in my hand, and he shuddered against me as I rubbed my thumb along the silky head of his cock.

"Ah," he said, his voice sounding strangled. "I won't last long if you keep doing that."

"What, this?" I said, and did it again. I liked seeing him this way, out of control, his eyes glittering and wild in the low light of the room. But then he turned the tables on me, flipping me over so I was pinned on my back, and he kissed his way down my throat, stopping to suck one aching nipple in his mouth, roll his tongue along the swell of my stomach before he found my clit. I bucked involuntarily, my hips grinding into him as if my body knew it needed more even before my mind did. He licked and sucked, his tongue doing wicked things inside me, until there was no way I could hold myself back even if I wanted to. I clenched at the sheets, gasping as I felt my orgasm shockwave through me.

When I caught my breath again, I hooked my thigh around his leg, rolling on top of him so it was my turn to be in control. "Condom?" I breathed against his mouth.

"Nightstand drawer."

I ripped open the packet with my teeth, faltering only slightly when I saw the way one corner of his mouth twitched, something more than sex passing between us, a reminder of that shared moment we'd had back at his party. My fear in having a fling was that it would feel empty, but this didn't feel that way at all, and maybe that was scarier.

But then I didn't have any more time to think about it, because I'd rolled the condom on and sank onto him in one fluid motion, feeling suddenly so *full* that I let out an involuntary sigh.

"*Fuck,*" Sam said. It was the first time I'd ever heard him say the word. His hands squeezed my hips, my ass, as I rode him until we were both sweaty and spent, collapsing against his sheets.

We lay there for a minute, the only sound our heavy breathing. I felt suddenly shy, unsure what to say. Sam rolled toward me, brushing strands of hair away from my face as he pressed a soft kiss to my temple.

"That was amazing," he said. "You're amazing. How do you feel?"

Why did he have to ask me *that* of all questions? My body felt tired and sore and sated in all the best ways, and there was a part of me that was still floating on a cloud, a cloud of Sam telling me I was beautiful and the rasp in his voice when he'd said that single profanity. But my mind was already starting to come back down to earth, questioning things, like *Will it be weird now?* and *Did I leave my bra in the pool?*

"Exhausted," I said, because it was the most honest response I felt capable of. I gave him a smile and a kiss on the corner of his mouth, hoping I didn't sound as conflicted as I was inside. I'd pushed this, after all. I'd kissed him first. I'd encouraged it every step of the way.

"Then stay," he said. "You can sleep here."

I meant to protest. The last time I'd spent the night at a man's house had been . . . pre–grad school? It definitely wasn't with the few-and-far-between flings and fuck buddies I'd been with since. Plus I had so much writing to get done tomorrow, and I was beginning to worry we'd left some of the paint out, and I was positive at this point that my bra was floating in his pool . . .

But the bed was so comfortable, and Sam's arm was so warm around me, and it had to be at least three in the morning by this point. I closed my eyes, and let myself drift off to sleep.

I WOKE UP to the distant sound of a knock, which in my dream I'd turned into another sound. It instantly disoriented me, especially when I rolled over and realized I wasn't in my bed at home, when I saw the still-sleeping Sam next to me.

He had a small scar above one eyebrow, I noticed. Nothing major—probably a childhood scrape that hadn't healed properly— but it was the kind of detail about his face that I felt like I could only absorb now that we were so close.

I wanted to trace it with my fingertips, but instead I shook his shoulder as the knock came again.

"Sam," I said. "Someone's at the door."

"Mmm," he said without opening his eyes, snuggling closer. His erection was pressed against my leg now, and I felt a spark deep in my gut, desperate to kindle into a full-on flame, but then it was doused as it hit me just who was probably outside. I shook his shoulder again.

"*Sam,*" I said. "I think it's my brother."

That got him to open an eye. "Why would Conner be at *my* door at . . . what time is it?"

Given that I'd told Conner to bring me lunch today to make up for skipping out on painting yesterday, I hated to think what time that meant it was. Later than I'd slept in a while, that was for sure.

"He probably tried to call," I said, groaning. This was the last thing I wanted to deal with. "But I did it again—left my phone back at the house. I can't just blow him off. He'll worry."

"Okay," Sam said, getting up and giving me a delicious view of his naked butt as he reached into dresser drawers to retrieve clean underwear and jeans. "Do you want to borrow something to wear—a T-shirt and some boxers, maybe?"

"That would be great," I said. "And then if you can just distract him, I'll sneak out the back and go through the fence to let myself in next door. It should take me a few minutes, tops—ask him what video game has the most intuitive gameplay. That'll get him going for a while. Then you can say that you haven't seen me, but maybe I just didn't hear his knock and he should try again."

Sam frowned. "Why don't I just let him in, and you can come out when you're ready? Or I can tell him you're still sleeping, if you'd rather not face him. I know it's a little awkward, but we're all adults. He'll know we're together eventually anyway."

The silence that hung between us after that was coiled with tension. I could see the moment it dawned on Sam what my lack of response meant, and some light in his eyes flickered and died. It killed me, not being able to explain that it wasn't personal, it was just that I preferred not to get shit about this from Conner, preferred not to have more people who might get invested in whatever this was, might ask me about it once it was over. But there wasn't time. I tried to plead with him with my expression to please just understand and help me out.

"Intuitive gameplay," he muttered. "Right. Boxers are in the top drawer, shirts in the second. Make sure I've closed the front door behind me before you come out, or he'll probably spot you in the background."

"Thank you," I said, but he'd already left. I could hear him open the front door, the murmur of conversation as he talked to Conner, and then a click as he apparently closed the door behind him to talk to Conner on the front step.

I grabbed a pair of red boxer briefs and the first T-shirt my hand landed on, which was bright yellow and had a picture of a cartoon rocket ship with the words LAUNCH INTO LEARNING! printed on it and the name of a school I assumed to be Sam's employer. Put together, they were the brightest clothes I'd worn since probably toddlerhood. But I didn't have time to second-guess my choices, so I got dressed in a hurry before sneaking out the sliding glass door to Sam's backyard.

Just as I'd suspected, my neon purple bra was floating in the middle of the pool, a reminder of the turn our night had taken. I wanted to fish it out but settled for grabbing my clothes from the porch instead. There would be time to process everything later, after I dealt with Conner. But then I remembered that look that had crossed over Sam's face, disappointment and something else, something deeper that I didn't even want to think about, and I wasn't so sure.

SIXTEEN

C OLD TACO BELL was a dish best served . . . well, never, but it was my own fault. I'd gotten back to my house just in time to throw on some pants over Sam's underwear, then change out of the bright yellow shirt for a clean bra and black T-shirt of my own that didn't scream *I slept with an elementary school music teacher!*

"I knocked a hundred times," Conner said as he squeezed a packet of hot sauce onto his burrito. "*And* called you. Seriously, Pheebs, you're the one who fills my head with stuff about how the best motivation to keep a clean house is the thought of the grainy crime scene footage they'll show in court later. The neighbor must think I'm insane, always going over there to check for you."

"Sorry, I was in the shower." I realized that my hair wasn't even wet, and that saying I'd already taken a shower would hurt my chances to take one after lunch, which I desperately wanted to do. "About to take a shower," I amended. "What did Sam say?"

"Just that you weren't there, obviously," Conner said. "And then he asked me some weird stuff about video games. I'm going to have to make that guy a list of my top ten, because he's barely played *anything*. I brought up *Mass Effect* and he looked at me like I was an alien. *Mass Effect!*"

"Ha," I said, trying to think of a way I could subtly ask questions like *How else did he look?* and *Did he seem mad at me?* But obviously that was impossible.

"While we're on the subject—" Conner set his wrapped burrito precariously on his knee, reaching into a bag next to him to pull out a black rectangle wrapped with a power cord. "I brought you a present. I know it's old, but I figured it was better than nothing, and it already has *Crash Bandicoot* and some other games loaded on it. There's the small TV in Dad's room you could hook up out here. I can't play right now with my wrist. This way you can have something to do for when you get bored."

I thought of all the ways I'd spent my time since I'd arrived—cleaning and packing and painting and reading and writing. And Sam. Most of all, I thought of him. I thought of how much I liked seeing the red climb up his neck if I said something suggestive, the look in his eyes when I'd been on top of him last night.

I was a lot of things, but bored wasn't one of them.

Still, it was sweet of Conner to think of me, and I took the old PlayStation from him so he didn't have to keep holding it in his one good hand. Somewhere in the exchange he hit his burrito with his elbow, and sent it to the floor with a *splat*.

"I knew that would happen," he said almost cheerfully, like he was more happy to be right than to have his food intact. He reached down to wipe up the mess with one of the rough brown napkins, but I waved him off, going to the kitchen to get some cleaning spray and paper towels.

"You got way more done than I expected," Conner said, glancing around the Linen White walls. "It's starting to look almost HGTV in here."

"Yeah, well. Sam came over and helped. Did you know he spent three whole summers painting houses back in Chicago? He did all this trim freehand."

"Huh."

The tone of Conner's voice made me look up from my cleaning. "What?"

"It's just weird," Conner said. "When I talked to Sam earlier, he said he hadn't seen you. He didn't even mention being over here to paint last night."

"Dude, this isn't an episode of *The Confession Tapes*," I said. "It wasn't that big a deal, and he probably assumed you meant if he'd seen me *today*. Which, obviously, he hadn't."

That was the first outright lie I'd told Conner, if I was keeping proper track. It didn't feel great. And it didn't feel great that I'd asked Sam to lie to Conner, too. But when I thought of the alternative—how Conner would tease me about being obsessed with the neighbor, even more than he already did, how I'd get questions till the end of time about whether I was still seeing Sam, and was I going to bring him to the wedding, and when was *I* going to have a wedding . . . Conner could grind something like this with the same persistence he applied to his video games.

"All right," Conner said. "You don't have to attack me about it. I just thought it was weird. Oh! I remember what I wanted to ask you. Do you have plans for the Fourth?"

Never before had I been as thankful for my brother's sometimes short attention span. "Yeah, I'm going to bake a three-layer red-white-and-blue cake and throw our country a birthday party."

"Really?"

"Fuck no," I said. "It doesn't deserve it. Why, what do you have planned?"

"I'm going to propose to Shani," he said. "And I want you to be there."

Why did that get me feeling all emotional, like for one horrifying second I might actually cry? I must be about to get my period. I hated the idea of public proposals, of such a personal moment being put on display, but for some reason Conner wanting to include me had me feeling honored. Touched, even.

I cleared my throat. "Sure," I said. "Of course. How are you going to do it?"

I mostly listened as he described his plan—apparently, he'd talked to the guy who did the fireworks across the river, the ones we used to go see sometimes when we were kids. And the guy had said for some money he could do a special display that would spell out Conner's proposal, arranging the timing ahead of time so Conner could be sure to get down on one knee in front of Shani. It all sounded very sweet and very expensive.

But my mind also kept drifting back to Sam. Wondering what he was doing. Wondering how he was feeling about last night, if he regretted it. Because as conflicted as I felt today, I definitely didn't regret it.

After Conner left, I paced around the house, restless. I tried to sit down at my desk to work on my dissertation, but the only thing I ended up drafting was an apology email to Dr. Nilsson, telling her I hadn't been feeling well but would get her the Capote chapter soon. I opened up her notes on the *Helter Skelter* chapter but the sheer amount of tracked changes overwhelmed me and so I closed them up again. I could tackle those later.

I wasn't going to feel right until I talked with Sam, however scary that might seem. I needed to know where we stood.

Of course, right as I opened the front door to leave, that damn cat darted in again, making another beeline right for my room. After days of hoping she'd show up and being disappointed when she hadn't, now here she was, no doubt looking to camp out under my bed again while I plied her with delicious food. Well, not this time.

I did go back and fill a shallow bowl with water, setting it in the middle of my bedroom floor for her to drink from. I wasn't a monster.

"That's all you're getting for now, Lenore," I said aloud to the room. "If you want food you're going to have to be sociable." Then, after thinking for a moment: "Actually, I would hate for my sustenance to be tied to my ability to relate to other people, so fuck it, stay under there if you want. Just *don't* use the bathroom. Got it?"

Something told me she didn't have it. But I left anyway, sending a brief prayer to the feline gods that she wouldn't claw and spray everything in sight or whatever cats did when humans left them alone for ten minutes.

I knocked on Sam's door, my heart in my throat as I waited on the step to see if he'd open it. I guessed I couldn't blame him if he didn't, after the abrupt way I'd left earlier. I was fifty-fifty on whether I would've.

But I was banking on Sam being more emotionally well-adjusted than me, and I was right, because he finally came to the door. He still hadn't bothered to put on a shirt, which was totally fine—it was his house—but which would make trying to talk to him that much more distracting. I could make out a small circular mark above his left nipple from where I must've given him a hickey. My gaze shot up to his face, which was unreadable.

"Hey," I said. "Can I come in?"

He stepped aside, letting me follow him through the door until we were both standing in his living room. I crossed over to the pictures above the piano, pointing to each face in turn. "Let me guess," I said, pointing first to a woman who looked about a decade older than Sam. "That's Tara, that's Jack in the Cubs hat, Megan is in between, Erin's got the pink shirt on, and that's Dylan with his arm around you." I squinted closer at the picture. "Are you wearing a shell necklace? What year is this from?"

It was a cheap parlor trick, but I thought maybe he'd be impressed by my memory. I'd always had a knack for those first-day-of-school games where we had to go around the room and name every student who'd come before us and the one fact they'd told about themselves. Plus, I wanted to show him that I'd been listening. That I cared.

"You switched Megan and Erin," he said, not seeming as impressed as I'd hoped. Not seeming much of anything. He was more of a stranger than when I'd stood on his doorstep to drop off a package. "But otherwise, yeah. Did Conner leave?"

"A few minutes ago," I said. "And the cat came back. Just like you said she would."

"Great."

The problem was that my first instinct was to try to kiss him, to see if I could get him to melt into me the way he had last night. But I knew that would be a mistake. The physical stuff wasn't the issue here.

"Sam . . ." I swallowed, wishing I knew what to say, wishing there was some magic formula where I could give him as much of me as he wanted, but hold enough back to avoid being vulnerable. I had a sneaking suspicion that the formula didn't exist; that it was an unsolvable equation.

He glanced toward the table, where I saw there was a half-eaten sandwich on a plate. I'd interrupted his lunch, too. God, I was the worst.

"It's my fault," he said finally. "I guess after last night I thought . . ." He shrugged, as if it didn't matter, even though it clearly did. "If you don't want to tell your brother yet, I get it. It's more that I can't figure out what you *would* tell him."

"Not any of the details, that's for sure," I said. "My mother once told me about an incident with my stepdad involving a sex swing, and I'll never be able to bleach that image from my brain. It's made Christmases with them unbearable."

Sam smiled a little, but I could tell his heart wasn't in it. "I mean, what are we doing? Am I your boyfriend now, are we friends with benefits, was that a one-night stand . . . ?"

The way he said *boyfriend* sent a thrill up my spine. Which was ridiculous, because that was the last thing I wanted or needed right now—especially when I wasn't even planning to be in town for that long. But suddenly he said that word and I was back in tenth grade again, doodling my crush's name in the margins of my math homework.

"I definitely want more than one night," I said.

His eye contact was all-consuming. "So do I."

"After that . . ." I shrugged helplessly. "Can't we just be two people? Two people who live next door to each other and hang out and hook up sometimes—preferably a *lot* of times—but who don't have any expectations beyond that for now?"

"So, neighbors who hook up."

"Exactly," I said. "It's like friends with benefits, but less of a commute."

I was ready to put this plan into action right there, right then, but I could tell that Sam was still thinking about it, turning something over in his head. Then there was his poor forgotten sandwich on the table, and I already felt bad for the way this day had gone after last night had been so perfect.

"Look," I said, "no matter what, we can still be friends, right? Conner invited me to this Fourth of July fireworks thing—he's actually going to propose to Shani that night, but you didn't hear it from me—and you should totally come if you don't already have plans. What do you say?"

Sam ran his hand through his hair. "I may have something," he said, in a way that made me think he didn't. "Can I let you know?"

"Sure," I said, trying not to feel hurt. Fourth of July was pretty much the worst holiday, anyway. I hated fireworks and unquestioning patriotism. And I couldn't blame him for not being super psyched to spend time with the woman who'd bailed on him this morning. "We can keep it casual."

He gave a little laugh, more an exhalation of air than an actual sound of humor. "I think that's where we have a disconnect," he said. "But I'll let you know."

WHEN I GOT back to my house, I plopped down on my bed, both because I was still tired and because I was running out of places to relax in this place. I had completely forgotten about Lenore under the bed until she came out, meowing at me from the floor. She eyed me warily and then leapt up onto my stomach, her small paws starting to knead at my T-shirt.

"What is *that*?" I asked her. "What are you doing?"

I wished I could reach the cat book from the library, so I could look up what this behavior meant. I assumed it wasn't an act of aggression, because she didn't seem tense. She'd started to purr, actually, and licking the spot where she'd been kneading. I could feel the roughness of her tongue through the damp fabric.

Was she trying to *nurse* on me?

"This is a little weird," I said. "Not gonna lie."

But I let her keep doing it, because it seemed to make her happy. I reached out an experimental hand to give her a single stroke down the length of her back. She startled a little, as though not sure she liked it, and then went back to sucking on my shirt. Eventually, I was able to rest my hand on the top of her head, giving her a few firm pets that she didn't seem to mind as much.

"You're probably riddled with fleas," I said. "And I bet you go through people's garbage, don't you, you dirty trash cat. I'm going to call you DTC instead of Lenore."

She didn't seem bothered by the name change at all, just continuing her disgusting and a little endearing licking of my shirt. But I immediately felt bad, and had to correct the record. "I won't really," I said. "And I mean *dirty trash cat* with the utmost respect for your time on the streets. I'm just saying, we need to get you to the vet and get you cleaned up a bit."

I reached into my pocket for my phone, snapping a quick picture of Lenore that came out like a smudge of black on top of me. Still, I hoped Alison would understand what she was looking at as I sent it over to her. Her reply came back in minutes.

So cute!!!! Glad you decided to keep her.

I ran my fingers over my phone screen, feeling the jagged edge of one of the cracks. I sent my response back before I could second-guess myself too hard. **Have no idea what I'm doing. Would you be able to meet up with me sometime after work to help me buy supplies?**

If she said no, I wouldn't be offended. She was probably really busy, between work and the lure of another Epcot food festival or whatever else it was that got Disney people all riled up. And I could probably figure out what to buy on my own—there may even be a list of suggested items in the library book. As soon as Lenore stopped doing her bizarre licking and kneading thing, I'd get up and check. My shirt was already soaked through.

But Alison's reply came back with a gif that made me laugh, of Mr. Burns steepling his fingers together. I'd forgotten just how much *Simpsons* we'd watched in middle school. She said it was her day off, and could I meet her at the pet store next to the old Dunkin' Donuts, the one that had the pink elephant and red camel statues out front?

I surprised myself by knowing exactly the place she was talking about.

SEVENTEEN

A LISON TRIED TO explain to me some nuances of cat ownership as we stocked up on basic supplies—litter box, food, cat carrier—but it was hard to stay focused when I kept thinking about how I'd left things with Sam. Alison even had to take my phone from me and finish making the vet appointment, because I kept stuttering and stammering over basic information like how old did I think the cat was and what was the best number where they could reach me.

"Hey," she said after she'd hung up and handed me my phone back. "You can do this. I promise it's not hard. Cats are fairly low-maintenance, except when they're vomiting up hairballs or knocking over your drink. Want me to go to the vet with you?"

"You've already done too much," I said, when really I wanted to say, *Yes, thank god, please help me because I'm drowning here.* "But let me buy you a coffee, at least, if you think we have time before that cat destroys the entire house."

"Oh, it only takes cats about point two seconds to do that," Alison said, and then laughed when she saw my widened eyes. "But I highly doubt Lenore is getting up to much mischief right now. It sounds like she's still intimidated by the new surroundings."

We loaded all the supplies in my car and then headed next door to grab some coffee, Alison chattering on about cats the whole time. She showed me at least thirty pictures of hers at home by the time we got to our table.

"That must be Maritza," I said, pointing to one picture of a woman making kissy faces at the gray striped cat. She had dark curly hair and a beauty mark on her cheek. "Good of you to slip at least one picture of your wife in there. She's pretty."

Alison smiled, swiping back to her phone's home screen to show me a picture of the two of them together. They really were adorable. Ugh, would I have to add them to my suddenly growing list of healthy couples? It had been much more fun back when I'd been going down Wikipedia rabbit holes trying to figure out which postconviction relationships lasted after the inevitable book deal. Sondra London had dated not one but *two* convicted murderers and written books about or with them. Now that was commitment.

"She used to make fun of me for all the cat pictures," Alison said, "but then she moved in and ended up getting attached. I bet your phone will be just as bad in a couple months. It's encouraging that Lenore was kneading on you like that. It shows she trusts you."

"At least someone does," I said.

Alison's brows drew together. She was wearing another pair of hip glasses today, these ones wire frames that made her look extra librarian-ish. "What are you talking about?"

I wasn't going to talk about it. I hadn't wanted Conner to know, and I didn't see any reason to discuss my personal life with Alison, either. But she was a lot less connected to the rest of my life, and it had been bubbling up in me all day. I was dying just to get it out.

"I slept with Sam," I said.

"Your hot neighbor?" she said. "I mean, I figured."

"Yeah, it just—" I stopped, her words registering for the first time. "Wait, what?"

"The way he mentioned what you'd named the cat," she said, lifting one shoulder. "I don't know. I figured you were together."

"Well, we weren't *then*," I said. "And we might not be now. I think I fucked it up."

There was a mom and her young son at the counter, buying donuts, and I suddenly got paranoid that they could hear every word of our conversation. I sank lower in my seat, but the mom just handed her kid a sticky jelly donut and a napkin, focused more on wiping something off his cheek with her own spit than anything we were talking about.

Alison gave me a dry look. "I am admittedly not an expert on heterosexual intercourse, but it has been shoved in my face in movies and books for years, so I think I can say with some confidence that it is highly unlikely you messed anything up."

"I think he wants a *relationship*," I said.

Alison's eyes traveled from one corner of the coffee shop to the other, as though she were actually scanning the room for what the problem was. "And that's bad?"

I enumerated the reasons on my fingers, as much for my benefit as for hers. "One, I'm here for only another month or so. After that, it's back to North Carolina. And after I graduate in December, who knows where I'll go—my advisor said it was best to keep my options open. I could do a postdoc at the University of San Diego for all I know. I could be an adjunct in Pawhuska, Oklahoma."

"Well, they have . . . what does Sam do again?"

"He teaches music at an elementary school."

She made an exaggerated *aw* face. "That's adorable. I love that." Then, perhaps realizing she was *not* helping, she shook her head. "Sorry, okay. I'm just saying, they have music teachers in Pawhuska, Oklahoma. Or you could do long distance. Or you could break up. But that doesn't seem like a reason not to try, if you really like him. And it seems like you do."

That last part wasn't a question, so I didn't bother answering it. "*Two,*" I said, holding up my fingers like it was important that she understood there were now multiple reasons it wouldn't work. "He's, like, sickeningly well-adjusted. He comes from one of those big families where you just know they all fly in for Christmas to surprise Mom, and she's so happy to have all her kids in one place that she doesn't even *need* presents, but they all chipped in to buy her a necklace with each of their birthstones on it anyway."

"Is that from a commercial?" Alison said. "And I don't think those necklaces are that expensive, actually."

It was, in fact, from a commercial. "My point is, he doesn't even know what he's getting into with me. I hate when people say children of divorce are from broken families, but in my case it's pretty on point."

"So? Who cares. I'm adopted, which some people might think means I have some unresolved attachment issues or whatever. I'm sure that's the case for some adoptees, but not for me. On the other hand, it was an interracial adoption, which brings up other issues that those same people might not even think about. Maritza came into our marriage with baggage from one side of her family who weren't as accepting of same-sex relationships. We all have something."

I knew that what Alison was saying made logical sense. I also knew that she, of all people, should know just how fucked up I was. After all, she'd been the one who was there when I was fifteen and threatening to kill myself in internet messages. I'd always said it was just a joke, and it *had* been, in a way. But jokes had also always been one of my safest ways of expressing myself—sometimes allowing me to skate around what I wanted to say, other times allowing me to crash right into it and then later deny I'd meant to.

"If I can make one more observation?" Alison said. She'd already said a lot, so I waved her on. No reason to hold back now.

"You've always been kind of . . ." She turned her to-go cup of coffee around in her hands, as though she were trying to figure out the exact order to put her words in. "All or nothing."

She gave me a look through those wire glasses, and her meaning was so clear that I had to glance away. Because wasn't that essentially what had ended our friendship? I'd taken her intervention phone call to my mother as the ultimate betrayal, and had allowed that one incident to poison all the years we'd had together. I knew she was right. It didn't mean it was easy to hear.

"So this thing with Sam," she said. "Maybe just keep an open mind. You don't have to be in a relationship, if you're not ready for it. But don't be aggressively *not* in a relationship, either. You know?"

I wished I could say I didn't. There were a lot of double negatives in that sentence. But I knew exactly what Alison was saying, because it was true—the minute I'd woken up next to Sam, I'd immediately started thinking about ways to make it clear that this was just sex, I was *not* emotionally involved. It was a defense that put me on the offense, and I'd done it before.

"Okay," I said. "Now that you've solved *that* issue, tell me. Where am I supposed to put Lenore's litter box?"

Alison gave me a grin that I did not like the look of at all. "By now, she's probably pooped in some corner of the house," she said. "I would suggest you put it right there."

———

IT TURNED OUT that was exactly what Lenore had done. After I cleaned it up and muttered a few more choice words to her, I set up the litter box in the spot where she apparently liked to do her business.

"This is now your designated area," I said. "When we get to know each other better I'll show you the *Dateline* where the girl slips and says *designated area*, after she's been saying the whole time that they never planned to kill her boyfriend's ex when they all went out to the salt flats together. Keith Morrison jumped right on it. He should've won an Emmy for that episode alone."

The book had recommended I mostly ignore Lenore, to give her space as she figured out her new surroundings. That part was easy enough. To encourage your cat to play, it said to stay on the floor, idly flicking a string or other toy while talking in a friendly manner. It didn't specifically say to talk about your favorite true crime programming, but it didn't say not to, either.

The whole time, I was listening for the sound of Sam's truck. It had been gone from his driveway when I got back from coffee with Alison, and I was anxious for him to come home so I could talk to him.

I hadn't even yet fully planned out what I would say. An apology was as good a way to start as anything. He'd told me I was beautiful, called the sex amazing—which it *had* been—and asked me to stay the night. While I'd told him I was exhausted, taken some of his clothes, and hightailed it out of there as soon as I could.

I didn't need the internet to weigh in on this one. I was the asshole.

Eventually, Lenore did venture out to where I was waving a toy back and forth on the floor, some stick with feathers at the end that Alison assured me she'd go nuts for. The cat gave me a slit-eyed look, like *You thought I'd fall for this shit?*, and refused to pounce, but she was watching, so I kept up the steady movement of the toy.

"I get it," I said. "You have too much dignity. This is beneath you. You probably want the *New York Times* Style section."

A flick of the tail. Maybe she was more of a current-events kind of cat.

"That's us, alone in our dignity." A rumble came from outside, and I sat up straighter, my ears perked up like I was the cat. But then the sound got louder, before quiet again, like a car had driven by the house but kept going. I slumped back, the toy forgotten in my hand.

Lenore slunk away to the kitchen, where I could hear her rustling at the bowl of food I'd set out for her.

"Okay, just you," I said. "I have no dignity left anymore."

———

I DIDN'T SEE Sam the next day, either. Clearly he'd come home at some point, because he'd put his trash and recycling out, which was a good reminder that I needed to do the same.

My neighbor on the other side, Pat, poked her head around her open garage to watch me as I walked up the side of the house for the cans. She always had her garage open and nine times out of ten would be in there sitting on a foldable lawn chair, chain-smoking. If I had really thought about it, *she* would've been the one to bust Sam for any serial killer activity long before I arrived on the case. There wasn't much she seemed to miss from her nosy position under the shadowed eave of her garage.

I lifted my hand in a wave, since by this point we'd clearly established eye contact and it would seem weird *not* to. But I had to respect Pat, because she didn't give a shit about any such social nicety, barely acknowledging me even as she continued to stare.

"A real Aileen Wuornos energy to that one," I muttered, grabbing the cans to drag them to the street.

The very thought made me stop, turn around to study the shed on the back of Pat's property. Maybe her watchfulness had less to do with her distrust of other people and more to do with protectiveness over her own secrets. She could have all kinds of clues to her crimes, or even a whole secret family living back there, and who would know? I didn't want to be the person living next to Jaycee Dugard without suspecting a thing.

"My condolences." A gruff voice came from beside me, and I jumped.

There was a whole hedge between me and Pat, but still I felt prickly and threatened by her approach. "Sorry?"

"About your dad," she said. "My condolences."

"Oh." It occurred to me that she'd lived next to him for decades, but between how insular he was and how antisocial she was, they probably had barely spoken a word to each other. One hundred percent they could've each lived next to a certified horror house and would've both prided themselves on minding their own business.

I cleared my throat. "There's a cat," I said tentatively, "who's been coming around my house lately. Black and white, pretty small? Is she yours?"

This felt like the right thing to do, but there was a part of me that still kicked myself for asking a question I wasn't sure I wanted the answer to. What if she said *yes*, and I had to give Lenore back? I was surprised at the vehemence with which I rejected that option. At the same time, I wasn't looking to be the subject of some Nextdoor post about how there was a cat thief in the neighborhood.

Pat gave me a look like I was from another planet. "Those cats don't *belong* to me," she said. "They don't belong to anyone. They're animals."

"Right," I said.

There was the sound of a car coming around the corner, and I turned, automatically looking for Sam even though I already knew it hadn't been the rumble of his truck's engine. By the time I turned back to Pat, she was carefully stubbing out her cigarette against the thick denim of her jean shorts, sliding the butt into her pocket when she was done.

"People don't belong to anyone, either," she said cryptically, and disappeared back into her garage.

Was she referring to me and Sam? Under her watchful eye, I had no idea what she would've seen or what conclusions she might've drawn.

Either way, I thought as I dragged the trash and recycling to the curb, that didn't seem to be a sentiment you'd expect from a woman who was keeping a secret kidnapped family in her shed. I supposed I could cross that one off my list.

AT LEAST I no longer had to worry about Pat getting some kind of revenge on me for doing things like feeding Lenore or taking her to the vet. At the first appointment, I learned to my surprise that Lenore was probably at least three years old, and that sometimes cats could be so demonic while they were getting shots that the vet tech had to wear special gloves and still came back looking a little rattled.

"All set!" she said, but with no additional praise about what a good kitty Lenore had been. Was this what having a cat would be like? Was I doomed to feel a spurt of indignation when other people tagged their cats with *#bestcatever* on Instagram?

Yes, Alison responded when I texted her that.

"Well, *you're* the original DTC," I said to Lenore through the door of her carrier as I set it back in the car. "No one can take that away from you."

The scent of ammonia immediately hit my nostrils.

"Nice," I said. "Thanks for that."

Conner had been texting me about the fireworks tomorrow, asking me questions about what I thought he should wear and whether it would be tacky to get a little stoned before. (**Just wear a button-up over a nice t-shirt without some funny saying on it. And I would recommend going into this with all your faculties intact.**)

It was cute, how nervous he was. I found that I was nervous, too—for Conner, but also because I still hadn't had a chance to confirm with Sam whether he'd be coming along or not. I really wanted to see him again. Aside from wanting to make things right, I realized that this was the longest I'd gone without seeing him in a while. I'd gotten used to having him in my days.

Finally, I ripped off an old sheet of stationery I'd had since I was a kid, *From the Desk of Phoebe* written on the top and a cartoon gumball machine on the side, and scribbled a quick note.

Sam—I was an asshole. I'm sorry. Picnic/fireworks at the park by the river tomorrow around seven. Meet us there?—P

I wished we could drive over together, since that would give us some time to talk, but Conner had me running around picking up stuff for the meal he'd planned. Apparently Shani had gotten obsessed with fancy charcuterie boards on Pinterest and he was now determined to re-create one for her. As touched as I'd been to be included, I did try to point out to Conner that something like a full-on picnic with his girl's favorite fancy cheeses might be better enjoyed as a one-on-one–type affair. To which he'd typed out an all-caps response about how he would not be able to make any semblance of normal conversation and would end up fucking it all up, and could I *please* just make sure to pick up the Brie.

I responded the only way I knew how, the exact way that little shit would've replied to me if the roles were reversed.

Dude. Chill.

But then I added a smiley face, because he was obviously stressed, and he was my little brother.

EIGHTEEN

THERE WERE STORM warnings for the Fourth, and the sky above looked gray and angry as we laid out our blanket on an open spot of grass. Conner kept glancing up at the clouds, as though he could will them to drift away if he worried about it enough. Shani was oblivious, wearing a yellow strappy sundress that looked amazing against her brown skin, happily sipping on a wine cooler we'd poured into Conner's corporate water bottle.

"It's going to get rained out," he said.

"You know how Florida is," I said. "There are storm warnings practically every day. Even if it rains, it'll probably only be for half an hour. We can take cover and then come back. They haven't canceled the event—all these other people are here."

Conner looked around at the crowd that had started setting up around the grass, seeming to take some comfort from that at least.

"If they cancel, we'll just go home," Shani said. "We have the Versace house episode to watch, anyway."

"See," I said to Conner. "Silver lining."

"Not helping," he said. "And what's gotten you all jumpy?"

"What? I'm not."

"You've glanced at the parking lot like twenty times. Is it a towaway zone or something? Do I need to move the car?"

"No, it's just . . ." I was debating about whether to tell Conner I'd invited Sam out or not. I knew he wouldn't mind—he seemed to have a *the more the merrier* approach to his impending marriage proposal. And he genuinely seemed to like Sam, lack of knowledge about *Mass Effect* notwithstanding. But I didn't want to tell him and then have Sam not show up. It would be worse than Conner finding out we'd been together in the first place— him finding out that now we weren't, and I was sad about it.

But then I saw Sam coming over the grass, his hands in his pockets. He was wearing a soft blue T-shirt and jeans, his hair pushed to one side and sticking up in the back, like he'd been running his hands through it. He was scanning the crowd, look- ing for . . . me. And when our eyes connected, something in his face eased, and it felt like the fireworks were already starting somewhere behind my rib cage.

"I invited Sam," I said to Conner quickly, in a low voice. "I figured . . ."

"Hey," Sam said, coming up on us. He gave me a smile before turning to Conner. "Phoebe told me you were watching the fire- works from here. Hope you don't mind if I join you."

"Not at all, man," Conner said, gesturing toward the meats

and cheeses already laid out on the blanket. "We brought more than enough to share."

"Hi, Sam!" Shani said, waving from her spot next to the Brie. Conner was right about how much she loved the stuff. I think half the wheel was already gone and I hadn't even sat down yet.

"Hey, Shani," he said, and damned if his eyes didn't seem to have an extra twinkle to them, a *You don't even know what's going down tonight*. It was incredibly cute.

I wanted to tell Conner I'd invited Sam there as my . . . what was the right word? Date? Or would it be better to show, not tell, to reach for Sam's hand and let them draw their own conclusions?

Except he still had his hands in his pockets, and his body language and the tone of his voice definitely had a *just friends* vibe to them. Did he not know this was a date? Or did he not want it to be, after I'd treated him so shabbily a few days before?

"This weather," Conner said, giving the sky another worried look, "does not look good. They're going to cancel, I can just feel it."

Shani shrugged. "Fireworks are whatever anyway," she said. "They're so loud."

My stomach sank like *I* was the one planning to propose. "I love fireworks," I said, and now it was my voice that was too loud. Conner gave me a look, like *Dial it down*. I cleared my throat. "They're just so . . . majesty."

From next to me, Sam choked on a laugh. "Purple mountain majesty?"

"*Majestic*," I said. "I meant majestic. Don't you think so?"

"They're gorgeous," he said, his gaze on mine.

Okay, that was it. I was jumping him right here, right now,

and I didn't care about my brother and his soon-to-be-fiancée or the family set up on camping chairs only a few feet away.

But then Sam sank down to sit cross-legged on the blanket, reaching for a slice of prosciutto, and I was left to wonder if I'd imagined that brief moment. By the time I sat down, he was deep in conversation with Shani about a funny story about one of her patients at the hospital, laughing in all the right places.

Conner was looking at his watch. "Shouldn't they start them early?" he said. "If there's going to be bad weather later?"

The fireworks weren't supposed to start until eight thirty, after it had gotten dark. I tried to assure my brother that everything would be fine, but it took all my energy trying to keep his anxiety at bay while also not letting on to Shani that anything was up. I was leaning back on my hands in the grass, watching the sky because I'd promised Conner I would so he could actually talk to the woman he was planning to marry, when I felt a light brush against the back of my hand.

"Hey," Sam said from next to me. His voice was low, and his thumb slid across my wristbone, sending a shiver through me. "I just wanted to let you know that we're cool. And we don't have to tell your brother or anything."

Was it terrible that the first thing I felt was relief? But after that came confusion, because I really didn't understand why Sam would be so chill about it all now when he'd seemed upset before. "But I was such a jerk," I said. "I didn't even tell you how good the sex was. Which I totally meant to do, by the way, because that whole night . . ."

I glanced over to see if Conner and Shani were paying any attention to us, but Conner seemed engrossed in feeding Shani more Brie. Reason number eighty-five why I thought it would've been better without me here.

"A-plus," I finished. "Definitely."

"A-plus-plus," he said, but his gaze was on my face, as if searching for something there. Finally, he turned, giving me his profile. God, how I loved the imperfect bump of his nose, the soft curve of his lower lip. I wished we were here alone so we could just talk and make out or do whatever we wanted.

"I'm glad we can still be friends," he said finally. "I've really enjoyed hanging out with you this summer, Phoebe. It would be a shame to let one night wreck that."

I heard his words like a record scratch in my head. They made me feel ridiculous—for going to Alison for advice, for waiting for his truck, for wearing my hair down in hopes he would come tonight.

"Right," I said. "Totally."

Suddenly I was as impatient as Conner for the fireworks to start so we could get this whole night over with. The air was heavy and humid, the way it always felt right before rain, and the mosquitoes were starting to come out. Or else they'd *been* out, and were only now starting to drive me crazy, which was probably more accurate.

The family next to us took another look at the sky and started packing up, which I could tell made Conner anxious. I cut my eyes from Sam to Shani, trying to send him a telepathic message to distract her with some conversation. Thankfully, he seemed to receive the message, because he turned to her and started asking polite questions about what her plans after nursing school were.

I grabbed the sleeve of Conner's shirt, pulling him closer. "Listen, just tell yourself it's not going to happen."

"What?"

"I'm serious," I said. "Tell yourself right now, oh well, tonight's not the night. I'm going to propose, but it's not going to be during the fireworks."

"But I set it all up," he said. "I *paid* for it."

"And we'll get you your money back," I said, "if I have to write a strongly worded letter to do it. Just say it after me. *Tonight's not the night.*"

"Tonight's not the night," he said, sounding miserable.

"Great," I said, letting go of his shirt. "So now, if it rains, it rains. We'll grab the Brie—whatever's left of it—and run. And on the very slim chance that the sky clears and the fireworks go off without a hitch, you can get down on one knee and still live out your fantasy clickbait romantic moment. But we're going to treat that like a distant possibility and just enjoy the night for what it is, okay? You're here with your girl and she loves cheese and loves you. Now, why don't you take her for a walk down by the water while we wait to see if there are pyrotechnics or proposals in our future."

Conner blinked at me, a little taken aback by the vehemence in my speech, but then he went over to lean down to Shani and say something in her ear. She beamed at him as he pulled her up, and they went walking off together toward the river.

Sam scooted a little closer to me. "Tough love?"

"Managing expectations," I said, watching them until they disappeared behind the crowd. "If he's smart he'll propose to her right there by the water and get it over with."

"Spoken like a true romantic."

I glanced at him. He hadn't said the words with any particular rancor, but given the recency of our own romantic conflicts, I couldn't blame him if he had.

"I was straight with you the other day," I said. "I do want to be with you, as more than friends. We don't have to define it as anything yet, but I can be open-minded."

Sam yanked a couple blades of grass from the ground, twisting them between his fingers. "I think I have to do some managing expectations of my own. You're looking for something casual, which makes sense. I just don't know that I can be casual about you."

"So . . . no kissing?"

He gave me a sad smile. "Not unless you mean it."

I've meant it every time, I wanted to say, but I didn't. "You've always been a relationship guy, huh?"

"I guess so," he said. "I didn't have my first real girlfriend until college. I know, pathetic, right? But I was so shy in high school. I barely talked to anyone. I've dated a little, here and there, but mostly if I'm with someone it's because I hope for a future with that person."

A future. It was a nice idea, but I couldn't even imagine what that would look like, with Sam or otherwise.

"Like Amanda," I said.

He frowned, as if he wasn't quite sure why I was bringing her up again. A part of me felt like I was testing him, poking at a wound to see if it still hurt. It was a horrible thing to do, probably. I didn't even know what result I wanted. If he was obviously still hung up on her, it would give me an out in a way—I'd be able to tell myself that *that* was the reason why it never would've worked between us, not because of anything to do with me. But if he was obviously still hung up on her, it also made me feel jealous and sad.

"Amanda was . . ." He'd pulled more grass and was braiding it now, without looking. I didn't even know if he knew he was doing it. There was going to be a bald patch by this blanket when we left. "Well, I've already told you. It was always a lot of effort with her. Like I could feel that she wanted me to be a certain way, and I could feel all the ways that I was constantly letting her down. But it kept me busy, keeping up with it, and so when she broke up with me it came as a surprise even though it shouldn't have. I'd known it wasn't right almost the whole time. It was like getting off a treadmill and your head is spinning and your feet on solid ground just *feel* wrong, but then you're like, wait, I didn't want to be on that treadmill in the first place. I should've stopped it a long time ago."

"That is a *very* relatable example," I said. "Fuck treadmills. If I'm running it better be because the Sunrise Slayer is after me."

"I thought you said he died in prison."

"And you didn't actually date a treadmill," I said. "I thought we understood we were being metaphorical here."

Sam smiled at that. "So what about you?"

"What about me?"

"I've given you a full dossier on my last relationship," he said. "I want to hear about yours."

"Isn't this a bad idea?" I asked. "Trading stories about exes?"

He shrugged. "Just two friends talking."

"Okay, okay." I mentally sorted through the last few guys I'd been with, discarding all of them as not really a relationship. I knew if I asked Sam to define exactly what that word even meant I'd only be opening myself up to more questions, so I finally settled on a boyfriend I'd had after college, which meant it was . . . six years ago. Yikes.

"His name was Brandon," I said. "He actually worked part-time at the vitamin supplement place in a nearby mall, so he was way into fitness. I think he would've dated a treadmill for real. We met through mutual friends who seemed to think we'd hit it off, although I can't think why because it turned out we had very little in common. He was generally a pretty sweet guy, but I think he was looking for a girlfriend who would be more . . ."

I shrugged, not totally sure how to finish that sentence. But of course I should've known that Sam wasn't going to let me off the hook.

"More what?"

"Demonstrative, I guess?" I said. "Affectionate? I didn't laugh much at his jokes, because I didn't know he was making any, and I didn't randomly massage his shoulders when it seemed like he'd had a rough day. Meanwhile he was always trying to massage me, and that shit *hurt*. He'd really dig in there and put some torque in it. Dude would eat protein powder without even mixing it into a shake first. That's just not right."

Sam laughed a little, leaning back on his hands in the grass, our pinkie fingers almost touching.

"We were just total opposites," I said. "He even said it himself when we broke up. He had a hard body and a soft heart, whereas I . . . well. You know."

I could feel Sam's gaze on my face now, but I squinted and

looked away, scanning the water for any sign of Conner and Shani like it was the most important thing I had to do. I actually did spot them, walking hand in hand, starting to make their way back up the grass. Conner seemed a lot more relaxed, smiling and saying something to Shani, even though the sky only looked more likely to open up at any minute. I tried to figure out if maybe he *had* proposed to her on their walk, but somehow I didn't think so. They looked happy, but not like taking-selfies-with-the-ring happy.

"That's such bullshit," Sam said.

"This body is pretty soft," I said, poking myself in my not-flat stomach.

"Your body is bangin'," Sam said, "and to the extent Bench-press Brandon meant any insult with that comment, I hope he chokes on his protein powder. But I meant the heart thing, too. You don't have a hard heart."

I shrugged. "You don't know me that well."

"I know you're *here*," he said. "Providing moral support because your brother asked you to, even though you hate fireworks. I know you let him call you *Pheebs* even though it gets under your skin. I know you took in that cat because you hated to think of her not having a home. I know you're here, back in town in a house that makes you sad, because you didn't want to leave it for your brother to handle by himself."

A raindrop hit my arm with a splatter, and then another, but I was barely conscious of the weather or the fact that people around us were starting to pack up and leave in earnest. Sam's outburst had left me speechless. How did he know I hated the nickname *Pheebs*, except when my brother used it?

"Sorry," Sam said, rubbing his hands on his jeans. "We should probably—"

He was starting to push himself up to his feet, but I grabbed a fistful of his shirt and pulled him to me instead, crushing my mouth against his. It didn't start out as the most graceful kiss—I think I stabbed his cheek with my nose—but what it lacked in finesse it made up for in feeling. *I mean it I mean it I mean it.*

His hands were in my hair, cradling the back of my head as he deepened the kiss. But then he pulled away, and I saw his gaze dart nervously behind me. "Shit," he said. "Conner and Shani, six o'clock. Or your twelve o'clock. I have no idea how this works."

"I don't care," I said, and kissed him again. We were both getting rained on at this point, but I didn't care about that, either.

I did manage to pull away and straighten my shirt—somehow, there was a warm imprint on my side in the exact shape of Sam's hand—before Conner and Shani walked up. I wasn't a total PDA psycho, although my brother of all people would deserve it after the tableaux of love he'd subjected all his social media followers to over the years.

"Get a room," Conner said as they walked up, but he was grinning. He turned to Shani, reaching into the pocket of his cargo pants, and for a minute I worried that he was going to propose *right there*, which would've been awkward. But instead he withdrew his wallet, pulling out a twenty-dollar bill and slapping it into Shani's outstretched hand.

"You called it," he said.

"Called *what?*" I demanded, although it was pretty clear from the gleeful thumbs-up she gave me exactly what Conner had meant. This was why if I had my way, I wouldn't tell them *any-*

thing. To the extent I'd ever dreamed of my own wedding—which was approximately never—it had always been a courthouse affair for health insurance purposes where we told no one and continued to live in separate houses.

At least Conner wasn't still freaking out about the proposal-that-didn't-happen. He seemed back to his usual relaxed self as he started gathering all the food and putting it back in the cooler. The rain was coming down harder now, soaking through my shirt and plastering my hair to my cheeks, but Conner seemed to have no sense of urgency. Meanwhile, I was dying to get out of there for numerous reasons, only the least of which was the rain.

"Uh," I said, "I'm probably just going to get a ride with Sam . . ."

"Yeah, get outta here," he said, waving me off. "I'll text you tomorrow about coming over to go through Dad's room."

A task I was emphatically not looking forward to. "Sounds good."

Sam had already stood up, offering me his hand to pull me to my feet. I could've dropped his hand immediately after—it's not like I needed to be led through the park like a child—but it felt nice, his warm palm against mine, our fingers interlaced. He pulled me closer to him as we half ran toward the parking lot, sheltering me at least partly from the rain with his body, and we were soaked and laughing by the time we climbed into his truck.

"So," he said.

"So." I gathered my heavy, sodden hair in a ponytail at the nape of my neck before releasing it again. The adrenaline was coursing through my body with such intensity that I could power this car myself if I could figure out how to plug in somewhere.

"Are we going back to your place, or do I have to ravage a public school teacher in his truck?"

"I'm glad one of us is thinking of my role as an upstanding community member," Sam said. "I can't say that's where my head was at." He turned the key in the ignition, the truck bouncing over a divot in the pavement as he backed up and drove us home.

SAM AND I barely made it inside his house before we were all over each other, clothes quickly discarded in a trail to the bedroom, where we made it to a wall, at least, if not the bed.

"Tell me this doesn't feel casual for you, too." Sam's hands circled my wrists, pinning them gently to my sides, as he kissed his way down my neck. "God, Phoebe. I like you so much."

I'd been about to make a joke, with the dim part of my brain that was even capable of rational thought. Something about how we were at least up to *neutral professional* by now, although nothing about this felt neutral or professional. But Sam's declaration lodged somewhere in my chest, feeling somehow bigger even than if he'd used the word *love*.

"I like you, too," I whispered, and then his tongue was in my mouth and I didn't think about words again for a while.

SAM TRIED TO convince me to stay the night, but I was worried about leaving Lenore that long.

"Not that she pays any attention to me," I said. "But she's actually using the litter box and I'm convinced she'll stop just to be a brat if I'm not there to monitor her."

"Sounds about right."

We were lying in his bed, his arm under my neck, his fingers idly playing with my hair. It would be so tempting to roll over and go to sleep, but it seemed important to make this distinction somehow, and not just because of the cat. One of my fears with having a boyfriend—if that's what Sam was—was losing myself, focusing so much on the relationship that I let go of important parts of me. And then if the relationship ended—*when* the relationship ended, an insidious voice whispered in the back of my head—would I be able to find those parts of myself again?

"I can hear your brain working," Sam said.

I rolled over, propping myself up on my elbows so I could look down into his face. He smiled at me, a little bemused, until he seemed to sense that my thoughts were veering down a more serious path. His hand dropped from my hair, and already it scared me, how much the loss of that brief contact caused something to hollow out in my stomach.

"I need to finish my dissertation," I said.

"Okay."

"I had a chapter due to my advisor like, a week ago," I said. "And then I still have another chapter after that, and a bunch of work on the conclusion and the bibliography and god, the formatting, it'll be a nightmare because I've been copy-and-pasting citations in as I go . . . and Conner is coming over tomorrow to help with the house, and I know he's going to want to debrief about the proposal fiasco and brainstorm new ways to do it. All I can say is if he's planning a flash mob or anything involving equestrian dressage, he's on his own, because I don't dance and I'm not getting on a horse."

"You'll get it done," Sam said. "And if I can help, I will. Not with the dissertation, because my only contribution would be to Select All and then make the font the same, and I assume you know how to do that yourself."

"I do," I said. "They taught a whole class on it my second year."

"Well, there you go. I've already proved my ability to edge a tight corner with paint, and I'd welcome the opportunity to show off again. If that's me swinging my dick around too much, just let me know."

I gave a surprised snort of laughter. Already I could see what a bad influence I was on Sam. I would've made that kind of crass comment when we first met, just to shock him. But now here he was, although even in the dark I felt like I could see the color slant across his cheeks. I hoped he never lost that.

"I'm just saying I may need some space," I said, suddenly more serious. "Not in a Taylor Swift kind of way. I do want to be with you . . . I just have a lot going on. I need you to understand if I have to hole up next door for a couple days to finish a draft or whatever."

"Phoebe," he said. "I get it. I don't expect you to drop everything to be with me. We can take it slow, okay?"

I nodded, swallowing around the lump in my throat.

"If you still want to head back next door, though, you should probably do it. That position is not conducive to me giving you space."

I glanced down. My arms were pushing my breasts together, making my cleavage look even deeper than usual. "Oh my god," I said. "My tits look amazing."

"I know," Sam said. "That's my point."

"They may never look this good again. Take a picture."

"Don't tempt me."

I slid up against his body, until I felt the hard length of him on my thigh. "We can start with the space thing in, like, twenty minutes," I said.

"Forty-five?"

"An hour, max."

"I can work with that," he said, and grabbed my ass with both hands, pulling me on top of him.

NINETEEN

I DID EVENTUALLY MAKE it back to my dad's house, although not until two in the morning. So when Conner showed up bright and early—without bothering to text first—he didn't quite get the reception he'd obviously been hoping for.

"This is dedication," he said, holding up his injured wrist, which was now wrapped in a simple bandage. A full cast had ended up not being necessary, or else Conner hadn't wanted to pay for it. It wasn't clear. "If I could've been this responsible in college, I wouldn't have failed so many eight a.m. classes."

"How many did you sign up for before you realized eight in the morning was too early?"

He scrunched up his face, thinking. "Four? To be fair, I only failed one. I dropped two others and skated through another with a B-minus. The prof even stopped coming by the end of that one."

I'd been so focused in college, determined to take as many classes as possible and maintain a mind-boggling number of lists to keep everything straight. Sometimes it felt like the only semi-wild thing I'd done was the time I'd performed a parody version of Ke$ha's "TiK ToK" for a fundraising event for the undergraduate literary magazine. I'd consumed an uncharacteristic amount of liquid courage beforehand, so all I could remember was the first line of the song. *Wake up in the morning feeling like Joan Didion / I grab my laptop I'm out the door I'm gonna write some fiction.* After that it was a blessed blur.

"So," Conner said, waggling his eyebrows like something out of a cartoon. "The neighbor, huh?"

"I can't believe you and Shani took a bet on it."

"After the party, Shani was like, oh, *now* I see why she's so obsessed with him," Conner said. "Which I was fine with, because I'm secure like that. She said she bet there was more going on there than just your supposed fear of being mutilated in your sleep, and I said, nuh-uh, you don't know my sister. She really does think about serial killers that much."

Bizarrely, I was kind of touched by Conner's defense of me. But I didn't feel like giving him that ammunition, and I *really* didn't feel like discussing Sam. So instead I turned my attention to the pantry, trying to see what paltry breakfast I could scrounge up. I wasn't normally a big breakfast-eater, the occasional Waffle House trip notwithstanding, and the leftover groceries at this point appeared to be mainly Pop-Tarts or granola bars.

"No cinnamon brown sugar?" Conner asked, then shrugged as he opened a packet of strawberry frosted and popped them in the toaster.

"Whoa, look at you," I said. "Actually toasting your Pop-Tarts. How nouveau riche."

"I'll have you know that we made enough on-time payments that the electric company took us off their EZ-Pay plan," Conner said. "It's ACH all the way now, baby."

"I thought you had that glow about you."

"But seriously," Conner said, taking his breakfast from the toaster with the corners pinched gingerly between his thumb and forefinger. "You don't toast yours? You know they're made to be toasted, right? It says so on the box."

I shrugged one shoulder. "Mom didn't really like me snacking too much," I said. "So if I did, it was usually something quick snuck into my room."

"Oh." He seemed to think about that for a minute. Then, as if we'd been debating the topic and he needed to make one final point, he said in a burst, "That's the main reason I picked to live with Dad, you know."

"Because he let you have the run of the toaster?"

"Because he'd let me do whatever," Conner said. "You remember how he was. If I'd wanted to go to Busch Gardens with my friends, Mom would've wanted to know who they were, who their moms were, had I cleaned my room, did I have my own money saved because she wasn't about to give me twenty bucks for food, and on and on. Dad didn't care. I think he was relieved if I was out of the house, or playing video games all day, or whatever, as long as I didn't bother *him*."

I did remember that about our father. It had been one of the most paradoxical things about him, in a way. He could be the most generous person; he wanted you to have everything you'd ever wanted. But if those wants pushed some invisible boundary he didn't want you to cross, that's when he could get cold, and angry, and mean. Eat all the marshmallows you can stomach. But if he reaches in the bag and there's none left, he'll lose his mind.

"Well, ironically, Mom did get a little looser once she met Bill," I said. "New lease on life or whatever."

"True." Conner had had the opportunity to see a little of that when he'd come over every other weekend per the custody arrangement, but of course it hadn't been the same. We'd spent at least one of those days playacting as a Family, filling our time with board games or mini golf or, once, a Pink Floyd laser light show that must've been Bill's idea. There had been some legitimately fun times, but it also felt like we were always *doing* something, like we never had time to just talk and be.

It was going to be a long day if a sugary breakfast snack was already causing this much self-reflection. Conner went to take a bite, recoiling when he got too much of the hot filling at once.

"It's like watching Icarus fly too close to the sun," I said, shaking my head. "Come on. Let's go see what we're dealing with."

———

ALL THIS TIME I'd built up my father's room as the great white whale, and it turned out that it was just . . . stuff. Some personal stuff, for sure—clothes I remembered him wearing, bills and other paperwork, old *Auto Trader*s that still had faded pencil circles around cars he'd probably never planned to buy. But a lot of it was junk that could easily be stuffed into garbage bags.

I surprised myself by being sentimental enough to set aside one of his flannel button-up shirts, a blue plaid one I'd bought

him one Christmas. I wasn't naive enough to assign any significance to the fact that he still had it hanging in his closet—it had
been the ultimate practical gift, after all, and my father was never
one to throw much away. But hanging on to it seemed like the
right thing to do, and I waited until Conner was on the phone
with Shani to fold it up and shove it to the bottom of one of my
suitcases in my room.

"Sorry your proposal last night didn't work out," I said once I
came back, seeing that he was off the phone. "Did you talk to the
guy yet about getting a refund?"

"I didn't have to," Conner said. "He actually sent it right to
me through the app with a message that if I hadn't proposed by
New Year's, we could try again."

"That's not a bad idea," I said. "New Year's could be cool."

Conner shrugged. "At this point, I'm starting to think I
should just drop to one knee when she gets home from work one
day and do it right there in the apartment."

The low-key approach I'd been advocating since the beginning, but something about seeing my brother so dejected made
me swallow my usual anti-romantic sentiment. "Maybe give
yourself a few weeks to think of something. And if you can't
think of a good idea—or the moment just feels right—then I say
go for it."

There was a knock at the front door, and I had a brief jolt of
my usual *Judgment Ridge* before I realized that it was probably
Sam. Sure enough, there he was, holding a cardboard carrier with
three coffees.

"Hey," he said, leaning in to give me a quick kiss that made
my toes curl. I still wasn't used to casual affection like that. It felt

more dangerous than the sex, in a way. "I saw Conner's car here and I figured . . . sorry, I didn't know how you guys took your coffee, so I just grabbed a bunch of creamers and different kinds of sugar."

It was a truly impressive array when he laid it out on the table. "You cleaned them out," I said. "If I see this on the local crime blotter later, I'm turning you in."

"But now you're an accessory after the fact," Sam said, pointing to where I'd just dumped two raw sugar packets in my coffee. "I think I can count on your silence."

Conner, I was relieved to see, had just pushed his coffee toward me so I could have two. He was a self-proclaimed "simple man," which meant his tastes ran to Mountain Dew, Red Bull if it had been a true all-nighter. It had been thoughtful of Sam to get him some coffee, nonetheless, and I gave Sam's arm a squeeze of thanks, trying out some casual affection of my own.

It wasn't so bad. It was kind of nice, actually—Sam's arm warm and hard under my hand, his immediate smile letting me know he appreciated the contact. I might've never let go, except Lenore chose that moment to come out of hiding and make her grand appearance for the day.

Sam crouched down to greet her, putting his hand out for her to sniff, and the little traitor actually did it. I supposed technically, she *had* known him longer, since they'd been neighbors longer than Sam and I had been. Still, I couldn't help but mutter under my breath.

"What?" Sam said.

"Nothing."

"She said *Judas*," Conner said helpfully. "Not sure if she meant you or the cat."

I glared at him. "Well, now I mean *you*. See if I assist with your next harebrained proposal scheme if you're going to throw me under the bus like that."

"That reminds me," Sam said, now fully petting Lenore, who was, if not actively purring, at least *tolerating* the contact. Was it wrong that the image of him petting the cat was low-key turning me on? "Phoebe mentioned a flash mob the other night. If that was something you wanted to do, I think I might have an idea."

"Dude, yes," Conner said. "Hit me with it."

Sam proceeded to explain how he'd taught his third-graders a coordinated dance last year, apparently mostly consisting of some emotes in an online game that a lot of the kids played, which made Conner's eyes light up because he was basically a giant kid himself. They went back and forth on a few of the moves included, which sounded like pure gibberish to me but which seemed to get Conner more and more into the idea.

"I could send an email out through the PTA," Sam said, "see if any of the parents would be down to meet up with us at a local park or something. There's only one small issue, and I'm not sure how you'll feel about it."

"It all sounds great," Conner said. "Shani will flip."

Lenore finally slunk away without giving me so much as a backward glance, as if she was tired of this conversation. I heard her lapping up some water in the kitchen, so at least I was doing one thing right in my cat caretaking so far.

Sam stood back up, reaching for his coffee to take a sip.

"Okay," he said. "But the kids learned the dance to a specific song, and I don't think I could teach it to them with another song in time. Especially because it's summer, and everyone has plans—this would need to be a one-and-done deal, you know?"

"That should be fine," Conner said. "Even if it's a song with some *you don't know you're beautiful* messaging, I can always explain to Shani that it's okay if she esteems herself, and it doesn't take away her overall beauty."

He shot me a finger-gun gesture with a little *click* out of the side of his mouth, and I rolled my eyes. At least he'd been listening, I guessed.

"So what's the song?" I asked. I had no idea what you'd teach third-graders to dance to. "Let It Go (Club Remix)"? Some Kidz Bop version of a song that reframed any desire for sex as a desire to play marbles together or something?

"'Tubthumping,'" Sam said. "By Chumbawamba."

I actually choked on my coffee. And it wasn't a cute sitcom spit take, either, but a full-out down-the-wrong-tube coughing fit. Sam rubbed my back while I got myself together enough to give them both a thumbs-up so they'd know I wasn't dying.

"Sorry," I said. "But what *year* is it?"

"That song is a classic," Sam said. "And it teaches resilience. You get knocked down. But, you know, you get up again."

"Maybe I could work that into my proposal somehow," Conner said, already on his phone, probably looking up the lyrics.

"'Shani, with you I will drink a whiskey drink, I will drink a lager drink,'" I suggested dryly. "Is that song even appropriate for kids?"

"The alcohol references don't even touch some of the stuff

kids sing along to without even knowing what they're saying," Sam said. "Or some of them do know; that's even worse."

"Okay, I'm in," Conner said. "Put out your Chumbawamba call to action or whatever you need to do. Maybe for this Saturday? This is going to be *sick*."

I left them to work out the details, heading back into my dad's room to make more headway on the mess. It felt wrong, somehow, to refer to it that way, but that's all most of it was to me. I'd love to say I found a box of handwritten letters to me he'd kept in a box, unsent but heartfelt, but this wasn't a movie. I was separating out more clothes in *donation* versus *trash* when Sam came in to say goodbye.

"I have to teach a couple guitar lessons," he said. "But I should be back around two. Want to hang out later?"

I wanted to say *yes*. It almost surprised me, how much I wanted to. But I knew it wasn't the best idea for my productivity, and there was some perverse part of me that still wanted to assert a boundary just as a reminder that I could. The fact that I knew Sam would accept it unquestioningly only made it feel shittier, in a way, that I was doing it mostly to prove a point to myself. "I really, *really* need to work on that chapter," I said. "I'll come over if I finish before dinner, but I might not."

"Okay," he said. He wanted to kiss me—I could just tell. He'd leaned forward in the doorway a bit, his fingers drumming on the wood frame. But I was behind a tall mountain of clothes, my hands busy with taking things off hangers, and I didn't make any move to meet him halfway. We'd already kissed once when he came over, and he'd brought me coffee and petted the cat and solved my brother's problem, and I'd touched his arm and gently teased him about his musical taste . . . if we added anything else to today, it might give him the wrong idea.

And what idea is that?

I mentally told myself to get a grip, and gave Sam a smile that I hoped seemed breezy and unaffected. "See you later," I said.

After Sam had gone, Conner wandered back in the room and half-heartedly tried to pick back up where he'd left off. I could tell he'd be useless to me the rest of the day, though, now that his brain was all filled with proposal plans again. He also forced me to listen to "Tubthumping" three times through, which eventually prompted me to tell him to go home so I could work on my dissertation in peace and quiet.

Part of the reason it had taken me so long to write this chapter on *In Cold Blood*—besides the usual issues of distraction and procrastination, of course—was that I was intimidated by it. Capote's book was basically *the* prototype for the genre, after all, and had been analyzed before by people smarter than I was.

One argument I'd made in my introduction was that true crime was ultimately about place, and time, with the criminal acts themselves just the lens through which an author sought to understand the broader cultural context. In that way, it wasn't just what Capote was trying to say about the Clutter murder, what relationship he'd developed with Perry and Dick while he researched his book, but his perspective on middle America in the early 1960s as a whole.

I thought it was interesting that, in addition to spending a lot of time giving the flavor of Holcomb, Kansas—a town in a time where still only one person was known to lock the door to their house, an unusual enough practice to be remarked upon—Capote also made sure that every major character in the book *wanted* something. The scene where Dick takes Perry to buy wedding clothes for a made-up event, a ruse just to pass off a fraudulent check scheme, is particularly affecting because it shows you just how badly Perry wishes it were true. He allows himself to believe, only for a second, that Dick's lies are reality, and that he has the love of a good woman waiting for him, the chance to have a child, make a life. It's the American Dream in its most distilled, bittersweet rendition, and then you had to reconcile that with the fact that these are the same two men who ended four other American Dreams with close-range gunshots.

I was on a roll, my fingers flying over my laptop keys, when Lenore jumped up and walked right across my keyboard, putting her asshole in my face.

"Thanks," I said, making sure my progress was saved before her kitten paws replaced all my work with *asno;wiwn;;aj.* "Very helpful."

The pulsing heartbeat of true crime, of all human stories when you got right down to it, was we all wanted and hoped and dreamed and loved, but we had no control over what happened in the end. There was a reason why even the most sensationalistic supermarket paperback would tell you that the victim loved animals and wanted to be a veterinarian, or that another victim was three days away from her birthday.

"These books promise closure and justice," I said to Lenore, scratching her under the chin. "But ultimately they reinforce the reality that so many lives are interrupted, so many dreams unfulfilled."

She looked at me through slitted eyes, a slight tilt of her

head the only sign that she wanted me to continue with the scratching.

"That's why you gotta live in the moment, DTC," I said. "To want something is to set yourself up for disappointment."

The flick of her tail seemed to say, *Bitch, I invented living in the moment,* and, *Three thousand words of analysis on Capote's classic and you've reduced it to an Instagram quote on a picture of a sunset?*

I wondered what Sam was doing.

TWENTY

"OKAY, HERE'S THE deal," I said to him ten minutes later, after I'd shown up at his front door with my laptop in my backpack. "I have to finish this today, so I'm going to keep working. But I don't want to be distracted, and the best way is if you are also doing something productive and not just, like, watching Red Hot Chili Peppers concert DVDs or whatever you normally do."

"I don't even like them that much," Sam said. "I just respect their musicianship—"

I had already hung my backpack up on the back of one of his dining room chairs and unpacked my laptop to set it up on the table. "The point is, I think it would be a good idea if *you* spent time working on that guitar you've been trying to build. Then we can check back in in, like, an hour?" I frowned down at the wall, where a two-by-two shelf filled with records appeared to be blocking where the outlet would be. "Where can I plug in?"

"Other side," Sam said. And of course, there was an open outlet in the same spot on the opposite wall. Some graduate-level critical thinking there.

"See, dropping RHCP song titles even now," I said. "You can't help yourself."

"Can't stop."

I rolled my eyes at that one, sitting down and pointedly putting my earbuds in. I only half expected Sam to actually follow my direction about the guitar. I had no idea what he'd been doing before I showed up, after all, and I wasn't the boss of him. But I was aware of him disappearing into the garage, the door shut behind him while he did . . . well, whatever building a guitar entailed. Something with wood and strings, I imagined.

When I'd finished and emailed the chapter to Dr. Nilsson—rough as hell but *done*, at least—I ventured out there, not sure if I should knock first. Even though I now knew that the garage wasn't some secret serial killer lair, I still had this squirmy feeling in my stomach about bothering Sam there. But he glanced up from where he was working, giving me a smile as I came in.

"Done?"

"With that part, at least," I said. "And I emailed this local professor my advisor wanted me to meet with, to set that up. Then I had to text Alison to see if she could help me look for a blazer." I waved a hand, figuring it was all pretty boring. "Whatever. I hate shopping. What are you marking that up for?"

Sam had been measuring out distances on the raw wood body, penciling in a few dots along a straight center line. "I still haven't decided on the scale length of the neck," he said. "But if I go with twenty-five point five, I think this is where the bridge'll go, and then the pickups will be here."

He was pointing at various spots on the guitar, but I had no idea what half those words meant, so I focused more on how good his hand looked as he swiped some eraser dust off the wood, how much I liked hearing the energy in his voice when he talked about something that excited him.

"I have an old electric from high school," I said. "The strings have a really bad buzz to them now, though."

"Could need to have the frets leveled," Sam said. "Bring it over and I'll intonate it for you, put new strings on."

"Cool, thanks," I said. "Don't be scared if the only song I can play is 'Doll Parts.' It's just super easy so it might be the only one I remember. Personally, I don't think Courtney had anything to do with what happened to Kurt."

"Courtney Love doesn't scare me," Sam said. He put the pencil down, looked at me. "You're used to intimidating people, aren't you?"

I shrugged. "You have to admit. When you first met me, you were scared."

"Because you threatened me with Mace," Sam pointed out. "And called me *my dude* in a way that suggested imminent violence. I still thought you were cute. Meanwhile you thought I was a six on your serial killer scale."

That seemed so long ago already, a time when I didn't know Sam the way I did now. The way his eyes lit up when he found something truly hilarious. The way he sometimes pressed the tip of his tongue to the corner of his mouth when he was concentrating. The way his hands clenched my hips when he was about to come, as though he wanted us as close as possible.

On my serial killer scale, Sam was now comfortably at a one.

But on a scale of how much he scared me? It was starting to climb the charts. Because this was supposed to be a brief, fun summer thing . . . so why did it already feel like more?

"I'll probably leave for North Carolina in about a month," I said. I realized it was a non sequitur in our conversation, but in my head the through line was perfectly clear. "I should be able to find another apartment in the same complex where I was renting before, but I still need to get everything settled."

"Okay," Sam said. "Teachers go back the first week of August, so if it's before that I can help you move."

An altogether confusing response. On the one hand, my brain couldn't help but interpret that as an eagerness to see me gone, although I was the one who'd brought it up and my leaving had never been in question. On the other hand, he wanted to help me move? Like, drive ten hours, go through my storage unit with me, unpack a bunch of boxes of books I probably didn't *need* but was never going to get rid of?

That sounded like more commitment than a summer fling.

"We'll see," I said. Then, because I couldn't stop myself, I blurted, "What about the next few weeks, then? What are we doing, if we know this is going to end?"

Sam cradled my jaw in his hands, his eyes searching my face, as if he were looking for some answer there. From his expression, I couldn't tell if he'd found it. "We know it's going to change," he said, resting his forehead against mine. "That doesn't necessarily mean *end*, unless you want it to. You have my full attention, Phoebe. I'm not going anywhere."

The joke was on the tip of my tongue, something about how *I* was the one going somewhere in this scenario. But I swallowed it back, not wanting to shift out of this moment just yet. I pushed up on my tiptoes to press a kiss behind Sam's ear. "My dude," I said.

SAM AND I ended up spending the rest of the night watching movies—somehow, I convinced him to let me put on *Silence of the Lambs*—and eating some pasta dish he'd whipped up that I was very impressed by.

"It has, like, five ingredients," he'd said. "Checkers, not chess."

I would've happily stayed in that bubble, taking turns going down on each other on the couch before going for another nighttime swim, but I still didn't like the idea of spending all night away from Lenore, no matter how much she ignored me.

Plus, the next day I was supposed to meet up with Alison to try to find a blazer at the mall. I already knew it was going to be a futile search. There were too many brands that acted like you should be grateful if they went up to an L, too many stores that stocked a million size 4s and then one size 16 somewhere on the clearance rack. And a blazer was one of the worst items to fit of all, considering that I had to contend with shoulders and sleeve length and whether it pulled weirdly because it had failed to account for the fact that some women have breasts.

"The shoulder fit is the most important," Alison said as we were going through the racks in one department store. "You can always get any clothing item tailored, but it's harder to adjust that part. You have such nice, straight shoulders."

"I'm not going to send some fifty-dollar polyester thing to a *tailor*," I said. "That's just throwing away money."

Alison shrugged. "Obviously it's better if you start with a high-quality item to begin with," she said. "But I know you're on a time crunch so we'll work with what we have."

I wanted to point out that all this was easy for her to say. She had the kind of figure that they made clothes for—thin and straight—and everything looked amazing on her. But then I also knew I was being churlish, because that was exactly the reason I'd asked for her help. If left to my own devices, I'd half-heartedly try on a single blazer in Target and then walk out of there with it, only to find out later that it didn't really fit.

"How are things going with Sam?"

"I took your advice," I said, "and am keeping an open mind."

She handed me three hangers that held the same blazer, but in different sizes. "And more importantly, how's Lenore?"

"A little brat," I said. "*She's* the one who seemed to want in the house so bad. *She's* the one who was trying to suck on my shirt like I was a surrogate cat mom. And did I tell you the vet said she's at least three years old? She's just small, maybe from mal-nourishment from living on the harsh suburban streets. It's like the plot of that movie, remember the one, where the couple adopt a child from Russia but she turns out to be an adult with some rare hormonal disorder that stunted her growth? And then she tries to kill them all?"

"That doesn't sound like a movie I'd like," Alison said, wrinkling her nose.

And of course, I remembered that Alison never liked scary movies, and she really didn't care for any media that depicted adoption in either an overly negative or overly inspirational way. I felt like an asshole for even bringing it up.

"Sorry," I said. "Anyway, Lenore's fine. We're still getting used to each other."

"It'll take time," Alison said. "It's actually very encouraging that she's taken to being in the house so well. I was worried she'd be a bolter, since she's spent her whole life outside."

"To bolt, she'd have to *come out*," I said.

"Remember that one hamster you had," Alison said, "that would only stay in the little house-bed thing you'd bought it? It was like a hamster recluse."

I'd creatively named the hamster Rocket, because the day I got him was the same day my dad bought Conner a rocket set to launch in the backyard. The antisocial creature would only come out to eat, and if I tried to reach my hand in to get Rocket out to clean his bed shavings, or god forbid to pet him, he'd nip at my fingertips.

"When he died, I buried him in that little house," I said.

Alison put a hand to her chest. "Aw, that's so sweet. He gets to spend eternity with the thing he loved most."

I'd meant it more as a spiteful *if you love it so much, here, take it* gesture, but Alison's version of events made me sound a lot better, so I left it.

"I was such a jerk when I was a kid," I said.

"Aren't all kids, in a way?" Alison said. "Like when we do

story time at the library—don't get me wrong, the kids are *adorable*, and way preferable to their parents in most respects. But they're self-absorbed. It's developmentally unavoidable. If they want to stand up to get a better view of the book and block the kid behind them, or pet your feet while you're reading—there's one girl who will do this, and I can't even begin to tell you how creepy and weird it is—or snatch the rest of a cookie out of another kid's hand . . . well, they're kids. That's what they do."

"But you're talking about *toddlers*," I pointed out. "If I snatched a cookie out of your hand right now, you'd think I was rude as hell. Or like the way I just cut you off, the way I treated you after you were trying to help. That was a jerk move."

There. I'd said it. I hadn't even known I was going to, but the minute I had it felt like a relief. It had been great, getting closer with Alison again over the last few weeks, but it always felt like there was this one thing between us. Maybe it was time to talk about it.

Alison had been rifling through some multicolored cardigans, careful to only lift enough to see the size sticker on each one so as not to disturb the neatness of the stacks. She definitely had a librarian's desire to leave everything exactly as she'd found it, and a librarian's need for more and more cardigans. Now she paused.

"You were so angry after your parents split up," she said. "And since you'd moved away and neither one of us could drive yet, I felt like I was losing you. To the distance, but also just to . . ." She gestured vaguely out to the ether.

"Depression?" I supplied. "I know. I was in a black cloud around that time. Sometimes I think I have a bit of a gray cloud, at least, that still follows me around. I know people's parents get divorced, and every teenager is practically required to go through a stage where they shop at Hot Topic and say things like *You laugh because I'm different, but I laugh because you're all the same.* But it felt like too much to deal with, and I shut out a lot of people, including you."

"I could tell you were going through a lot," Alison said. "When you said that thing, about swallowing a bottle of pills . . . well, it sounded like you could be serious. I didn't want you to get in trouble, but I also knew I'd never forgive myself if you ended up doing something and I *hadn't* acted on it. I knew you were at your dad's that weekend, but also knew that you weren't that close with him, so I thought it was better to call your mom's apartment. I'm really sorry if that ended up being the wrong thing to do."

It had ended up becoming another fight between my parents, a piece of evidence as to why *she* wasn't doing a good job raising me and why *he* wasn't doing a good job of supervising me when I was back in his care. It meant my mom spent the next year randomly asking to read my chat threads or watching me especially close on major holidays—she seemed to think that New Year's in particular would send me over the edge, which was actually pretty astute. It meant my dad had burst into my room while I was chatting with Alison and yelled, *Not in my house!*, the only thing he'd ever directly said to me about the entire incident, which left me with the distinct impression, however false and overdramatic, that he cared less if I killed myself and more that I didn't do it during the forty-eight hours when I was his responsibility. It meant that I'd decided, fine, not in your house, and arranged it so I never spent another custodial weekend in that house again.

But none of that was Alison's fault.

"I was mad at you at the time," I said. "But deep down, I think I was mad at myself. I knew I wasn't actually planning to do anything, that it was just a cry for attention. And I hated myself for it."

Alison's brows drew together. "But what's so bad about needing attention? Especially if you're in pain, or struggling."

I shrugged. "Call it being a Capricorn," I said. It was a deliberately simplistic response, because how else could I express it, the way my skin crawled at the idea of saying baldly to someone, *I'm in pain, I'm struggling, I need you.* It always blew my mind, when people on social media posted things like "I'm having a bad day, please send compliments!" I loved that for them, being so open, but I'd rather saw off my own foot.

"Either way," Alison said. "I'm glad you came back and we were able to reconnect. I missed you."

"Same." Then, before it could get any mushier than it already had, I held a charcoal blazer I'd found up to my body. "What do you think?"

"That could be a good color," Alison said. "It lets you wear it with black without worrying about matching exact shades."

"Truly the bane of my existence," I said, adding it to the growing pile over my arm. "Speaking of, time to hit the dressing room."

TWENTY-ONE

———

I ENDED UP WITH two different blazer options—the charcoal and a black one—and a new pair of shoes. Considering that I'd effectively found almost half my outfit for the interview and hadn't broken out into frustrated sobs once, it was a successful trip.

I let myself into the house and hung the clothes up in my closet, automatically clicking my tongue against my teeth the way I did when I was trying to see if Lenore would come out. She rarely responded, but it felt like something I had to do, regardless, a *Hey, honey, I'm home.*

The house did seem extra quiet. It shouldn't—even if Lenore was there, she'd be under the bed or on the windowsill behind some blinds in my dad's room, watching the birds through the window. It was her favorite place to be lately, although she'd jump down and scurry into the closet if you came into the room.

I got down on the floor to peer under the bed. No Lenore.

Still making the clicking sound, I walked slowly through the rest of the house, my gaze sweeping every corner. Since we'd moved so much stuff out, there really weren't that many places for her to go in the common areas. It must be an incredibly boring place for her to hang out, compared to the variety and stimulation of outside. Why hadn't I thought about that before? Gotten a fucking cat climbing tree covered in carpet or whatever that book had recommended?

She wasn't on the windowsill. She wasn't in the closet. Her food bowl was still mostly full. And the more I thought back to that morning, the more I thought about how I'd gone to my car only to realize that I'd forgotten to bring the shirt I planned to wear for the interview, like Alison had told me to. I'd run back in to grab it, and I may have left the door ajar. That didn't sound like me, especially after I'd read about the Vampire of Sacramento and how he'd never hit up a house with a locked door, feeling it was a sign he was unwelcome. But it had been for only a few seconds, and I was pretty sure I'd left the door open.

Sam's truck was in his driveway, so I went over and knocked on his door. He opened up almost immediately, giving me a wide, lazy smile. "You don't have to knock," he said. "Just come on in."

Obviously someone wasn't as versed in the Vampire of Sacramento as I was, but there was no time for that now. "Lenore's gone."

His smile fell. "Are you sure? Maybe she's under the bed."

"I checked there, and all her usual places," I said. "I was in a hurry this morning, and I think I left the door open for a minute. Of course she ran—why wouldn't she have run? She probably saw it as a heroic escape. Like that 'dead giveaway' meme, remember that one, after those women finally escaped that guy's basement in Cleveland?"

Sam reached out to grasp me by the upper arms, massaging my shoulders. "The good news is that she's a savvy little cat," he said. "She knows her way around. She's lived out here for years, and always found her way back to this street. We'll find her."

"I'm just going to walk around the block a few times, see if I spot her."

"Give me a sec," Sam said. "I'll come with you."

I waited for him on the front step, unwilling to take my eyes off my own house next door in case Lenore somehow came walking up right at that moment. But by the time Sam had put on his shoes and locked the door behind him, she was still nowhere to be seen.

"I know this is irrational," I said after we'd walked a little ways. "To be worried about her, I mean. Like you said, she's lived in the elements for years. She probably saw a strip of blue sky and was like, *My wild heart can't be tamed!* and shot right out that door. It's my own fault, for trying to pin her down."

"Are you still talking about the cat, or a cowgirl lover?"

I nudged him with my shoulder. "Shut up."

It was quiet outside, most people probably in the middle of eating their dinner, and sometimes we passed by houses with open blinds that showed a flickering television inside. The sun had set but it wasn't dark yet, the dusk making me second-guess every shadow, thinking it could be Lenore.

"Did you have a good shopping trip?"

"It was . . ." I'd been about to say *fine*, the highest compliment I could pay any trip to the mall, but I realized it'd been better than that. I'd found some clothes, and I'd ended up having a really good conversation with Alison that had been a long time coming. We'd just had fun, too, going into the novelty gift store to laugh at the inappropriate refrigerator magnets and grabbing orange chicken and chow mein at the food court.

"Yeah," I said finally. "It went really well. How about your dance practice?"

Sam had met up with Conner and a few of the kids and their adult chaperones at a local playground, planning out the logistics of the flash mob. I'd teased him with a couple *Dance Moms* references, but I'd only ever seen the ads for that show, so I'd run out pretty quickly.

"Great," he said. "The kids are really excited."

"And Conner?"

"I said *the kids*," Sam said, "specifically to be inclusive of your brother. He's 'beyond stoked,' to quote him directly."

"I don't know where he gets that shit from. Like he's a surfer from the eighties or something."

"He also invited me to play his wedding," Sam said. "I had to tell him I was out of the live music game, except for the tambourine. If he finds a band that's *almost* there but missing that little something extra, I would come out of retirement."

As we walked by one house, I saw a flash of fur dart behind a car, and I pulled on Sam's arm to stop. "Did you see that? Was it her?"

"I think it was an orange cat."

"Could've been her," I said. "Orange and black look really similar in the dark."

"If I had a choice between wearing a black shirt to bike around the neighborhood at night, or wearing orange, I feel like one of those choices is smarter than the other."

"Maybe save color theory for the art teacher," I said, but then the cat emerged from under the car, scurrying back into the woods behind the house. "Okay, that cat *was* orange, though."

Sam didn't say *I told you so*, which was to his credit. He just put his arm around me, drawing me closer to give me a quick kiss on the head, before releasing me again, as though he knew I was hit-or-miss on physical contact. The problem was, though, that with Sam I was pretty much always *hit*. I thought back to my conversation with Alison, the novel idea that if you wanted something sometimes all it took was to *ask* for it. But I just couldn't bring myself to do it.

"I feel like the worst cat owner on the planet," I said instead. "Cat mom? I don't know what to even call myself. Whatever it is, I'm the worst."

"You're not."

"I buried my hamster in his little spite house," I said. "Seriously, I shouldn't have pets."

Sam actually stumbled a little over a crack in the sidewalk. "Jesus," he said. "How *old* were you?"

"Maybe ten?" Then I saw Sam's face, and saw the miscommunication that must've happened. "Oh god. The hamster was dead. I didn't bury him *alive*."

"You do have that thing with Edgar Allan Poe," Sam said. "You can't blame me for jumping to conclusions."

"I'm just not cut out for this." It was straight-up dark by now, and I worried we'd never find the damn cat. And sure, maybe she'd come back tomorrow, lying in front of my door flicking her tail, looking up at me like, *What are you so upset for?* But maybe she wouldn't. Maybe she'd get hit by a car, or attacked by a coyote, or get so lost she couldn't find her way back. Maybe the brief domestication I'd foisted upon her was the worst possible thing I could've done, a way to dull her best street instincts just when she'd need them most.

"I can't take care of something else," I went on. "I can't worry if she's eating right, or if she needs to socialize with other cats, or whether I'm fulfilling her existential need to roam. I can't watch her get older and wait to see what the vet has to say about the weird bump. Sam, if I take in this cat, I'm basically saying I am going to watch her *die* one day. That is insane. My mom was totally right not to let me bring home that sick Russian blue, because that is some existential shit. It might even be for the best that she got out? Maybe she's truly happier out here, and we were never meant to spend our lives together. It's like one of those movies where at the end the two characters don't end up with each other, and at first you're like, *the fuck?*, but then you realize that it was literally in the title and the marketing and even the musical cues told you this was going to be a story about people who were in each other's lives for a short time just to help them learn something about life or love or whatever—"

"Phoebe," Sam said.

"I hate those movies. Especially when one of them dies in a truly freak accident. The fuck outta here with your emotionally manipulative shit."

"*Phoebe*," Sam said, with more emphasis this time, his hand on the small of my back as he pointed toward my house. We'd made a complete loop around the neighborhood and I'd been too wrapped up in my own thoughts to even effectively look for the cat I'd gone out to find.

But there she was, draped across my front step, licking her paw. She looked up at us with a *took you long enough* expression, as though this had been a game the whole time.

"She came back," I said, and burst into tears.

I CRIED A disproportionate amount for a cat who'd been lost for a few hours, an amount that suggested that it probably wasn't all about the cat. It all hit me at once—my dad dying and the years I'd lost with my brother and the way my friendship with Alison had ended and now this stupid cat, who immediately scurried to her place at the windowsill the moment we were in the house.

There was nowhere to *sit* anymore, except my desk chair and my bed, so as if by mutual agreement Sam and I went into the bedroom, where he sat next to me on my narrow twin mattress.

"Hey," Sam said, rubbing my back. "It's okay. She's here. She's safe."

I shook my head. I wanted to explain that it wasn't just the cat, but I didn't know how to put it all into words. My throat was tight and hot, and I swiped at my eyes, trying to will the tears to stop coming.

"You *are* cut out for this," Sam said. "You're doing just fine. She got out. It happens. But you've already taken her to the vet and switched foods once because she didn't seem to like the first food, and you obviously care about her."

He was so close I could see the pulse in his throat, the way his overlong hair curled at the nape of his neck. It was wild, that someone could be a complete stranger, and then just weeks later be one of the most important people in your life.

"I can hear your brain working," Sam said, so softly it was almost a whisper.

I leaned forward to press my lips to that spot in his throat, the jump under his skin.

"I don't want to think," I said. "I just want to *feel*."

I pulled on the hem of his shirt, impatient until he lifted it over his head and tossed it on the floor, forgotten. He had such a great chest, warm and strong but not overly muscled; no protein powder for Sam. I splayed one hand over his heart, feeling the rhythmic beat beneath my fingertips.

Sam reached up, encircling my wrist with his hand, his thumb at the pulse point there, pressing my palm harder against his skin. "Phoebe," he said, and there was something different in the way he said my name. He wasn't telling me to stop, and he wasn't telling me to go. It was more like he was telling me to stay right here, in this moment. Like there was something special about it.

Inexplicably, tears pricked the back of my eyes, but I was done crying. I didn't want Sam to see me like this. *I* didn't want to see me like this. My gaze dropped to his mouth, almost hesitant, as if asking for permission. When I looked back up, his blue eyes were a definite *yes*. They were his sexy bedroom eyes, dark and hungry, but there was more behind them than just sex. There was more to his *yes* than just this moment.

My hand still on his chest, I slanted my mouth over his in a slow, deep kiss. The corners of my lips were damp from the tears, and Sam licked away the salt with his tongue, his hands sliding up under my shirt like we were two teenagers making out after school. Which was a little how it felt, being with him like this in my childhood bedroom, the same quilt still on my bed from when I was fifteen.

Maybe Sam felt that, too, because his hands under my shirt were working maddeningly slow for someone who'd already seen me naked multiple times before. They slid up my rib cage, brushed against the sensitive skin under my breasts, flicked once against my nipples, which were taut and aching under my bra. But then he skimmed back down my sides and gave my leggings-clad thighs a squeeze, leaving me hungry to feel his hands on my bare skin.

"What do you want to feel?" he murmured, his breath warm against my cheek.

Everything. But instead, what came out was, "Taken care of."

He broke off the kiss, his eyes blazing as he looked down at me. "Take off your shirt," he said.

I crossed my arms at the hem of my shirt, pulling it over my head in a motion that left my hair wild and tangled over my face. Sam brushed it away from my forehead, my temples, his expression almost contemplative despite the heat in his eyes. "Now your bra," he said.

I wasn't used to this bossy side of Sam, but it struck me what he was doing. The way he seemed to know that part of not wanting to think was not wanting to have to make any decisions, not wanting to have to tell my limbs what to do. He had taken that part over for me, and it was incredibly hot but also, strangely, incredibly sweet.

I reached behind my back to unhook my bra, letting it fall to the floor next to the bed.

He ran his hands along my shoulders, the ridges of my collarbones. His fingers sank into the tense muscles of my upper back, massaging in deep, sensual circles that caused a moan to escape my mouth.

"You deserve to be taken care of," he said, and then his hand was on my hip, directing me. "Here. Let me do this properly."

I turned around, scooting back until I was nestled in between his thighs, and he resumed his slow ministrations, his thumbs digging into the space between my shoulder blades. "Tell me if I'm too rough," he said quietly into my ear, but I could only shake my head. It felt amazing.

He ran his nails down my back, the sensation sending a delicious crackle down my spine, before calming the activated nerve endings with a rub all the way down to my lower back. His fingers hooked in the waistband of my leggings, my underwear, before tugging at the stretchy material of the leggings. "Now these," he said. "Only these."

I had to stand up to comply with that command, rolling the leggings down from my hips and stepping out of them. It gave me a chance to see Sam's face, his eyes hooded, watching me. Any questions I may have had about whether this was only about my pleasure were answered in that look, and further by the hard ridge of his jeans against my ass when I took my place back between his thighs.

I half expected him to touch me in a more explicit way than a massage of the shoulders, but he simply returned to the slow kneading of my back, no more improper than what you might ask a friend to do, albeit with fewer clothes. It made my body scream to be touched—I wanted his hands everywhere, on my breasts and in my mouth and in between my legs. I ground my ass against his erection through his jeans, trying to send him a message.

"Shhh," Sam said against my ear, less a command to be quiet and more a soft sound of indulgence. "We have time. We have all night."

He reached around to squeeze my thighs, massaging the skin there, too, his fingers brushing tantalizingly close to the edge of my underwear. I should feel self-conscious, in this position. There was enough moonlight coming through the window that he'd be able to see the dimples in my pale thighs, and sitting up made my hips and belly curve over the elastic waistband of my underwear. But somehow that part of my brain turned off with Sam, and I could focus instead on the way it felt as his hands spanned my inner thighs, urging me to spread them further.

Finally, he scraped just his knuckles along the pulsing core of me, the friction intensely erotic through the damp fabric of my underwear. My body jerked involuntarily at the touch, but then just as suddenly it was gone. He curved his hands under my ass, gripping my cheeks as he shifted me closer. I heard his sharp intake of breath at the contact, and I relished it, that sign that he was just as turned on as I was.

He cupped my breasts, rolling my nipples between his fingers in a way that instantly made my breathing shallow. "I love how you fill my hands," he said. "I could come just thinking about your tits. I *have* come just thinking about your tits."

"You have?" I barely recognized my own voice.

"Mmm," he said. "That night after I jumped your car, I came home and thought about you. Just the feel of when you'd brush against me, when we were walking side by side."

"Wow, you're easy." But it gave me a thrill, knowing he'd thought of me that way, even then.

He continued fondling one breast while his other hand slid down my belly, under the waistband of my panties, stroking me down my wet slit.

"Oh," I breathed when he finally slipped a finger inside. "Fuck, Sam."

"I like it when you say my name," he said, and I said it again and again, until he added another finger and the strokes became faster, deeper, and I stopped saying anything at all.

I leaned back against him, my hair splayed out across his hard chest, my head resting on his shoulder, my throat exposed.

"You feel so good," he said, his breath hot on my neck.

It was pornographic, the scene we made. Me with my knees up close to my chest, my legs spread, his fingers still working in me. Somehow the fact that he was still wearing his jeans, that I could only see the outline of his knuckles through the thin cotton of my underwear, only made it feel more so. But it was a vulnerable position, too, the way I was so open to him, the rasp of his voice in my ear. When I came it was so sudden it surprised me, my body clenching around his hand even as I grabbed his wrist, holding him there until the last of the aftershocks rippled through my body.

Finally, his hand skated back up over me, leaving a streak of wetness on my nipple from where he'd been inside me. I watched Sam's profile from under my lashes. The way his mouth parted as he rubbed that wet nipple with his thumb, the way he bit down on his lower lip.

I leaned all the way back until I was lying on the bed, pulling

Sam down over me for a long, deep kiss. I was trying to tell him something with that kiss, and I didn't even know what it was. It vibrated through me, in my tongue in his mouth and my fingers pulling at the button of his jeans, desperate to get them off. It was a low hum in the back of my throat as I laughed a little when I couldn't, and he reached down to undo the button with one hand and slide them down his hips. There was an awkward moment where he was working on that while I was trying to kick my underwear off, all while directing him to the box of condoms I'd recently bought and stashed under the bed. It could've spoiled the mood, but somehow it didn't. Sam pressed one more hungry kiss against my mouth, and then he entered me in one fluid motion, and stole my breath.

When I looked up, his eyes were open, his gaze on my face. One corner of his mouth hitched in a smile, but it didn't seem like an expression as simple as pleasure, or even a leftover from the silliness of the logistics from a few moments before. It was more like . . . awe. Like I could feel some glow come from the center of his chest where I'd unconsciously flattened my palm.

I was scared of what he might say, with an expression like that. I was scared of what *I* might say. So I ran my hands up his arms, my nails up his back, my fingers in the hair at the nape of his neck as I pulled him toward me. At the same time, I lifted my hips, inviting him to move with me. The rhythm was exquisitely slow at first, then built until the wrought iron headboard of my bed was banging against the wall.

"Right there," I gasped, reaching up to grasp two bars of the headboard as Sam thrust into me. "Right there, Sam, oh god."

This time when I came, it was gentler than before, rolling

through my body like a wave. I could tell Sam was close, and I clenched around him, urging him to keep going, to fuck me until we were both strung out from it. I watched his face as he came, the way his jaw clenched and then went slack, the way his Adam's apple bobbed as he gulped air, as though he'd forgotten how to breathe for a second. I'd never done that before—watched a partner climax during sex. It had never even occurred to me to open my eyes. But with Sam, I wanted to pay attention.

He took care of the condom and then climbed back into bed, our bodies nestled close on the narrow twin mattress.

"I think we may have broken it," I said, reaching up to rattle the headboard.

"It seems pretty solid."

"Well, we definitely embarrassed it at least. This was my childhood bed."

"I don't think furniture stands in any kind of judgment. It's inert."

I smiled at that. Sam's head was on my chest, and I ran my fingers through his soft hair. "I spent a lot of time in this bed daydreaming about what my life was going to be like."

He was quiet for a moment, his breath so even on my skin that I thought maybe he'd fallen asleep. But then he said, "What did you imagine it would be?"

"I thought maybe I'd be a writer," I said. "Or an editor. Something with books. I wanted to live in a big city, in a cool apartment like they always have on TV. One with a view of the skyline and a quirky doorman. Oh, and a cat. I always thought I'd have a cat, actually, although in my daydream my cat was more of a purring lap animal than a feral street beast."

"Glad to see you've recovered from almost losing Lenore," Sam said dryly. "What else?"

"It all sounds so generic now. It was probably the same thing every kid dreams of because we all watched the same movies. I thought I'd lose all my baby fat and turn from an ugly duckling into a beautiful swan. I thought that would make my mom like me more, and we'd grow up to be that mother-daughter pair who drink mimosas together at Sunday brunch."

I swallowed. "I always imagined that I'd get at least one moment when my dad would be really proud of me, and I'd be able to tell. He never would've said it—that wasn't his style—but just some moment where I *knew*."

And now I would never have that. I hadn't realized what a different kind of grief that was—the loss of all the potential moments that would never be, not just the past moments that already were. I'd focused so hard on that past, where my relationship with my dad had been so complicated, but forgotten that I used to dream of a day when it wouldn't be that way.

"Did he ever mention me?"

I hadn't known I was going to ask the question until it was out of my mouth. It was so raw, there was no hiding it, and I immediately wanted to snatch it back. Of course my father wouldn't have mentioned me, a daughter he barely spoke to, a daughter he'd probably written off.

"Your dad wasn't a big talker," Sam said, his voice a rumble against my chest. "As you know. But I feel like I could tell, from the way he checked his mail, that he was super proud."

I bit the inside of my cheek. "Could not."

"Oh yeah," he said. "You should've seen it. He'd do this shuf-

fle down the driveway—it *screamed* that his daughter was about
to become a doctor, he was obnoxious about it, to tell you the
truth—and then he'd open the mailbox and peer inside. Then
he'd pull out the envelopes and start sorting them like he was
reading through the paper you presented at the pop culture conference last year, the one about masculinity and monstrosity in
The Shining—"

I propped myself up on my elbows. "Wait, how—?"

"I Googled you," Sam said. "Anyway, then he'd amble back
up the driveway, his gait making it clear to the whole neighborhood that his daughter was strong and empathetic, smart and
hilarious, and gorgeous. When he chucked all the mail directly in
his outside garbage can, his regret was painfully obvious, that he
couldn't find a way to tell you all those things himself."

My throat burned as I said, "All from a walk to the mailbox,
huh?"

"He did it every day," Sam said. "What can I say, I'm obser-
vant."

I snuggled into him, pressing a kiss to his shoulder. "You're
sweet," I said.

"Sweet on you."

I groaned at the cheesiness of that line, giving him a playful
swat. But the truth was that it wormed its way into my heart regardless. It made me dream, for one night at least, of something I
hadn't even dared to as a young girl lying in this same bed—that
all the pink heart valentine, sappy love song stuff might be real,
and be something I could have.

TWENTY-TWO

THE MORNING OF Conner's proposal dawned with about sixty-eight texts from Conner about the logistics, when I was going to pick up Shani to take her to lunch, what time we had to be at the park, even what I should wear. (**I know you have a lot of goth shit, but maybe for the pictures a color???**)

It hadn't even occurred to me that *I* needed to be in any pictures. The eventual wedding was going to be fun.

Sam was very cutely excited and nervous, too, and he had to leave early to get everything set up. Not only had he arranged the thirty-something kids who were going to do the dancing, but he was bringing out his sound system and hooking it up so "Tubthumping" could be heard at a suitably horrifying volume.

"I need to pick up some cheese and crackers and apple slices at the store, too," Sam said, typing it into his phone. "Something both the kids and parents will eat. Maybe some water and Capri Suns."

"Make sure they're Pacific Cooler," I said, folding myself into the chair at my desk and opening up my laptop. Dr. Nilsson had said she'd get me comments on my last chapter by today, and I was hoping to have a chance to take a look before all the festivities started.

"Phoebe," Sam said. "I've been working with kids for years. Trust that I know the superiority of Pacific Cooler by now."

He came from behind to press a kiss to the top of my head, and then he headed out, leaving me alone with Dr. Nilsson's email and Lenore, who'd graduated at least to hanging out in the same room as me. I'd turned an empty box on its side, and she liked to crawl in and out of it before eventually settling down to rest.

"Let's see what we have here," I said, opening up the email. I couldn't deny that I'd still talked to myself before Lenore, but her presence definitely made it happen more often. Only now I could justify it as talking to her.

Dr. Nilsson started with a bit about how she'd heard from Dr. Blake and was happy I'd set up the interview, et cetera. Then she launched into her feedback on my *In Cold Blood* chapter, and it was my own blood that immediately turned cold. Phrases like *not your best work* and *rambling and disjointed* and *needs more robust scholarship* flashed before my eyes before I could even bring myself to read the whole block of text from beginning to end.

I double-clicked the file to read her comments, and the sheer amount of red made my eyes tear up, whether from stress or the harsh glare of the color itself on my laptop screen. There were positive comments in there, too, although Dr. Nilsson tended to be fairly brusque with those—a *Good* in a little bubble next to a single point could count for a lot—but mostly I saw all the places where she'd slashed something as tangential, or asked for more evidence from outside the text itself to back up an argument. At the very end, she'd included one final comment.

> As sheer textual literary analysis, this isn't bad. But it fails to make the necessary connections to theory and cultural context that would elevate it to doctorate-level rhetorical study. You're in the home stretch—don't let yourself go off course now.

Those words created a pit in my stomach that lasted all through getting ready and into lunch with Shani, although I did my best to present a happy face in front of her. She was so pleased that I'd invited her out, making several comments that she'd always thought we should see more of each other, that I felt guilty that it had never occurred to me to do so before my brother had asked me to as part of his ruse. She really was a good person, and fun to talk to, with lots of stories from her job at the hospital or the many times my brother had been an idiot.

That idiot is going to propose in less than an hour, I kept wanting to say, but I was very proud of myself for keeping the secret. If I blew it at the last minute, I'd never forgive myself.

My pretense for stopping at the park was supposed to be that I remembered it from childhood and just wanted to drop by and take a walk down memory lane. **But it used to be nothing but trees and a couple benches,** I'd typed back to Conner. **Why would I care that they put a playground in here now?** To which he'd replied, **SHANI WON'T KNOW THAT BUT SHE EATS UP NOSTALGIC SHIT**

JUST DO IT PLEASE. In case I was wondering if he'd gotten any more relaxed with the second go-around.

Still, I felt obvious as hell when I rolled by the park and turned my car in at the last minute. "I hope you don't mind," I said. "I used to love this place when I was a kid, and I just wanted to check it out."

"Cool," Shani said. "Conner never mentioned that. He did say that you used to take him to a playground in another neighborhood sometimes, until someone asked you if you lived there."

I'd completely forgotten that, but now it came flooding back. I did used to take Conner when he was about four or five, and I was eleven or twelve, to this small playground the next neighborhood over. It only had a swing set and the tiniest jungle gym that could still be classified as such. It was in a fairly new neighborhood, and the tree cover wasn't great, so inevitably by the time we went home Conner would be a little sunburned and probably dehydrated, but he still begged me to take him. Then, one day, some random grown-up had asked me if we lived there. My *no* was honest but also self-protective—like I'd ever tell some stranger where I lived.

"Then you're not allowed to play in this park," the grown-up had said, her tone as serious as if she'd caught us shoplifting. If I could go back in time, I'd be, like, the fuck we can't, and keep taking Conner there every day until someone forcibly removed us. But at the time, it had spooked me enough to keep us away.

Those memories continuously surprised me, reminding me that there had been a time when Conner and I *had* been close, or at least I'd taken care of him a lot. But I couldn't get wrapped up in that right now. I needed to stay focused. There were a bunch of kids playing on the equipment today—more than the number I suspected were involved in the flash mob plan—and my palms were already so sweaty I had to wipe them on my jeans.

"Does it look like how you remember?" Shani asked as we walked up to the park.

There was Sam's sound equipment, set up next to a covered awning where a bunch of people were hanging out around a few picnic tables. Those must be the parents. I spotted more than one Capri Sun among them.

"Uh," I said. "Not really . . ."

There was a mark we were supposed to hit, that would signal the music to start and the dance to begin. I'd assumed Sam would want to do that himself, since it was his sound system, but he must've deputized a parent to handle it. It made sense that he wouldn't want to risk Shani spotting him, but I wondered where he was.

"Did you ever read that book on grief I gave you?" Shani asked.

Great. Fewer than ten yards from the mark, and Shani was asking the big questions. What was I supposed to do? Delay somehow and talk this through, while thirty-odd kids anxiously waited for their signal to start dancing? Already I noticed several kids openly staring at us. If we didn't get this show on the road, it was going to start looking like some *Children of the Corn* shit real fast.

"I haven't yet," I said. "Sorry. I will. What's your favorite thing to do at the playground? I always liked the swings."

I sounded like a first-grader trying to make a friend at school. Shani looked a little taken aback, but probably just figured that I really, really didn't want to talk about the grief book. Which was also fair.

"The swings are cool," Shani said, then perked up as she seemed to think of a better answer. "Ooh, you know what I liked? When they had a balance beam. I have *fantastic* balance. Does this—"

But we'd hit the mark, and all of a sudden the opening bars of the song started, the echoey, distant singing, and then right into the chorus. It made even me flinch back a little from the shock of it being piped through the park, and I'd known it was coming. As soon as the chorus started, a couple kids jumped off the jungle gym and started dancing in unison. I could see what Sam had been saying—they were almost more a series of poses than an actual dance, and one kid was half a beat behind, watching his friends do the moves first, but it was ridiculously cute.

"Do you see that?" Shani said, her smile wide with delight. "They must know each other or something. Where is the music coming from?"

She swiveled her head toward the pavilion, but by then it was on to the slower singing, the woman talking about pissing the night away in lyrics I still couldn't believe an elementary school would sanction. Once she came in, another group of kids started dancing toward us, doing another set of synchronized moves from the first group.

"This is unreal," Shani shouted over the music. "Have you ever seen this kind of thing?"

"Nope," I said.

Sam and I had watched several videos together of flash mob

proposals, and we'd convinced Conner that shorter could be sweeter in these situations. Sam had pointed out that ours would be made up of kids, which meant we should err on the side of brevity, and I'd pointed out that "Tubthumping" really was the same couple of parts repeated over and over, anyway. The plan was to keep the part until Conner came out under three minutes.

Still, I couldn't deny that it was a pretty magical couple of minutes. Each time the song shifted from the chorus to the verse, another set of kids added to the bigger group. There was a girl in particular I couldn't take my eyes off—chubby, with curly red hair and glasses, she was swinging her arms with the wildest abandon and lowest regard for anyone who might be standing near her. I almost saw her take out a skinny boy who kept glancing toward the pavilion, as if asking the adults what he should do.

Shani was entranced. At first, she clearly had no idea all this was for her—she was just enjoying the show. But by the second verse, it was obvious that the kids were forming a semicircle around us, and Shani glanced over at me like, *What is going on?* I just shrugged, but I couldn't help the goofy grin I could feel stretch across my face.

And then the chorus after that, Sam came out dancing with the last group of kids to join, moving closer to us with this footwork that involved them crossing one foot over the other, doing a shoulder shimmy, stepping back, then doing it all over again. His hair was plastered to his forehead with sweat—he'd been out there for the last couple hours, after all, while Shani and I had been eating Thai food—but he looked so joyful and confident I couldn't take my eyes off him.

I hadn't expected him to dance. We hadn't discussed it. But it made sense that he would've learned this routine along with the kids, if he was the one who'd taught it to them.

The dancers formed one big group around us now, and on the periphery I saw several adults filming on their phones—not just the ones who must be parents or guardians of the kids participating, but other adults, too. Sam led the kids in one final move, where they all did an almost frantic jog in place, starting low and then getting higher and higher until they threw their hands in the air and started free-dancing, bobbing and shaking their hips and doing the robot. Sam looked like something out of a 1980s music video, the way he twirled in a circle, tossing his hair out of his eyes with the motion. He was wearing a plain white T-shirt and light jeans, his red sneakers a bright blur as he danced, a strip of colored boxers showing when he lifted his arms.

Everyone was still dancing, but they parted to show my brother standing there, his arms clasped behind his back. He'd really wanted to give Shani flowers, but I'd talked him out of it— *she'll need her hands free to accept the ring*, I'd said—but I could see why he'd wanted them. It would've given him something to do with his hands, as he walked through the dancers toward Shani. But I thought it was better this way, more pure, nothing between them at all. The music was fading down, and I'd stepped to the side, letting them have their space.

"Oh my god," Shani said, audible now over the quieter music. She'd started crying the second she spotted Conner, and I could tell that my brother was having a hard time holding it together, too. I glanced at Sam. The kids were still dancing around him, other kids from the playground joining in. But Sam had stopped, and was watching my brother get down on one knee. I sensed his attention shifting to me, but suddenly I couldn't do it, didn't know if I'd make it through this moment unless I kept my focus solely on my brother and Shani.

"Shani," Conner said, then had to clear his throat. "I think you're awesome. The absolute luckiest day of my life was when I met you, and I feel like I just keep getting luckier." He'd taken the ring box out of his pocket but hadn't opened it yet, and now he frowned down at it. "Although, wait, that would mean that the first day couldn't have been the luckiest, if they kept getting better . . . but you know what I mean. I'm really lucky. That's the point I'm trying to make. Sorry. I'd planned out much better stuff to say."

I wished I could encourage him somehow, tell him he was doing fine. It was obvious he was speaking from the heart, and that was what mattered. Shani was shaking her head, hiccuping a little, but in the cute way that some girls can manage when they cry. I'd never been one of them. It was big ugly tears or gtfo.

"I want to have more and more lucky days with you, and not just luck but, like, work, too. Because it takes work to be in a relationship. Obviously. But with you it doesn't feel like work, and . . . anyway, Shani, I love you. Will you marry me?"

She nodded, as though that were all she was capable of, before saying, "Yes. *Yes!*" Conner stood up to wrap her up in a hug and kiss before realizing that he'd never actually opened the ring box, so he handed it to her, and together they opened it up and put the ring on her finger. Conner had been positive it would fit perfectly because he'd come up with a sneaky plot to borrow one of her other rings and take it to get sized, and he gave me a big thumbs-up when she slid it on, as though I'd been somehow personally responsible for making it happen.

I gave him a thumbs-up back, still wiping a stray tear from my eye when Sam wrapped his arm around my shoulder and pulled me toward him. "I think that went well," he said.

"Fuck yeah it did," I said, then glanced at all the kids around us. "I mean, yeah. It was pretty perfect. You're a good dancer."

"Not really," Sam said. "I've never taken any classes or anything."

"Still, you're so . . ." I couldn't think of the word I wanted. *Sexy* was true, but we were around all these kids, and anyway, that was only part of it. *Infectious*, maybe, like he was having fun and you wanted to have fun with him. It had almost made me want to dance and I never, ever did that. *Free*. Maybe that was the word.

He smiled down at me. "Hold that thought," he said. "I have to go talk to the grown-ups real fast, thank them and the kids for coming out. I'll be back."

I wandered closer to Conner and Shani, wanting to congratulate them but not wanting to interrupt their moment. I hadn't needed to worry, apparently, because as soon as they spotted me, they both attacked me with a group hug.

"I could not have done this without you," Conner said. "I mean it."

"It was mostly Sam," I said. "His sound system, his kids, his dancing." Then, just in case Shani now thought that my having lunch with her had solely been an obligation for this, I added truthfully to her, "I'm just glad I got to spend a little time getting to know you better this afternoon, now that you're going to be my sister."

Wow. That felt weird to say.

"No, not just today," Conner said. "All of it. I know you have your own life, and your essay about serial killers or whatever, but having you here this summer . . ."

For about the runtime of "Tubthumping," I'd managed to forget about my advisor's comments and the huge amount of work I'd have to do to get back on track, but now the pit of dread settled right back at the bottom of my stomach. "It's no problem," I said. "Actually, though, I do need to get some stuff done, if you don't mind me heading out . . . maybe we could plan a celebratory dinner this week?"

"Sounds good," Conner said. "Love ya, Pheebs."

"You, too." I smiled at Shani to let her know she was included in that sentiment, however poorly expressed it was.

I made my way over to the pavilion, where most of the people had dispersed, but Sam was crouched down, his elbows resting on his knees, talking to the skinny kid who'd almost gotten taken out by the joyous arms of the red-haired girl. I saw him as a teacher then, could picture the way he'd be in a classroom, encouraging kids to really go for it with the xylophones.

It was wild, how off my initial perception of him had been. The truth was that this Sam scared me more. He seemed like he was from a different planet, one where dancing was fun and families were big and happy. And I was from some other distant, lonely star, my lungs incapable of breathing his planet's atmosphere.

Maudlin thoughts, and I didn't know why I was having them. The whole day had been a roller coaster, from getting that email from my advisor this morning until Conner's proposal to Shani. What I probably needed was sleep, to reset from zero.

"I was trying to listen to the count in my head like you told us," the kid was telling Sam, "but I messed up. The slow parts are hard."

"They are," Sam said. "We talked about how that song keeps the same tempo, right?" He tapped one finger against his knee, counting out the beat of the song. "The words slow down, but that beat stays the same. It's tricky, but you did great."

"Is that who you're gonna ask to marry?" Marcus asked, glancing over at me. I hadn't even clocked that the kid was aware I was standing there, and I was startled to be drawn into the conversation. "We can do the dance again. This time I'll do the count right, promise."

Sam turned his head to look at me. "Someday," he said, his gaze still on mine. Then he was focused on the kid again, holding out his fist for a bump. "I really appreciate you coming out, Marcus. You excited about fourth grade?"

They talked a little more, before eventually the kid ran off to go back to playing, and Sam stood up. He started to clean up some of the leftover food and trash from the picnic table, and I joined in to help. He'd even thought to bring little lime green plates and napkins for the kids' snacks, a detail I would've one hundred percent forgotten.

"What did you mean by that?" I asked. "Someday?"

He didn't even look up, he was so casual about it. Just kept on picking up flattened Capri Sun pouches. "I mean *someday*," he

said. "Sure, I could see proposing to you. Not like this—
something tells me you wouldn't appreciate the public spectacle.
Somewhere quiet, just us. I'd go down on one knee and tell you
how I feel about you. I know that's a ways off, but it's nice to think
about."

I felt like I was missing about a thousand pieces to this conversation to make it make sense. "I don't even know if I want to get
married. Ever."

Sam shrugged, like that was no big deal, either. "Then we
don't."

Behind me was a cacophony of children's voices, raised in
high-pitched squeals and screams of excitement, the occasional
cry of a toddler who must've fallen down, the yell of a parent telling a kid to *stop putting mulch in your mouth* or *let go of your
brother.* "I don't know if I want kids, either."

He did look up then, and I tried to read anything behind his
expression when he said, "That's okay. I could go either way
myself."

That couldn't be how he really felt. He taught elementary
school, for fuck's sake. He would obviously make a great father.
He came from a big family. I made those points to him, but his
expression didn't change.

"Look, I like kids," he said. "Obviously, or I wouldn't do what
I do. But like you said, I'm around kids all day. I already have four
nieces and nephews and am the designated uncle to buy drum
sets for each, which my siblings will be thrilled by. I'm open to
talking through all this stuff—*someday* doesn't have to mean
today."

I shook my head. "I can't," I said.

That seemed to be Sam's first sign that I was serious, that we weren't just idly talking about the future. I didn't even know how to do that. Any projection into even months from now sent me spinning into doubt about whether my dissertation would get done on time, whether it would be enough to earn my degree, whether Sam and I would be able to last through a separation we both knew was coming.

He dropped the crumpled napkins he'd been holding, wiping his hands on his jeans before leading me away from the pavilion, under a couple of shady oak trees where we could have more privacy.

"You shouldn't leave all your equipment there," I said. "It looks expensive."

"It doesn't matter," Sam said.

"There's a kid standing close to it with a 'Baby Shark' gleam in his eye. I'm telling you."

"Phoebe," Sam said, a little impatient. "*It doesn't matter.* Talk to me. Tell me why you're freaking out."

"This whole thing feels like it's moving so fast," I said. "What are we even doing? It was supposed to be a summer fling, and now we're talking about marriage and kids? It's too much, Sam. I can't do it."

He stepped back, running his hand through his hair. The sweat had dried by now, and his agitated hands made the hair stick up around his ears. I could see from his face that the words *summer fling* had hurt him, and a part of me wanted to take them back. He'd told me multiple times that this wasn't casual for him, and the truth was that it hadn't felt casual to me, either, since after that first night. Since maybe before then, I didn't know.

But I also felt stupid and naive for thinking this could ever work out long-term. His life was here, and mine wasn't. He was made for a picket fence future—he *deserved* that future—and I didn't know where I fit into that at all.

"The kid asked me a question," Sam said. "And I answered it. What was I supposed to say—nah, kid, that's just my neighbor, we fuck sometimes?"

I flinched at his language, although I knew I'd asked for it, by rewinding us back to that first morning after, rewriting the rules of what we called whatever this was between us. "At least it would've been more honest," I muttered.

For a moment Sam just stared at me, like he didn't know me at all. I barely recognized myself, the things I was saying. I wanted to stuff them all back in my mouth and start over. I would've begged off, said I had a headache or wasn't feeling well, that I needed to focus on my dissertation for a bit and would talk to him later. This may have ended—it seemed inevitable to me, suddenly, that it was all going to end, any hope otherwise no more real than the fantasies I'd had as a kid about living in an apartment with a view of the skyline. But it didn't need to end like this.

"Honest," he said, almost more to himself than to me. "You're right, I haven't been honest. I'm falling for you, Phoebe. I've wanted to tell you that a million times. But I always worried I'd scare you off—that we'd end up having a conversation a lot like this one, actually—and so I held back. I know you may not feel the same way yet. I know the idea of being in a relationship terrifies you. I know it's complicated, with you only being here for the summer. But my feelings for you—that part's not complicated."

The shrieks of the playing children around us were an incongruous backdrop to this conversation. I wished we could some-how be transported back to his house, or mine. I wished I could be in a headspace where his words *didn't* freak me out, because he was right, they terrified me. *Falling* for me? Even the word choice implied pain, loss of control. He couldn't be falling for me, any more than I could be for him.

"It's been an intense few weeks," I said. "Hell, an intense *day*. It's been a concentrated incubation period, like when people meet at summer camp, or like Keanu and Sandra in *Speed*. But we barely know each other, when you get down to it."

"So tell me," Sam said, crossing his arms over his chest. "Tell me something big about you that I don't already know, something that would change my mind about the way I feel."

"You don't even know my middle name."

"I know it starts with an *R*," he said, then, at my expression, "You publish your papers under Phoebe R. Walsh. Rachel? Re-becca? Rumpelstiltskin?"

"It's Rachel," I said grudgingly, irritated that he'd guessed it on the first try. If he made any allusion to *Friends* I'd lose it.

"Mine is Copeland. Fun fact, all my siblings' middle names are Copeland. It's my mom's maiden name. So now that's out of the way."

"How old are you?" The most basic shit, and I didn't know the answer. It had never come up.

"Twenty-eight. Anything else?"

He was almost two years younger than me. There was no rea-son for that to be a deal breaker, but somehow it seemed to prove my point, of what little foundation we actually had to be making plans for any future.

"I'm leaving in a few weeks."

His eyes shadowed, but didn't leave my face. "I already know that. But we have phones, email, cars, access to air travel. I can take an extra day or two around Labor Day. I get the whole week of Thanksgiving off. We can make it work until you finish your graduate program, and then we can figure it out from there."

He made it sound so doable, so *reasonable*, but I'd never been able to sustain a relationship when we were both in the same city, much less when we were states apart.

"I'm sorry," I said. "I never meant to have this conversation today, especially after . . ."

I gestured toward his sound equipment, the pavilion, the playground. Suddenly it occurred to me that there could still be kids and parents here, that they could be watching this whole tableau play out, although thankfully they wouldn't be able to hear anything. Sam had done so much just to ensure that my brother's proposal was something memorable and special, and now here I was, ruining everything. It made me hate myself, but it only strengthened my resolve that ultimately this was the right thing to do, that I could only do more damage the longer we stretched this out.

"So when did you plan on having it," he said. It wasn't a question.

"I warned you," I said, my voice low. "I told you at the start of this that I didn't know if I could manage anything serious."

"You did," he agreed. "I guess I should've listened. I shouldn't have paid attention to all the small ways you told me that you care about me, too—the way you kissed me on the Fourth of July, or encouraged me to finish building that guitar, or let me hold you

after you thought Lenore was gone. Just be honest with *me*,
Phoebe. How do you feel about me?"

"Of course I care about you," I said, the words coming out
sounding stilted and false, even though I did mean them. "But I
can't be in *love* with you."

He looked away, his throat working as he swallowed. When he
dragged his eyes back to mine, they had a slight sheen. "Can't, or
won't?"

What was the difference? To love someone was to need them,
to open yourself up to pain and rejection and loss. Of course I'd
dreamed of finding the person I could fully trust, and of course
these last few weeks I'd harbored the occasional hope that that
person might be Sam. But when it came down to it, there was way
too much risk involved. I'd been on my own for so long, and I
knew exactly how to make that work for my life. Even my advisor
had said it—I'd let myself go off course this summer. It was time
to get back on.

"I just can't," I said. "I don't have it in me. I'm sorry."

Sam gave a little laugh, a humorless sound. "Well, that was
honest," he said. "I have to admit, I didn't see this coming."

"I know," I said. I was trying really hard not to cry myself,
because it wouldn't be pretty. The only thing I could do was stare
at the empty Capri Sun box still on one of the picnic tables until
my eyes blurred, trying not to think about how everything had
been just that morning, full of hope and excitement about Conner's proposal. And Conner was going to want to debrief everything later, and he was going to be so happy, and meanwhile I'd
want to die inside . . . "I swear to you, I didn't plan any of this. I

know you probably regret it all, especially spending your Saturday doing this, now that . . ."

I couldn't finish that sentence. There was no way to properly convey how bad I felt that wouldn't make it worse.

"I don't regret any of it," Sam said. "Not the last few weeks, not today, not even saying *someday* to that kid if that's what set this off. I don't regret giving you my heart, Phoebe. I just wish you'd taken more care with it."

And then I was definitely crying, but it didn't matter. Sam was already walking away.

TWENTY-THREE

———

T HE DAYS FOLLOWING my breakup with Sam were rough.
Dr. Nilsson wanted the revised chapter within the week, but
the idea of jumping back into the thing I loved—analyzing true
crime—suddenly held no appeal. I'd slump over my desk for
hours, rereading the same sentence. Then I'd get tired and try to
write in bed, but even propping myself up with pillows against
the headboard brought back memories of Sam, and I couldn't do
it. Next I tried a change of scenery, getting out of the house to
write in a local coffee shop, but all I did was stare at neighboring
tables with unfocused eyes until eventually one college-aged girl
asked rudely, "Can I *help* you?"

"No," I said. "Sorry."

She and her friends were still laughing when I packed up my
stuff and left.

One morning, there was a box on my doorstep, and since I
hadn't ordered anything I felt my heart lift, hoping maybe it was

another misdelivery for Sam. I could use it as an excuse to go over there, and then maybe I could . . .

Well, I never had the chance to carry that fantasy through. The box wasn't *to* Sam but *from* him—unlabeled and sealed only with the flaps tucked under each other. Inside was my copy of *Savage Appetites* that I'd left over at his house, together with my purple bra, now clean and neatly folded. There was no note.

I'd done the right thing. My timing had been shit, but there had been no real future between me and Sam, no matter how many times I might've allowed myself to dream otherwise. It would've only gotten harder if we'd allowed it to stretch out all the way until the end of the summer, when I'd been about to leave.

But sometimes when I was lying in bed at night, I thought about him dancing. His face, flushed from the heat and exercise and joy. Then I thought about his face after I'd told him I couldn't love him. He'd looked crushed, and *I'd* done that.

I wasn't sleeping much.

One night, while I was still lying there, tossing and turning, Lenore jumped up on my stomach. Her eyes glittered at me in the darkness, as if she were assessing just how low I'd gotten. Finally, she kneaded my shirt for a few minutes, turning in a circle and then plopping down to stay there. She didn't want to be petted— if I even tried she'd jump right back down. Instead, she was almost like a paperweight, holding me in place. It was incredibly annoying. It was also oddly soothing, and became one of the only ways to stop my masochistic inner loop.

The last thing I wanted to do in this state—the absolute *last* thing—was meet with Dr. Blake about my future career in academia. But it was all set up and I had the stupid blazer, and I didn't want to let Dr. Nilsson down again in yet another way. So I dressed up in a black dress with a cute 1950s silhouette and topped it with the charcoal blazer and some red lipstick, hoping I looked better than the warmed-over death I felt like.

I closed the front door carefully behind me, making sure that Lenore hadn't gotten out, and was in the process of locking up when I heard Sam's truck pull into the driveway next door. I felt stuck on what to do—if I ran to my Camry and got in real fast, I would *look* like I was avoiding him. But maybe that was the respectful thing to do, since he appeared to be avoiding me.

I ended up standing stupidly next to my front door, my keys still in my hand, as he climbed out of his truck.

He'd gotten a haircut, so that now it was still long but not quite as shaggy as it had been. He was holding a bag of some takeout food, and he glanced over at me, giving me a tense smile. That seemed to be all he was going to do, which maybe was for the best, but I couldn't help myself.

"Hey," I said.

"Hey."

That monosyllabic intro out of the way, we both just stood on our respective driveways. The problem was, I couldn't think of what to say after that. My instinct was to start apologizing all over again, but clearly that wouldn't do any good. And even if I wanted to make small talk, I couldn't think of a single goddamn thing—not an observation about the weather, not a piece of true crime trivia, nothing.

I miss you. That was what I wanted to say most of all, but of course I had no right.

He reached up to scratch his eyebrow, his body language saying he couldn't decide if he was coming or going, until eventually he dropped his arm back to his side in resignation. "You look nice," he said.

"Thanks," I said. There was a small, perverse part of me that was glad he had the chance to see me this way, after a summer of me wearing my most casual, worn-out clothes. "I have that interview thing."

"I remember," he said.

"And what about you, still teaching lessons at Jocelyn's?" My insides were one giant Michael Scott *yikes* face gif repeating over and over. What a ridiculous question. He'd already told me he was, right up until school started back up again, and even then he said he might still do a few on the weekends for extra money.

Now, he held up the bag of takeout. "My food's getting cold," he said. "Good luck with your interview."

"You, too," I said, and luckily he'd already disappeared inside his house before he could see the cringe face I made at my own self. Our first interaction since that horrible day after Conner's proposal. It could've gone worse.

It definitely could've gone better, too.

I tried to put it out of my head as I drove to Stiles College and parked in a visitor's spot. Dr. Blake had said they'd meet me at a student-run café on campus, although they apologized that it would be closed for the summer still. But we can walk around the campus, and I'll show you around, their email had said, which made me wonder again exactly what the point of this interview was. Dr. Nilsson had been very clear that it was not a job interview, and I'd double-checked Stiles' website. There were no job listings, at least not for a professor in the English Department. If I could teach statistics it looked like I might've had a chance.

Dr. Blake gave off serious *if you haven't done the reading, I will call on you in class* vibes, but as soon as we started talking about some professors in my program I relaxed a little. They were treating me more like a colleague than a student, and even referenced a paper I'd written, complimenting me on the way I'd tied two seemingly disparate pieces of media together by looking at them through a feminist lens. It reminded me of Sam, and the fact that he'd actually taken the time to search for my work on the internet, but that line of thinking was dangerous. I forced my mind to focus back on Dr. Blake.

"Ultimately, being in academia is service work," Dr. Blake was saying now. "Our research, our teaching, our *mentoring* is all to serve future generations of thinkers. How do you intend to do that with your degree?"

Maybe it wasn't fair to hear the echoes of *studying true crime is not real scholarship* in their question, but that was my natural defensive reaction. I spoke slowly, wanting to really think about my answer as I gave it.

"I know studying literature or rhetoric in general can get a bad rap," I said. "There are a lot of people who ask what's the point, poring over words that were written twenty, fifty, two hundred years ago. And doing it again and again, after there's already been so much written on the subject. But ultimately I think it's about learning to pay attention. Learning to examine something closely, and ask questions, and place it in different frameworks to see how it might change. As a culture, we are what we write about, and examining those texts can teach us a lot about how we see the world."

I glanced at Dr. Blake beside me, but they were simply staring straight ahead, their hands clasped behind their back, as they listened to my answer. "True crime is a perfect example of that," I said. "At its heart, it's about *what do we know about humanity's capacity for evil* and *what should we be afraid of.* The answers to those questions can tell us a lot, especially when you look at the intersections of privilege and power, who are telling the stories, who are the subjects of them. I know a lot of people think true crime is a pulp genre, and not worthy of analysis, but the fact that it's so closely tied to mainstream fixations makes it *more* worthy. If I can help students to pay attention to those stories and the way they're presented or received, I'd feel like I'd done my job."

I had never articulated all of that before. It was shameful to admit, even to myself, but I hadn't given my *service* much thought. I enjoyed teaching, the energy of being in front of a classroom, the chemistry that could happen when you were firing on all cylinders and your jokes were landing and the students' faces were lighting up with recognition. But it could also be stressful and exhausting, and had to take a back seat to my own studies and research while I focused on getting my degree.

It had been seeing Sam, and the way he was about his own students, that had really made me consider my own teaching more. He exemplified more of what Dr. Blake was talking about—the idea that everything he experienced or learned could be funneled down to spark excitement for music in a kid, or teach them a concept about tempo or pitch.

He'd asked me, all those weeks ago, about why I was drawn to true crime. I had no idea what answer I would've given then, but I had more clarity now.

"I feel like I grew up afraid of so many things," I said. "There's just so much uncertainty in life, especially when you're a kid . . . you don't know why your dad is upset, or why your mom puts up with it, or whether you'll ever have a true friend you could talk to. It sounds twisted, but by the time I was a teenager, there was something almost comforting about reading about serial killers. It was like, here, be afraid of *this*. Focus on *this*. There's uncertainty, and open questions, but it'll all get wrapped up at the end. Justice will be served, the victims will be remembered, whatever. It was only when I started reading and rereading some of those books more closely that I started questioning what *justice* meant, or *truth*, or even *fear*."

"It's an interesting focus," Dr. Blake said, and it didn't sound patronizing at all, the way it sometimes did when people used the word *interesting* to describe my work. "Do you think you'd want to teach the rhetoric of true crime specifically, if you had the opportunity?"

"I'd love to," I said. "But I know it's kind of a reach. I'm definitely ready to do my time teaching composition, professional writing, whatever pays the bills. And then maybe someday I'll find somewhere that would let me propose my own class, where I could focus more on American true crime from the 1960s to present."

"*In Cold Blood*," Dr. Blake said.

"Of course. But there's so much more diversity and nuance to the genre now, too. *The Third Rainbow Girl. No Place Safe. The Fact of the Body* is one of my favorites. And it's not just murder, either. The narratives about white-collar crime can be really fascinating, like *Bad Blood* or *The Wizard of Lies* or *The Big Short*."

We'd been walking for so long down the central bricked pathway through the campus that I'd barely noticed we'd reached a small white house with green shutters.

"Well," they said, "as Dr. Nilsson probably told you, we do *not* have any job openings at this time. But I believe we will be opening up a visiting instructorship before next year, for a three-year contract in the English Department. As you said, it would be a lot of composition and other service courses, but there would be room for a class or two in the candidate's specialty. I think a class in true crime would be quite popular. We would be doing a standard search once the job opens up, so this is by no means a guaranteed offer, but I hope to see your application materials in the pool. When the contract ended, there would be a possibility for the position to become more permanent, but that wouldn't be guaranteed, either. What do you think?"

What did I *think*? "It sounds amazing," I said, trying to play it cool but failing miserably.

They smiled at me, as if they sensed my enthusiasm but hopefully found it endearing instead of immature. "The English Department is in here," they said, gesturing toward the converted house. "Come in, I'll make you a cup of tea."

By the time I drove home, I was feeling pretty good about how the interview had gone, and almost hopeful about my future post–graduate school. I still had to finish the damn dissertation, which I preferred not to think about, and even letting my mind wander around the implications of a possible job within a reasonable commuting distance, what it could mean . . .

Well, that made me feel more melancholy than hopeful. It wouldn't change anything significant, just because there was a slim chance that one logistical barrier would be removed in any relationship between me and Sam. That was all done now. I'd torched the bridge and I couldn't torture myself wondering if there was any way back to the other side.

———

THE NIGHT BEFORE I was about to leave to return to North Carolina, Conner came over. I'd invited both him and Shani out for one last dinner together, because there wasn't much left in the house, and nowhere to sit except the desk, which Conner was supposed to help me strap back to the roof of my car. But Conner had said maybe it should just be the two of us for dinner. "We haven't gotten to hang out as much as I wanted," he said. "Which, I get. You were busy with school stuff, and I had work. My calls are under seven minutes, by the way. But this job sucks. I think I'm going to wait until after the wedding and then try to find something where they don't make you lock your phone in a locker at the start of every shift."

Conner and Shani were planning a spring wedding, and it was already shaping up to be a much more involved affair than either of them had thought, once some of Shani's Indian relatives weighed in on the details of the ceremony and reception. Words were thrown around like *itinerary* and *second outfit change*. Conner was psyched about the clothes he'd get to wear, though.

When Conner showed up, I was finishing up my last edits to the *In Cold Blood* chapter, which was way better now that I'd focused more on Capote's credibility and depiction of "truth" throughout his book, as opposed to whatever rambling mess I'd turned in before. I was a little behind now, and would have to write my *Stranger Beside Me* chapter and the conclusion once the semester had already started, which wasn't ideal since my defense was scheduled for late October. But I knew I could make it work.

"Listen to this," I said, holding open to a page in the book. *"He is uncomfortable in his relationships to other people, and has a pathological inability to form and hold enduring personal attachments.* I'm tagged in this picture and I don't like it."

"What's that from?"

"A psychologist's description of Dick Hickock after he'd examined him for the trial," I said.

Conner came over and took the book out of my hands. "You need to get out of the house. Come on."

I said I'd drive, so we headed to my Camry. I paused for only a minute before I started the ignition, glancing over at Sam's house. His truck was in the driveway, but I hadn't seen him in days—not since before my interview. He must've been going somewhere and staying gone, because he didn't stick to his old pattern of back-and-forth from his lessons at Jocelyn's.

"Still haven't talked to him?" Conner asked.

I'd filled him in a little on what had happened—just that we'd broken up, to the extent we were together in the first place. I hadn't told him it had been at the park, right after the proposal. I didn't want to taint that memory in any way. Conner was still forwarding me new video clips when they popped up on social media.

"Not really," I said.

"I wanted to go over there, thank him again for everything he did for us," Conner said. "If you want, I can mention—"

"No," I said. "Leave it. Please, Conner."

He held up his hands in surrender. "Okay, okay. Anyway, where do you want to go? My treat, just not anywhere fancy like Outback. I don't have Bloomin' Onion money if I'm saving up for a wedding. My ceiling is fast casual."

"Actually," I said. "There's somewhere I've been wanting to go, and this might be my only chance. It's a bit of a drive, though—at least an hour."

"Let's do it."

We didn't talk much during the drive, just listened to the local alternative radio station, which I realized with a pang I would actually miss even though it seemed to interpret its own genre as One Very Popular Band or, in the alternative, Another Very Popular Band. I could tell Conner was getting suspicious once we pulled off the highway in a rural area where there were miles in between gas stations or any other marker of civilization.

Finally, I pulled onto a street in front of a run-down old house, set back and seemingly abandoned, surrounded by an overgrowth of weeds. I parked the car on the side of the road and unbuckled my seat belt.

"This was the Sunrise Slayer's house," I said. "Nobody's lived here for at least a decade, since the family moved."

"Uh," Conner said. "I was hoping for somewhere with curly fries."

"We'll find somewhere to eat afterward. I just want to check it out."

As clunky and overwrought as the writing had been in the Sunrise Slayer's daughter's memoir, one thing she'd done well was to bring the home where she grew up to life. I'd felt like I could map its layout, could peel the stickers off her walls with my own fingers, could hear the sound of bacon sizzling on the stove one morning when her dad cooked a rare breakfast. Of course, later she'd realize he'd been up early because he'd already killed a girl off the nearby running trail, but otherwise it had seemed like a usual domestic life. It had reminded me a lot of my own child-hood.

"Did he, like . . . do anything here?" Conner asked, traipsing behind me through the tall grass.

"No." The windows were fogged up, maybe from the humid-ity, and I pressed my face to the glass to see inside. Surprisingly, there was still stuff in there—an old couch that leaned to one side, a pile of what might have been clothes or wet cardboard or insula-tion from the ceiling, it was impossible to tell with the effect of time. This was what my dad's house might've looked like, if left alone.

As if reading my mind, Conner said from behind me, "You know Dad wasn't a serial killer, right?"

"Technically, we don't *know* that," I said. "But yes, I'm aware that it is highly unlikely, and that if he *was*, my interest in the subject would take on a macabre sort of irony."

"Okay," Conner said. "It just feels like you *don't* know that. He was just a dude. I think because you didn't have much of a relationship with him, the last ten or so years, that you built him up to be this malicious, horrible person. As far as dads go, he wasn't great. He got angry a lot for no reason, he took absolutely zero interest in stuff that you liked but he thought was dumb, like me with video games or you with . . ." Conner gestured toward the house, as though to say *this weird shit you're into*. "He made you think you were crazy or oversensitive or misremembering the way something happened, he could be really caustic and negative about the state of the world."

That last one hit a little too close to home for me. One of my biggest fears was turning out like my dad in some way, and his sarcastic humor was definitely one thing I'd inherited, for better or for worse.

"But he was just a dude," Conner said again. "A really sad dude, when you think about it. He had so many opportunities to have really close, meaningful relationships with his kids, and he never took any of them. When I told him I was moving out, do you know what he said? He said, *Don't take the computer, I paid for it*. When he'd bought some parts for my birthday and then never bought the rest that he'd said he would. Good riddance, you know? I'm not going to let that shit get me down."

I thought back to my first night in the house, those pieces of the computer strewn about the floor. That sounded exactly like my dad. He could be incredibly generous—he'd signed on to all of Conner's student loans, for example—but then he could take it back the next instant, or say he'd never meant you to have it in the first place. It had been such a disconcerting way to live, and it was no wonder that Conner and I still had whiplash from it.

"I don't think he told me he loved me once," I said. "Most of the time, I questioned whether he was even capable of that emotion."

"The opposite of love is fear," Conner said. "I think Dad was the most afraid person I've ever known."

"Shit." I stopped in my tracks, suddenly less interested in poking around this rather ordinary, depressing little house, and more interested in what my brother was saying. "You're really getting your money's worth out of that therapy."

"Oh, that was a line from a song Shani likes," Conner said. "It's true, though."

"I think I might be like him," I said. "Closed off. Afraid. Unable to love."

"You're not."

I shrugged uncomfortably. If he only knew how that last conversation with Sam had gone, he'd know what a monster I was. I couldn't even think of it without spiraling back into shame about the things I'd said, the way I'd hurt him. But I didn't know if anything I'd said was *wrong*. If anything, the fact that I could be cold enough to say it in the first place proved my point, that I wasn't cut out for that kind of connection.

"Pheebs," Conner said. "You're *not*. You're not like that *Cold Blood* guy, either. For one thing, you love me."

I rolled my eyes. "You're a pain in my ass."

"But a lovable pain in the ass."

I acknowledged his point with a grunt. We'd made our way to the back of the house by now, where there was a porch with no screen in it anymore and some charred wood at the bottom of one corner of the roof, as if there had been a grill fire at some point. Even the Sunrise Slayer had cooked bacon, or grilled out on the Fourth of July. He'd just also been killing women while he'd done it. What would that do to you, as a child, to find that out about your parent? And yet what did I want, for his daughter to never be able to move on from it, to have a life that was always tainted by this darkness she'd been a victim of, too, in her own way?

"I can't even say the words," I said. "They stick in my throat. I can't even *text* the words. I don't know why. Alison will drop it all the time, no big deal, and I just text back a smiley face like an asshole."

"So ease into it," Conner said. "Try ILY first. You can manage a few letters."

"I guess."

"Pull out your phone and do it," Conner said, gesturing toward my pocket. "Assuming you get reception in this godforsaken place."

"The last text she sent me was about a home organization show she'd started watching," I said. "I'm not just going to drop an ILY after that."

"Oh, I think Shani's watching that one," Conner said. "It's so boring it's like a lullaby. I could fall asleep to it every night. Look, you're leaving tomorrow. Just text something about that, then put the message at the end. Add an emoji if you want to soften it a little. What's the point of being a doctor if you don't know shit like this?"

I took my phone out. To my surprise, I did have reception. To my greater surprise, I actually pulled up the conversation between me and Alison, my thumbs hesitating over the phone while I considered whether to listen to Conner's advice. What was I so scared of, anyway? Rejection? She'd already said it a million times to me, so rationally I had no reason to believe she'd reject me if I said it back. If anything, *I'd* been the rejecter in this scenario, refusing to let her words pierce through my armor no matter how close we got otherwise.

Alison's last message hung there, an innocuous thing about how the couple in the first episode exemplified every terrible millennial stereotype. I'd already responded with a simple *ha*. I took a deep breath, and started typing.

> **Hey, as you know, I'm heading out tomorrow! I know you'll be at work, so just wanted to say thanks again for all your help w/ the cat and the blazer and all of it. ily!**

I tried it without the exclamation point, but then that actually made it seem *more* serious, so I put it back in. Then the letters just didn't feel like me, so I deleted and typed **love you!**, no personal "I," with a heart-eyes cat emoji. I hit "send" before I could second-guess myself.

"Nice," Conner said, reading over my shoulder. "Now can we please get out of here? I'm starving and I know exactly what I want to eat."

I FULLY EXPECTED Conner to pick the place that had what he'd previously called "the best curly fry game in town," but once we'd gotten back near the house, Conner directed me until we were pulling into a parking lot for a strip of stores that included a Starbucks, a nail salon, and the grocery store I never went to.

"You know I'm always down for coffee," I said. "But I don't

pay eight dollars for a soggy prepackaged sandwich unless I'm at an airport. Sometimes not even then."

"Not there." He nodded toward the grocery store. "We're going in."

My hand paused on the door handle. "No, we're not."

"If *you* get to drive me to the middle of nowhere to a literal serial killer's house," Conner said, "I get to make you go to the grocery store you avoid."

"Because our dad *died* there."

"Exactly," Conner said. "It's time we pay tribute. Come on."

From the outside, there was nothing sinister at all about it. An older couple were crossing the street slowly to enter on one side, a woman exiting the other side with one of those shopping carts that looked like a race car, twin toddlers at the two steering wheels that would be a bonkers design choice were it a real race car.

"Conner," I said. If I could've literally dug my heels into the pavement, I would've.

"I promise," Conner said. "This will be good. Five minutes. Okay?"

He looked at me, his eyebrows raised. And I knew, however irritating my brother could be, that if I truly said I couldn't do it, we'd turn around and walk right back to the car. But I also knew he was probably right. It was silly to avoid a grocery store. There may have been a small part of me, deep down, that had never fully put my father to rest, even after the funeral, even after going through all the things in his house. If this would help, then maybe it was worth it.

So I followed him through the automatic doors, past the sales items at the front of the store, and to the cleaning aisle. Conner seemed to know exactly where he was going, which surprised me. We'd never really talked about it, not even that night before the funeral when we'd both gotten drunk off our asses, but he'd been living only ten minutes away when it had happened. Possibly he'd been called to the store before the ambulance had left.

"Dish detergent," Conner said once we were standing in front of the display, picking up a bottle of blue liquid. "He always used the same one. It says it cuts more grease, so less scrubbing, but don't you think people kinda do the same amount of scrubbing no matter what? Like muscle memory. You don't slack off just because the detergent says it'll pick up more of the load for you. They're always saying that."

"Can't be trusted," I agreed, looking at the bottle. Such a mundane item. "Do you think he was in a lot of pain?"

"The doctor at the hospital—the one who told me he was dead—said no. Dad lost consciousness when he collapsed, and the doctor said it had all happened pretty fast. Maybe they're just trained to say stuff like that, but I think it was true. I doubt Dad had the chance to be scared or anything."

I think Dad was the most afraid person I've ever known. It was true, I realized, even though growing up I'd always thought that *he* was the scary one, the way his face turned red when he yelled, the way he could flip on a dime. It was a relief to think that maybe he hadn't had to be afraid when he died.

I hugged Conner then, wrapping my arms tight around him. "I do love you," I said. "You're a huge pain in the ass and not as charming as you think you are, but I do love you."

"You can put it all in your best man speech," Conner said. "Maybe more compliments, though."

"Wait." I pulled back. "What?"

"Best man," Conner said. "Or Best Person, I guess, whatever you'd call it. Of course it has to be you. You've really been there for me and Shani this summer. I don't want to stand up there without you. You're my big sister, Pheebs."

I hugged him again, and probably would've kept doing it for longer, only I could feel him trying to nudge the bottle of dish detergent into one of my hands.

"What are you *doing*?"

"Shani said I'm supposed to get you a gift when I ask you," he said. "Actually, according to this website she found, there are, like, a hundred gimmicky ways you can invite someone to be part of your wedding party, and she's planning something special for her friends. But I don't know, man, I'm tired! That proposal took it out of me. I need a break from that Pinterest shit. So maybe you'd take this dish detergent, and call that your gift?"

"I don't need any gift," I said. "But I don't know if I want a bottle of overpromising liquid that you've been waving around as a prop for the story of our father's death."

"Oh," Conner said. "When you put it that way." He placed it back on the shelf. "Want to grab a couple subs and some snacks, eat them back at the house? I left the small TV set and PlayStation there, so we could play some *Crash Bandicoot*."

"Sounds perfect," I said.

"Hang on," Conner said as we started down the aisle. "Is there still a toaster, or will I have to eat my Pop-Tarts like an animal?"

TWENTY-FOUR

B Y THE NEXT morning, I was all packed up, except for the desk and Lenore. Conner was supposed to help me load the desk on my car the night before, but we'd ended up staying up a lot later than we'd planned, talking and trying to beat every level of the original Crash game, even the ones that required secret keys to open. We hadn't succeeded, even after I gave up and looked up an ASCII art–riddled walk-through from the late nineties that explained which levels to beat for the colored gems and in what order.

Lenore was still prowling around the house, clearly unsettled and eyeing her carrier very suspiciously. I was delaying putting her in it for her sake, but for mine, too, because I knew once she was in she'd probably pee everywhere within the first hour of the trip.

I shut Lenore in a bedroom with her litter box and food, saying *sorry sorry sorry* and promising to find a cat treat she actually liked once we were in her new home. I'd already put down first, last, and security deposit on an apartment in the same complex where I used to live near the university, and my landlord had said he'd leave the key in the front office lockbox for me.

I managed to rock the desk back and forth on its legs to halfway out the front door before I gave up and texted Conner, trying to see if there was any way he could drop by on his way to work, just for five minutes. **Otherwise,** I texted, **I'll leave the desk here and it will be up to you to ship it to me by the start of the semester. Your call.**

"Need a hand?"

Sam's voice was gruff behind me. When I spun around, he was so close I could see the rings of navy around his irises. He was dressed in a new variation on neutral professional I hadn't seen before, this one with nice jeans and a forest green button-up shirt, rolled up neatly to just under his elbows. He was obviously dressed to go somewhere, and it was seven thirty in the morning.

Not that it was my business anymore. And he had no obligation to help me. Truly, maybe the best option was just to leave the monstrosity of a desk here and figure it all out later.

"I got it," I said. "Thanks, though."

"Phoebe. Just accept help, okay? You want this strapped onto the top of your car?"

"That was the plan . . ."

He grasped under the desk on both sides, hefting it up with a grunt. He had to walk slowly with it down the driveway, leaning back to distribute the weight, before he set it down next to the car.

"I always wondered how you'd moved it by yourself," I said. "That first night."

"Turns out it *is* heavy."

The exchange felt enough like one between friends to make my heart skip a beat; just enough like one between strangers to make my stomach twist with regret. "Sam, I—"

But he cut me off. "I am going to need your help getting it up top, though. If I take one side, can you get the other?"

I lifted the side closest to me while he did the bulk of the work angling the desk enough to lower it upside down on the roof of the car. When he asked for the straps, I popped the trunk and grabbed them from on top of the suitcases and boxes I'd wedged back there.

"So you should be in North Carolina by dinnertime or so?"

"If I drive pretty much straight through," I said. "But I may end up making a few stops on the way. It depends on Lenore."

"Can I say goodbye to her?"

"Oh," I said, blinking a little. "Sure."

He finished tightening the straps that he'd wrapped around the desk legs in an intricate crisscross, pushing against the desk and seeming satisfied when it didn't budge. I led him back inside the house, to my bedroom where I'd put Lenore.

She was under the bed, of course. I'd cleaned out a lot of the stuff in my room, but had left the bed because I'd still needed it to sleep on. I told Conner he could do whatever he wanted with it. We'd also never gotten around to repainting the black, but Conner said he didn't mind taking care of that and a few other remaining items, since he'd had to take a couple weeks off when he hurt his wrist. He mentioned that he'd already talked to Josue about possibly coming by to check out the house, and seemed to think it would sell by September. I didn't know that I had his confidence, but it was mostly the real estate agent's problem now.

"Did you know that in Florida," I said, "you don't have to disclose if someone died in a house even if it was a murder or suicide? You also don't have to disclose a haunting because none of those things are considered a material fact."

Sam was crouched down on the floor, holding his hand out as if to invite Lenore to sniff. "That," he said, "is an incredibly creepy thing to tell someone after you've invited someone into your room."

I felt my cheeks heat up. Of course, he was right. I hadn't even thought about that angle—just let my mouth run away with me as usual.

He glanced up, giving me a sad little smile. "It's okay," he said. "I'm used to it from you."

He stood, apparently giving up hope that Lenore would come out. He looked around the room, taking in the bare black walls, the bed still made up with sheets. I wondered what he was thinking. If he was remembering, the way I was.

"I should probably get going," he said. "I have a team meeting at the school."

Ah. That explained why he was dressed up. I was hit by a sudden panic, that this would be it, that I'd never see him again, that I'd never have a chance to tell him how I felt. I didn't know if this was love, this cold, sick feeling in my stomach, but I had to tell him how important he was to me, how much I'd valued our time together, how much I would miss him.

But the words stuck in my throat. It was different with Sam than with Alison or Conner. The stakes were so high. I couldn't expect anything *but* rejection from Sam. I would deserve it, too.

"Here," I said, reaching for my guitar, leaned against one wall. "Take this."

He raised his eyebrows at me. "You still want me to fix your guitar?"

"No," I said. "Keep it. You'd use it more than me, anyway."

There were still a couple stickers on the back of it—one from the Amnesty International club I'd joined in high school, the other for a band I was embarrassed to admit I'd barely listened to but thought their logo was cool. I didn't know if those made the guitar worthless, but it should still *play*, regardless.

But Sam didn't reach for the instrument. "I don't want it," he said. "No offense, Phoebe, but I don't want . . ."

He trailed off without finishing that sentence, which was cruel, considering he'd started it with two of the most dreaded words in the English language. *No offense.* He didn't want what? To have anything of mine in his house? To remember me? To care about me anymore?

"It would be painful," he said finally. "To see that every day."

Which made total sense. But for some reason, it was suddenly more important to me than ever that I give him *something* and that he take it, that there was some external acknowledgment of all that had passed between us.

"So use it for parts," I said. "Smash it up. That always looks really satisfying—when rock stars smash their guitars onstage. You can't get that kind of catharsis from throwing a tambourine, that's for sure."

He didn't smile.

"Please, Sam," I said. "Seriously, I won't use it. Take the pick-ups out of it or whatever you were talking about doing and then throw the rest of it away. Or put new strings on it and give it to one of your students who shows an interest. I don't care. But please, take it."

He grasped the guitar by the neck, hefting it in his hand. Then he set it gently back down on the floor, leaning it against the wall where it had been previously. My eyes felt hot and itchy as he stepped forward to envelop me in a hug.

His arms were warm and tight around me, his hands pressed in between my shoulder blades. I'd known he'd give great hugs, since that night of his party. I'd craved his touch, even then, wanted to feel his arms around me just like this. A sob caught in my throat, and I squeezed him back, resting my cheek against his shoulder.

I don't regret any of it, either, I wanted to say. *Except the very end. If I could go back in time and undo that last day, I would.*

"Drive safe," he said. Then he gave me one final squeeze, pressed a kiss to my hair, and was gone, the guitar left behind exactly where he'd put it.

Lenore finally crept out from under the bed, just in time to see me sniffle a huge bubble of snot from my nose.

"I know," I said. "I'm not a pretty crier. I'm disgusting. Shall we go be disgusting together, seven hundred miles from here?"

TWENTY-FIVE

T HE SEMESTER STARTED back up at the end of August, and it was a relief to get back into my old routine. Preparing syllabi for the last two classes I'd teach in my graduate career, finalizing my dissertation chapters for Dr. Nilsson's comments, filling out paperwork to stay on track for graduation in December. Everything was back to normal.

Except it wasn't. Now I had a cat, who seemed to only moderately like me more than she had in Florida, but who at least seemed to love the small screened-in balcony that came with her new home. And now I was having trouble sleeping, unable to fight off the melancholy if I had even a minute of unfilled time on my hands. I had a giant hole in my chest in the place where my heart should be, and nothing I tried seemed to fill it up—not reading, not writing, not grading papers, not mindless Netflix watching.

Conner and I talked on the phone at least once a week, and

he'd put Shani on for her medical expertise if I happened to mention anything about my sudden insomnia. Her advice was sound and in keeping with what the internet said—no caffeine after two, no screens after eight, no using my bed for anything but sleep. But instead I sat up in my bed all night, drinking coffee and reading unsolved mysteries Reddit threads on my phone.

We'd had a few people look at our dad's house, including Josue, who ended up saying it seemed like more work than he wanted to take on.

"It was the black bedroom," I said on the phone to Conner, leaning down to peer into my almost-empty fridge. "I told you we should've painted it."

"Actually . . ." I could hear rustling on the other end, like Conner was shifting around. No matter how many times I told him the mic on his earbuds was super sensitive, he insisted on doing things like refilling his cup with ice or playing a video game with full sound on while we talked. Once, I'd heard him taking a leak. I'd told him in no uncertain terms that he was ideally never to do that again while we were on the phone or, if he absolutely couldn't hold it, at least mute his phone like a normal respectful person.

"Shani and I were thinking maybe we could move in," Conner said. "We'd take over the payments, of course, and do what we need to in order to make everything right with creditors or your share or whatever. It'd be cheaper than our rent on an apartment now. And there'd be no need to repaint the room, because it's kinda perfect for a gaming space with all that darkness."

"You're going to turn my childhood bedroom into a *gaming space*?"

"At least I didn't say *man cave*," Conner said. "What do you think?"

Everything he said made sense. At the start of the summer, I'd assumed that Conner felt the same way about the house that I had—that it was filled with bad memories and not a place he'd ever care to return. But staying there even for a few months had shown me that it was just four walls and a roof and a few doors that were so swollen from humidity they didn't shut all the way anymore. If it could help him and Shani on their new life together, then I was happy for them to live there.

Except one thing. "Oh god," I said. "You're going to be neighbors with Sam."

"Yeah . . ." Conner said. "Awkward. I take it you haven't talked since you left?"

There had been one night, when I'd been feeling really low and I'd reached for my phone and I would've *definitely* sent Sam a text, ranging from anything as innocuous as a *hey* to as thirsty as a cute selfie I'd "accidentally" forward. Not that I would stoop to such tactics.

If I had his phone number. I realized that we'd never actually exchanged that information—we hadn't needed to. He was always right there, one knock away.

"Have you seen him?" I asked now, hoping my voice sounded casual.

"The other day, briefly," Conner said, then seemed to hesitate. "There was, uh, a girl with him. He introduced her as something like Gem, Gemma, I can't remember."

I *knew* that pretty clerk at the music store was into him. "Jewel."

"That was it!" Conner was quiet for a minute, Shani's voice coming through in the background. "Shani said I shouldn't have told you that."

"It doesn't matter," I said.

Only, holy shit did it matter, because for days afterward it was all I could think about. I'd never been a particularly jealous person, but the idea of Sam with another woman made me literally sick to my stomach. Every night I slept in his LAUNCH INTO LEARNING! T-shirt and red boxer briefs that I'd purposefully never returned. It was all completely unlike me.

The week of my dissertation defense finally rolled around, and that at least was back in my comfort zone. It was what I'd prepared for the last five and a half years, and I couldn't allow my focus to wander now.

I had one more meeting scheduled with Dr. Nilsson, although she'd assured me it was just a formality to go through a few last things about the structure of the defense. I'd turned in my conclusion and revised all the previous chapters based on her initial notes, and I knew the dissertation itself was in pretty good shape.

"Who's going to be there on Thursday?" she said toward the end of the meeting, when I thought we'd wrapped everything up. I wanted to say, *Hopefully, you and the rest of my committee?* but could tell she wanted more from my answer. I just didn't know what.

"Family, friends," she clarified. "You can invite anyone you'd like for the first part. It can be a nice way to show all the people who've supported you in this journey what you've been working toward. We know that doctorates aren't earned alone."

"A lot of people from the department should be there," I said. Some of them I considered friends, although I realized I'd spent the last few years focused on my work, and not really taking a lot of time for extracurricular friendships. The truth was that I *had* been alone, for a while. But it had always been the way I liked it, where I called all the shots and I was responsible only to myself. It had never felt *lonely*.

Now, suddenly it did.

"Mmm," Dr. Nilsson said. And I should've dropped it, but something about the way she hummed that syllable, a judgment I sensed there, made me bristle.

"You're the one who said I should keep my options open," I said. "Right? Not get too tied down in one place or with one person, keep myself flexible so I could be more marketable for academic jobs?"

She blinked at me, as if she were genuinely taken aback by the vehemence of my question. Probably she was. I doubted she even remembered having that conversation, but it had stuck in my head ever since.

"Yes," she said slowly. "That's true, to an extent. It can be a nomadic road at first, trying to find a tenure-track position that is the right fit for you. And I won't sugarcoat it—the market is more competitive than ever. But I apologize if I gave you the impression that you couldn't have relationships. This can be a hard road, too, and sometimes those connections are what you need to get through it. My parents flew all the way from Sweden to see my defense."

"Really?"

"Many years ago," she said wryly. "They didn't understand any of it. But it meant a lot to me, to look out at the people in that room and see their faces there."

I had the absurd impulse to make a joke, something about imagining people in their underwear when you get nervous. But I couldn't workshop it in my head fast enough—for the best, considering that Dr. Nilsson was not generally known for her sense of humor. Instead I just sat there like a potato, still trying to wrap my head around the soft expression on Dr. Nilsson's face when she thought back to her family's support decades earlier.

Dr. Nilsson smiled at me. "You're well prepared, Phoebe," she said. "Get some rest, and I'll see you Thursday."

UNFORTUNATELY, *GET SOME REST* was advice I rarely followed. Instead, I paced around my apartment while Lenore watched me from her usual spot on the back of the couch. I scrolled through my streaming options, trying to find something to watch that would let me zone out a little, and instead landed on an episode of *Disappeared* that I'd somehow never seen.

"I know, I know," I said to Lenore, giving her a few scratches under her chin as it started up. "This is not me making healthy choices."

The setup was classic—a young husband and wife, both working two jobs in their quest for the American Dream. I almost wished Conner was there, just so he could see how right I was about the narrative choices these shows always made. Because the couple were always working, there was plausible deniability as to why it took the husband three days to even realize his wife was missing, but still. Clearly this was going to end up another one of those *the husband did it* ones.

I leaned my head back against the couch, which caused Lenore to look at me slit-eyed before going back to her breadloaf nap. I felt such a sudden strong desire to have Sam there with me it was almost painful. He'd probably have convinced Lenore to curl right up in his lap by now, would find ways to give this *Disappeared* jabroni the benefit of the doubt as he described his frantic search for his missing wife. Hell, Sam wasn't even *here* and I was already breaking character to root for love in this episode. No way could the husband be involved. Why weren't the police taking him seriously, filing a missing persons report?

When the wife was found alive, the victim of a horrible car accident that might not have been discovered in time were it not for the husband's persistence, I was shocked to find myself actually tearing up. It was cathartic, the relief that she was okay after all—something true crime programming rarely gave you. But there was more to it than that.

Somehow, Sam had sanded down my cynical edges. I'd built up this armor for so long, and I'd always worried I wouldn't recognize myself without it. But it turned out that I *liked* who I was with Sam. Dr. Nilsson had talked about what a hard road academia could be, and I knew it was true even as I'd discounted her words. I wasn't afraid of traveling hard roads alone. I'd done it before.

But I didn't *want* to do it anymore. And with this dissertation defense, I'd practiced and practiced my presentation, tried to predict questions I might get and prepare brief, articulate answers to them. But I'd never really thought about how it would feel to actually be up there, staring out at a crowd of people there to listen to my research. Hadn't considered that there might be people I would want there, not because they were colleagues or future graduates, but because they cared about me, and I cared about them, and I wanted to share this part of my life.

I wanted Conner and Shani there, if it was at all possible this late in the game. I wanted Conner to give me a high five afterward and say something ridiculous about the one twisted detail he'd gleaned from my entire presentation. I wanted Shani to be there, radiating positivity and encouragement. I knew it was very unlikely that Alison would be able to come, but I would love for her to.

Most of all, I wanted Sam.

———

THE ARRANGEMENTS WERE easier to make than I'd thought. After I'd sent out a few texts, a poet from my teaching practicum last year said she'd be happy to come by and feed Lenore and clean out the litter box. It almost made me feel bad, how quickly she responded, because I'd considered her an acquaintance but had never thought we had much in common. It just highlighted the ways I'd kept myself in my own little bubble, thinking that there was no point in trying, when there were people out there ready to be friendly at the first opportunity.

If I drove straight through, I could be at Sam's house by midnight. That would leave me the next day to drive back to North Carolina, and then turn around and have my defense the morning after I got back. The first thing I did once I'd gotten on the highway was call Conner, and ask him if he'd want to come.

"Dude," he said. "Of course. I have sixteen hours of PTO saved up at this point, and Shani's next shift isn't until Saturday."

"You don't have to," I said. "I mean, I know it's late notice—"

"I *want* to," Conner said. "I would've asked to before, except you said it wasn't the kind of thing where people came to it. So I thought it would be like asking to sit in on a literature class or something."

"I can't promise you that it won't be boring," I said. "But it would mean a lot to me if you were there. I'll pay for your flights or hotel or gas, whatever you need."

"We'll figure it out," he said.

"How about at Waffle House, tomorrow morning?"

Conner laughed. "What do you think, we're going to leave *now*? We could maybe get there in time for a late dinner tomorrow night."

"No," I said. "I meant the one by the house. In Florida. Oh, and I may need somewhere to stay tonight. Although I hope I won't."

"What are you—" And then it seemed to dawn on him. "Oh. Shit, Pheebs, are you driving down to talk to *Sam*?"

"Yes, and don't try to talk me out of it. I don't care if he hates me or if he's dating someone new or if I'm about to make the biggest ass out of myself. I need to tell him how I feel, and—"

I suddenly couldn't hear anything but a high-pitched squeal, and I winced. Shani must've grabbed the phone.

"Oh my god, *yes*," she was saying, "I was hoping something like this would happen. You two are *perfect* for each other, and he hasn't been the same since you left. I don't care if that girl was over at his house, which I still don't think Conner should've told you."

I could hear Conner protesting in the background, and could picture Shani swatting him, telling him to shut up. "What do you mean, hasn't been the same?"

It was dangerous, the lift in my heart at the idea that maybe Sam had been feeling as wrecked and lonely as I had, that maybe he would welcome me back into his life.

"Just quiet," Shani said. "We've been over there quite a bit, starting to move some stuff into the house. If we see him he always says hello, but it's very . . . polite."

That sounded like Sam, at least the shy version I'd met at first, and then the reserved version I'd gotten at the end. It had been nothing like the real Sam I'd known in between, who was thoughtful and funny and open and kind.

"Has he—" I started to ask, but then Conner came back on the line.

"Don't overthink it," he said. "You're doing the right thing. Call if you need anything else, but otherwise, we'll see you tomorrow at the Waffle House, maybe around eight?"

"Sounds good."

"Bring Sam!" Shani shouted in the background, and I smiled, although my stomach was a twist of knots.

"I'll try."

TWENTY-SIX

I T WAS PAST midnight by the time I pulled up in front of Sam's house, the neighborhood dark with its lack of streetlights. The windows in his house were dark, too. I had no idea what time he went to bed on a weeknight, but he'd once told me the time his school started, some god-awful hour meant for unconsciousness. It made sense that he'd be asleep already.

I chewed on my bottom lip, wondering if I should just head next door, put off any confrontation until tomorrow. But I didn't have much time, if I wanted to get back for my defense, and I'd come all this way. I had to see him.

My first knock on his door was as quiet as possible, hoping he was awake enough to hear it. After waiting a few minutes, it was obvious he wasn't, so I tried knocking harder. I even did Conner's *shave-and-a-haircut* and hated myself for it, but it seemed like one way at least to convey that it wasn't the cops at the door. Finally, as a last resort, I tried the doorbell.

Inside, a light switched on, and my heart jumped into my throat. I'd had the entire drive to plan what I was going to say, practice speeches that were varying levels of groveling, but then I heard the door unlatch and it swung open and any plans flew right out of my head.

Sam was wearing a Tampa Bay Lightning T-shirt and sweat-pants, his feet bare, his hair all rumpled, a crease from his pillow still across one cheek. He looked so cozy and cute and warm, so *Sam*, that I immediately wanted to lean forward and wrap my arms around him. But his face was a kaleidoscope of emotions, ranging from irritated to wary to concerned. I took a step back instead.

Hi seemed inadequate. But after the seconds passed, with us just staring at each other, it seemed better than nothing. My tongue was stuck to the roof of my mouth, and I tried to get it to form the word.

"This is very *Judgment Ridge*," Sam said finally, his voice still hoarse with sleep.

"Actually, that's a fear more specific to daytime visitors," I said. "Especially ones pretending to be solicitors or surveyors."

He leaned against the doorframe, dragging his hand down over his mouth. I couldn't help but follow the movement, wishing I could just kiss him, put everything I wanted to say into that press of my mouth against his.

"Didn't they knock on a guy's door months before in the mid-dle of the night, pretend to have car trouble so he'd invite them inside? Only the guy thought something seemed fishy, so he wouldn't do it."

I blinked. "I think you're right," I said. "Wait, did you read the book?"

He opened the door wider, stepping back to let me in. I wasn't prepared for how immediately comforted I would feel, just being back inside his house again. I'd missed it. I'd missed *him*.

"Only the first couple chapters," Sam said from behind me. "Once the eventual victims were introduced I had to check out."

That seemed like an awful segue into asking him to come to my defense of a true crime dissertation. It had to be encouraging, though, that he'd even tried. Or was it? I wished I could ask, *When did you read it, before I broke your heart or after?* "You're probably wondering why I'm here."

"It did cross my mind, yes."

He was wearing a thin, braided bracelet that I'd never noticed on him before. It only occurred to me now that it would've been possible for him to have someone over tonight, that Jewel could be lying in his bed right now, which would make me coming over in the middle of the night extra awkward. But there had been no other car in the driveway, and the house felt empty, except for the two of us, standing in his living room.

"I like your bracelet," I said.

He glanced down at it, then gave it a nervous little tug. "A kid at school made it," he said. "I was touched that he gave it to me, until he got busted the next day for selling them around school for Shark Bucks."

At my expression, he added, "School currency, to be earned for good behavior. The principal doesn't see running an underground bracelet-selling ring as good behavior."

"Sounds entrepreneurial to me," I said. "And you should still be touched that he gave it to you. Unless he busted your kneecaps for Shark Bucks after?"

Sam shook his head. "So why *are* you here?"

"I wanted to see you."

He rubbed his chest through his shirt, looking suddenly as tired as a guy whose sleep I had disrupted. God, I couldn't seem to get it right. Maybe I should've written him a letter, something where I could think through everything I wanted to say and make sure I got it exactly the way I wanted, without the distraction of the way he looked in that T-shirt or how sweet it was that he obviously cared so much about the kids he taught.

"Phoebe," he said. "I know your brother's moving in next door. I figured that would mean I might see you again . . . I'd be lying if I didn't say it was a relief in a way, the idea that I'd see you again. But if this is going to be a thing where every time you're in town, you want to hook up . . . I just. I can't. I'm sorry, but I can't."

I drew my brows together. "You think I'm here for a *booty call*?"

That red slash across his cheekbones, another part of Sam I'd missed. Who was I kidding—I'd missed all of it.

"Maybe that was presumptuous," he said. "Sorry. I shouldn't have said anything."

"No," I said, taking a step toward him. "*I'm* sorry. That's part of what I came here to say, and I don't even know where to start. I'm sorry for waking you up tonight, for one thing, but most of all I'm so sorry, Sam, for the things I said and the way I treated you that day at the park. I was scared, and lashing out, and I hate that I hurt you."

He shrugged, a jerky gesture that wasn't completely natural. "You already apologized for that," he said. "Several times. But you feel how you feel, Phoebe. You don't need to be sorry for that."

"But I *don't* feel how I feel," I said, my voice coming out ragged. "Or I guess what I mean is that I *do*, but I lied to you, or I lied to myself."

"It's late," Sam said, "and I'm pretty beat. I don't think I follow what you're saying."

"I love you," I said. The words weren't nearly as hard to say as I'd thought they'd be, so I said them again. "I *love* you, Sam. I don't know exactly when I started loving you, but definitely by that day in the park. I just didn't recognize it, and I was scared to examine it too directly, to confront what that might mean. When I said I didn't think I was capable of love, that wasn't a lie. With the way I grew up, my relationship history"—here I hiccuped a little, an almost desperate-sounding laugh—"if it's not too generous to call it that, just the *way I am*, I didn't think love was for me."

He'd braced himself against the piano with one hand, and his finger slipped and hit one key. He was utterly speechless, just staring at me, but I chose to take that as an encouraging sign. At this point, I had no other choice.

"And now in two days I'm about to deliver the second-biggest presentation of my life, and I realized I want you there. I *need* you there. Which, obviously, is a huge ask, since I didn't send a save the date or anything, and you have work, and probably no interest in coming to North Carolina to watch me talk about a genre that freaks you out . . . but it's not even about that. It's just that I need you in my life. Which, by the way, is a sentence that would've literally shriveled my insides to even *think* about saying a few months ago. But now I feel like I'll shrivel up if I *don't* say it. Even if you don't feel the same way about me anymore, or have moved on with Jewel or someone else, I had to say it. So, I just drove for ten hours, got pulled over once, narrowly avoided spilling coffee all over myself, and showed up on your doorstep at the most ass-hole hour possible, to say it. I love you. I need you in my life. I'm sorry." I took a deep breath, my first for the last few minutes. "Not necessarily in that order."

This time Sam half sat on the piano, depressing several keys before standing back up. "Wow," he said.

"Good wow?" I asked hopefully. "Or bad wow."

I'd known before coming here there was a chance of rejection. I'd steeled myself for it, told myself that if Sam said it wasn't go-ing to work, I'd say I understood with some semblance of dignity, and then I'd go next door and cry myself to sleep. It was impor-tant to me to convey the way I felt to him, no matter what the outcome.

"There's just a lot to unpack," Sam said. "I should've made coffee. What was that part about Jewel?"

A little chagrined, I said, "Uh, Conner told me. That she'd come over once."

His forehead wrinkled, then cleared. "To pick up an old violin I helped refurbish for the shop," he said. "She was here for maybe ten minutes. I'm not interested in dating anyone else."

Anyone else. I allowed my heart to lift, just a little bit. "Oh."

"And you want me to come to your dissertation defense?" he asked.

I shifted, hearing how outrageous it sounded. "Yeah," I said.

"I mean, ideally, I'd love to have you there. Conner and Shani are going to come. But it's also probably totally weird for me to ask you, and a huge imposition, and I'd understand—"

"Is it the same thing you said was the ultimate milestone of your graduate career? I'm sorry if I'm being dense, but you called it your second-biggest presentation of your life, so I'm a little confused."

"Well, yeah," I said. "Because *this* is the most important presentation of my life. What I'm saying to you now. I'm sorry I didn't make a PowerPoint."

He crossed the space between us in only a few strides, and then he was kissing me, his hands cradling my cheeks, my back against the door. The shock of having his mouth against mine, the sheer *relief* of it, made me start to cry, which I tried to hide from him so he wouldn't stop.

But he pulled back, rubbing his thumb along my jaw. "Ah," he said softly. "Please don't cry. I love you, too, Phoebe. I always will."

I hiccuped a little. "I thought I'd fucked it all up."

"No," he said. "I'd told myself I would wait until the semester was over, and then I'd ask Conner for your number. I didn't know what kind of reception I'd get, but I wasn't ready to give up on us."

"Really? I was afraid you'd forget about me."

"Not possible." He gestured over toward the corner, and I turned, not sure what he was trying to show me until my gaze landed on my guitar, lined up with several others in a rack over against the wall. "Turns out it was more painful *not* to have something of you around, so I asked Conner if I could have it."

And the little bastard hadn't even told me.

"I still have one of your shirts," I said.

"I know. I was looking for it. We're supposed to wear previous years' themed shirts on Throwback Thursdays."

I winced. "Whoops. Sorry."

He smiled, giving me a kiss on the corner of my mouth. "Don't be. I liked imagining you wearing it."

"What about *not* wearing it?"

His hands drifted down my back, settling over my ass and pulling me closer to him. "Even better."

"I know it's late," I said. "And you're tired, and I've been driving for ten hours, but . . ."

"Oh, don't worry about me," Sam said, his eyebrow raised in challenge. "I'm calling out tomorrow. My girlfriend is defending her dissertation and I can't miss it." He gave me a cute little squinty-eyed face. "Is that okay to say? Girlfriend?"

"I'm not afraid of that word anymore," I said. "I'm still afraid of a lot of things, most of them very specific scenarios involving being taken to a second location. But I'm not afraid of *this*, of loving you or being loved by you."

"Some might say your reading choices have a lot to do with that," Sam said. "But does the bedroom count as a second location? Or is that okay?"

I tilted my face toward his for another kiss. "I'd go anywhere with you," I said. "Take me there."

EPILOGUE

C ONNER AND SHANI got married the April after I graduated, in a wedding that was ninety percent Shani's family,
nine percent Conner's friends I'd never met, my mom and stepdad, and then me and Sam.

I'd finished my Best Person speech and plopped down in my
seat, still feeling flushed and full of adrenaline and sentimental-
ity. Sam looped his arm around me from behind, pulling me toward him to kiss my hair.

"You nailed it," he said. "Although I didn't understand any of
the *Crash Bandicoot* references."

"I was playing to my judge on that one," I said, reaching up to
press his arm tighter to my chest, wanting to be as close as possible. After a lifetime of feeling awkward and prickly around contact with another person, with Sam, I was finding that I couldn't
be held too long or too tightly.

"You really think your mom liked me?"

Sam had been fretting about that from the moment I'd introduced them yesterday at the rehearsal dinner, and he'd inquired about their German shepherd dogs before being corrected that the breed was Australian shepherd.

"They both have 'shepherd' in the name," I'd assured him. "It's understandable."

"Yeah, but they look *completely* different," Sam had said.

"It's not like you went golfing with the dogs and then called them German shepherds to their faces. My mom thinks you're *very sweet*. Those were her exact words."

It had been a whirlwind couple of months. My defense had gone amazingly well, save for one sticky question where a professor on my committee had asked me to step through the chronology of true crime publications and I'd ended up on a tangent about my favorite Aphrodite Jones book that was perhaps a little off topic. Sam and I had spent Christmas in Chicago with his family, where his siblings had not pooled their twenty dollars to buy their mother a birthstone necklace, but where everyone was very loud and happy and hugged a lot. It had been surprisingly nice.

Now, I was living with Sam and working on a book proposal while I waited to see if Stiles would request an interview for the visiting instructor job that had just opened up. I'd applied to other jobs, too, in other cities, and Sam said he had no problems packing up and moving anywhere in the country. Despite that, I found myself weirdly hoping we got to stay in Florida. It was nice, living next door to my brother—although the number of times he came over to borrow stuff made me question just what he *did* buy when he went to the grocery store.

"That dude," I said now, nodding toward a tall white guy with floppy brown hair and glasses. "Doesn't he look a lot like Dennis Nilsen?"

"Is that a computer programmer from the early eighties?" Sam said. "Because that's who he looks like."

"No, it's the guy who—" I caught myself before I could go any further. Something told me that maybe my brother's wedding wasn't the best place to start discussing Scottish serial killers and the inadvisability of trying to flush human remains. "Never mind."

Sam stood up, holding out his hand. "Dance with me?"

"'Dancing is not a compliment I pay to any place if I can help it,'" I said, because falling back on *Pride and Prejudice* quotes was always a good way to get out of something.

One side of Sam's mouth hitched up. "You can do this slow one with me now, or 'Tubthumping' later. Your choice."

The only thing worse than slow dancing was *fast* dancing, so I put my hand in Sam's and let him pull me to my feet. The song had already started, and there were other couples on the floor as Sam rested his hands on my waist. I'd never quite known what to do with my arms while dancing—even at live shows, I just nodded my head and kept my hands in my pockets. Did I rest them on his shoulders?

"Around my neck," Sam said. "It's basically just a socially acceptable way for us to hold each other for four minutes. You do have to sway a little bit, to get away with it."

It was easy to find the rhythm with Sam, actually. Nice, to feel his hands warm on my hips, to be close enough to see a small nick on his neck from where he'd shaved, to look into his eyes, so blue they took my breath away.

"It's not so bad," I said.

Over his shoulder, I could see Conner and Shani dancing together. I'd never seen my brother look so happy.

"I could see doing this, at some point," I said. "Getting married, I mean."

"Yeah?"

"Sure," I said, linking my hands tighter behind his neck, letting my fingers play with the hair at the nape of his neck. "Someday."

ACKNOWLEDGMENTS

Much like Phoebe, I sometimes struggle with remembering that I'm not an island, I'm not alone, it's okay to ask for or receive love and support. Truly this book would not exist without the following non-exhaustive list of people, places, and things (so, nouns? I could just say proper nouns) I appreciate more than words can say:

Laura Bradford, Hannah Andrade, and everyone at Bradford Literary for being the best champions for my work I could ask for; Taryn Fagerness for advocating for this book internationally; Kristine Swartz, editor extraordinaire, for everything but especially for letting me keep the MacDonald triad reference (IYKYK); the rest of the team at Berkley, including Mary Baker, Colleen Reinhart, Sheila Moody, Jennifer Lynes, Christine Legon, Bridget O'Toole, and Daché Rogers; Jenifer Prince for such beautiful cover art and for the amazing sapphic work she puts out into the world (follow her on Instagram @jeniferrprince, you won't regret it); my family, including my mom, who would lovingly bring home federal trial transcripts for me to read in high school; early readers of the LTSK Google Doc, including Kim Karalius (fellow writer, playlist track supplier, James McAvoy thirst ambassador), Charis (daily support texter and supplier of cat names), Stacey and Sarah (romance superfans), and Brittany (what can I say, dude, you're my best sister); Erin for all those nights we've closed down chain eateries talking about anything ranging from astrological signs to how we want our bodies disposed of after death ("throw me in the trash!!!"); my longtime NaNo friend, Kristin; Marni Bates for all the writing support over the years; Chase for always believing in me; Rebecca Frost for all her advice on writing a dissertation on true crime (and for helping talk me down when I actually think about going back to school to do it); Lindsay Eagar for her Fast Draft course; Pitch Wars for giving me the kick in the ass I needed to finish this manuscript; Pitch Wars mentors Rachel Lynn Solomon, Rosie Danan, Ruby Barrett, Annette Christie, Sonia Hartl, and Anna Kaling for seeing something in this story and giving me encouragement, support, and industry advice when I needed it most!; the Berkletes discord chat, especially the NSFW channel, which is an endless fount of new information; Christine Colby for letting me write for articles for Crimefeed that made me wary of going camping ever again (it's cool, I didn't like it much anyway); the *You're Wrong About* podcast for showing what an empathetic, thoughtful approach to true crime can look like; Sarah Marshall specifically for lunch and the Patty Hearst book; USF and the relationships that help me justify my student loans (including but not limited to Dr. Fleming, Liz, Christine, Bryan, Jessica); Carmen and Ann for hosting an amazing YA book club and generally being bright ambassadors in the book community; an anonymous someone where all I'll say is that if I mention *Judgment Ridge* in passing and then you read it and report back, I take it as the highest possible compliment; the Ask a Manager blog for being my favorite morning ritual; my two bosses, who I do appreciate even if I would appreciate them never reading this book; my local public library for taking me back even after I kept *Simon vs. the Homo Sapiens Agenda* for years, and especially for the curbside pick-up that kept me sane during the pandemic; the *Crash Bandicoot* games, especially the Hog Wild level; Janeane Garofalo when she dribbles beer down her dress in *Romy and Michele's High School Reunion*; Hayley Williams for releasing new music right when I needed it most; Tegan and Sara for the time they told me to go back to work in a Twitter AMA; Phoebe Bridgers' songs but especially that line in "Kyoto" about how 25 felt like flying; Apple Music's Metric Essentials for when I was too lazy to make a playlist of my own while writing; Chrvches' entire discography for the same reason; that part in the "Anna Sun" video where they all start dancing; the Etsy shop where I got some delightful goth stickers to mark every thousand words I wrote; untoasted cinnamon brown sugar Pop-Tarts; and *you*, if you've picked up this book and somehow made it through this prose poem of acknowledgments. I appreciate you.

And, of course, the biggest, most heartfelt thanks of all to Ryan, August, and Kara, who show me every day that love is real, and that the world is full of it. I love you guys.

ALICIA THOMPSON is a writer, reader, and Paramore superfan. As a teen, she appeared in an episode of *48 Hours* in the audience of a local murder trial, where she broke the fourth wall by looking directly into the camera. She currently lives in Florida with her husband and two children.

CONNECT ONLINE

🐦 AliciaBooks
📷 AliciaBooks

Ready to find
your next great read?

Let us help.

Visit prh.com/nextread